Everybody Got A Secret

2

A Drama-Filled Romance

By

Princess Diamond

Twitter & Instagram: @authorprincess
Facebook: @authorprincessdiamond
Pinterest: princess diamond

Everybody's Got A Secret 2: A Drama Filled Romance
Copyright © 2017 by Princess Diamond

Text COLEHART to 22828 to sign up for the mailing list &
for updates on New Releases. Also, Check out Cole Hart
Releases at www.colehartsignature.com

Acknowledgements

I give all praises to God who anointed me with this wonderful gift of writing. Through Christ I can do all things.

To my father in heaven, you passed away too soon. You have never seen any of my work, but I write in your memory. Love always.

To my mother in heaven, I still can't believe you're gone so soon. I miss you every day. I wish you were here with me. My biggest supporter. Love Always.

To my family and friends, I couldn't have done this without your endless days of listening to me talk about my stories, offering ideas, and giving me advice. You all are my rock. Thanks for everything.

To all the authors that have helped me. From giving me advice to supporting my work to the positive interactions. Much love.

To my readers, without your support, there is no me. I appreciate you all.

A special thanks to my sisters. Your input is priceless.

XOXOX
Princess Diamond

Princess Diamond's Books

Element of Surprise

Element of Surprise 2: Lust Unleashed

Put My Name On It

Dream & Drake Series

Everybody's Got A Secret Series

Chapter 1

Pebbles

Gabriel and I stepped off the plane like a power couple, hand in hand.

"Do you want to say goodbye to your family?" he asked.

He was so sweet. "Nope. They're good. I'll see them later or text them. Right now, I just want to be with you." I smiled.

He smiled back. "You sure know how to pump a brother's head up." He kissed me right in the middle of the airport. Gave me all kind of tingles down below. "So what was all that junk you were talking on the plane?"

I perched my lips. "What you talking about?"

He put his arm around my neck. "About how you was gonna blow my mind."

"Boy, I'm gonna give it to you so good, you'll be telling people your name is Pebbles."

He chuckled hard. "I don't know if I want that then. It sounds toxic." He laughed again. "I can't be bitchin up."

I giggled, and then turned around, shaking my butt in his face, like I was on the pole. "It's nuclear, baby," I said, looking over my shoulder, winking at him. "Once you get a taste of my goodies, you won't ever think about another woman again."

Gabriel gave me a sexy stare. "You're something else. You know that right?"

"So, I've been told."

While I was dancing in front of him, he scooped me off my feet, acting as if he was about to undress me right there in baggage claim. "Put your money where your mouth is."

"Stop," I squealed, playfully hitting him. I knew he was only joking around. Real talk, my body was banging. I had no problem showing it off. Yes, even in the airport full of people.

"There's your luggage," I told him, pointing as it came around.

Gabriel dropped me to my feet, yanking both bags off the carousel. He leaned over and kissed me on the cheek. "If I missed my bags that was going to be your ass."

I stuck my butt out, rubbing it against him. He smacked it. "Oh, shoot, there's my luggage."

Gabriel lightly bumped me out of the way, yanking my luggage off too. "I see things are going to get physical between us later."

I got all in his face. "Yeah. Well just know that I'm going to win. I always do." I stepped back away from him with a smirk on my face. "Try me, baby."

He stared at me lustfully. "We'll see about that, beautiful."

After we got our bags, we strolled towards the shuttle. His car was parked at the airport. While I was thinking of all the different ways to put my game down, I heard someone call my name.

"Pebbles! Pebbles!"

The voice was faint, but it was getting closer. As if they were running or something. Scanning the crowd, I just so happened to see Juicy jogging towards me. What the hell did she want?

"Where you going?" She looked at me, and then at Gabriel with her hand on her hip. "Dang, you cute. Who are you?" And then as if she suddenly remembered, she pointed her pinky finger at him. "Oh, yeah, I remember you. That dude from the bar that night. Um, um." She snapped her fingers at him.

"Gabriel," he said finishing her sentence.

Everybody Got A Secret 2: A Drama Filled Romance

"Yeah, I was just about to say that. If you would have given me a chance." She sighed. "Where y'all going?"

"What do you want?" I was trying to have some freaky fun with Gabriel. Not babysit her ass.

Juicy sucked her teeth. "Don't be like that. You know I need a ride home. Getting brand new cuz cutie is here." She twisted her lips, rolling her eyes hard. "I came with you, I'm leaving with you. That's what it is."

Now, it was my turn to suck my teeth. "Ugh! You killing the fuck outta my vibe."

I promise, I was about to call her out of her name when Gabriel offered to take her home. "It's cool. I can drop her off."

I looked at him like what the hell are you doing?

Juicy smirked at me, throwing her hair over her shoulder with an attitude. "Thanks, Gabriel. You're a keeper."

I was about to go in on Juicy when this bitch whipped pass us in a red Porsche Carrera, splashing water everywhere. She better be glad the water didn't hit me or I would have beat her ass. The car stopped a couple terminals down from us.

I needed to see this hoe because if she was ugly, I was going to clown her ass. She stepped out the car looking like a model.

"Better had," I said, as if she could hear me. "Cuz I was about to dog the fuck outta your ass."

"Who?" Juicy said, zeroing in on her. "That bitch in the red Carrera?"

We both gasped in shock.

Did this bitch just call out Stoney's name?

"Aww, hell no. This hoe just called out for Stoney." Juicy said, straining her neck to see what was going on.

The sun was shining in that direction so it was hard to see. I would put on my shades but it was cold as fuck. I wasn't about to dig in my carry on and freeze my damn fingers off.

"Did you see that shit?" Juicy yelled, hitting me in the arm.

"I see it, Juicy. Damn." She was talking about the kiss Stoney just gave my sister right in front of the chick who stepped out of the red sports car. "He's a bold muthafucka. That's all I got to say."

"While this dumb hoe is striking a pose in the middle of the street. I can't stand stupid bitches."

"C'mon girls," Gabriel said, signaling for us to go in the direction of the shuttle that just pulled up.

Me nor Juicy moved.

"Let's go, ladies," Gabriel said again, ushering us towards the bus.

We both put a pep in our step, struggling to get on with our luggage. Being the gentleman that Gabriel was, he helped us both with our bags, securing them on the bus. The ride on the shuttle was quick. Gabriel must've paid some coins cuz his car was in the first lot. We filed out and made our way over to a Lexus GS 350.

"This is nice," Juicy said, admiring his cocaine color ride.

I hopped in the front, melting in the heated leather seats. "Ah. I could live in here."

Gabriel smiled. "The seats got you, didn't they?"

"Yes," I said, relaxing. "I think I'm feeling the car more than you." I giggled.

Gabriel grabbed his dick. "Not for long. Wait until you get some more of this beef."

Oh, I love that kinda talk. It got me hot. I couldn't stand an uptight nicca who couldn't take a joke. The more I got to know Gabriel, the more I realized that I wanted him to be mine. I still wasn't totally over what Chip did, but Gabriel was the type of nicca that could make me easily forget.

"Where do you live?" he asked me.

"In Chatham. Off Ellis." I rattled off the address.

Out of nowhere, Stoney and that fake bitch pulled right in front of us, nearly clipping Gabriel's nice ride. I couldn't even hate cuz that car was bad as shit. If that were my ride, I would be showing off too.

"Damn, that's a serious whip," Juicy said, leaning into the front seat to get a better look.

4

Everybody Got A Secret 2: A Drama Filled Romance

"Would you sit your ass back? And put your seatbelt on before we get pulled over."

Juicy sucked her teeth and leaned back. "You think that's Stoney's car? Cuz I don't know. He don't seem that paid to me."

I thought for a minute, watching Stoney leave us in his dust. "I think he's paid. I can tell by his clothes and jewelry. Oh, by the way." I looked into the back seat at Juicy. "Marcel said he wanted us to perform at his show."

"Bet," she said, juking in her seat. "About to get that coin." She stopped dancing. "He is going to pay us, right? Cuz I'm not dancing for free. I needs my ends."

I ignored her, speaking to Gabriel. "I need to run inside and get a few things, if you don't mind."

"Nah, that's cool. Oh snap!" Gabriel quickly pulled over to the side of the road as a police car sped pass us. "I thought he was going to run right into me."

"Shit! It's too much going on. Hurry up and get us away from O'Hare. All this commotion is making me nervous."

Gabriel laughed. "What do you have to be nervous about, pretty?" He rubbed my thigh. "Unless you're trafficking." He laughed again. "I can't see you as that type."

"Boy please. As much as your cousin had a hard-on for me in customs, there's no way that I smuggled shit from the Bahamas."

"Looks like your boy just got caught up," Gabriel said, referring to the cop that just got behind Stoney.

"Oh, well. He shouldn't have been showing off." I didn't care one way or another. "That's what he get for trying to stunt."

"Man, that ticket is going to be ugly. He had to be doing at least a hundred."

"Whatever. I could care less," I said as we drove pass.

Gabriel shook his head. "That's a nice ride though. I hope he's not riding dirty. Cause they'll impound that one-hundred thousand dollar ride."

"That's how much that car costs?" I asked. Shit. Stoney is doing better than what I thought. I should have gotten a little friendlier with him.

"Yeah. I'm pretty sure. I saw one at the car show. That's a hot car right now."

"You can say that again," Juicy said, straining her neck looking out the back window to see what was going on with Stoney.

"Literally," I said, cosigning.

Gabriel wasn't driving the speed limit, but he wasn't a maniac driver like Stoney either. It took us forty minutes to get to my place.

"Alright, Juicy, peace out. Don't tear my shit up while I'm gone."

Juicy dug in her purse, then smacked her lips. "Can you let me in?"

"Dang, you ain't got your key again?"

"No," she said, standing on the curb with her luggage.

"I'll be back," I told Gabriel.

Gabriel backed into a parking space and got out to help me get my luggage out the trunk. "You need me to carry it up for you."

"Nah, boo." I squeezed his dick through his pants. "You just stay nice and hard until I get back." I kissed his sweet lips and strutted towards my apartment. When I looked back, Gabriel was still staring. I really switched my hips then, giving him something to look at.

"C'mon," Juicy said holding the elevator door open with her hand. "Before this broke shit closes. Then you gonna have to carry that luggage up all them stairs."

For once, she was right. I stopped being cute, hauling ass with my luggage before it closed and I was fucked. The last thing I wanted to do was carry two heavy suitcases up to the third floor. Sliding through the closing double doors, I made it just in time. "Damn these muthafuckas raggedy."

"You feeling Gabriel, ain't you?" Juicy asked leaning up against the elevator wall.

6

Everybody Got A Secret 2: A Drama Filled Romance

I just grinned. Normally, I would have something smart to say. Not this time. "Yeah, a little."

Juicy smiled too. "I say go for it. I can tell he really likes you. Plus, he's cute and cool. His whip is nice too. I say put it on him."

"You think?"

Juicy nodded her head. "Yep. I sure do."

"Hey, Pebbles."

"Hey, Rondo." He was right outside the elevator when we stepped off.

He stared at my butt. "How was your trip?"

"Good. You missed me?"

"Of course. I'd like to see you later, if you're not busy."

I put my hand on my hip. "I don't know, Rondo. You know I stay busy."

He gave me a sexy smile. "I see. Just get at me when you're free then."

"Ok."

Shoot, I didn't have time for Rondo. I was going to be all on Gabriel's dick. I wheeled my luggage into my apartment, to my room. "You're on borrowed time," I told Juicy. "You were supposed to have found a job by now. I need help with these bills. These muthafuckas don't pay themselves."

"That's what these niccas for. You better hit up Gabriel. He doesn't look broke to me."

I snaked my neck back looking at her. I was about to cuss her stupid ass out. She was lucky something came over me and I changed my mind. Either she gets her act together or I'm throwing her stupid ass out. I don't have to argue with someone who is staying in my shit.

Besides, I didn't want to keep Gabriel waiting for me. Quickly, I took off these borrowed clothes that Jayson gave me and jumped in the shower. After clipping my hair up, I threw some clothes and personals in an overnight bag, and rushed back out.

"Sorry, it took me so long," I said, getting back in the car with Gabriel.

"It wasn't that long." He leaned over kissing me. "You look so beautiful."

"Thanks, boo." I don't know what he was looking at. I just threw these clothes on. Some cut up jeans, a mid-drift shirt, sneaker wedges, and a leather jacket.

His kiss was so inviting that I pulled him back to me for another one. Our tongues danced while our hands explored each other's bodies. I squeezed the bulge in his pants while he slipped his hand under my top, fondling my breasts.

"We better stop," Gabriel said, moving away from me. "I'm getting pretty worked up." He looked down at his erection and I did too.

"We don't have to stop," I replied, unfastening my pants, wiggling out of them. "Let's get in a quickie."

Gabriel looked around, checking out the surroundings. "But we're parked right in front of your apartment building."

"I know," I said, tugging at his jeans. The button came undone when I pulled on his zipper. "You got tint."

"It's not that dark."

"It's dark enough," I said, putting my mouth on his tool.

Gabriel stopped protesting the moment I began working my jaws around his pole. I bobbed my head fast. Slurping on it like a Popsicle.

Gabriel moaned, taking the clip out of my damp hair. "You trying to make me cum fast?"

I didn't answer. I showed him that I meant business by cupping his balls and deep throating his dick. When I felt like Gabriel couldn't take much more, I stopped, straddling his lap. Pulling my thong to the side, I slid down on his tool.

He grabbed my waist, ramming into me.

"Shit!" Arching my back, I reached behind me, holding onto the steering wheel, working my coochie muscles as I came. "Shiiiiiiiiiit. Gabriel. Yes! Yes! Yes!"

Once I came, Gabriel pulled me closer to him, kissing me. "You do something to me."

Everybody Got A Secret 2: A Drama Filled Romance

"You do something to me too," I said, rocking my hips sensually.

Gabriel surprised me, rocking his hips to my tempo. He lifted my top, sucking on my breasts.

"Aaaaaaah! Sssssssssssss. Gabriel. You're about to make me cum again."

"Cum on it then."

He leaned the seat back a little. That gave me just enough room to really work my hips. I rolled my hips in a sensual grind while squeezing my vaginal muscles as tight as I could.

"Fuuuuuuuuuck!" Gabriel yelled.

"You're so damn sexy," I said, sucking on his bottom lip.

He stared at me with those sexy honey-colored eyes before sticking his tongue in my mouth again.

"Oh! Oh! Oh! Oh! I'm cumming." His dick was the shit. I wanted to hold out longer but I couldn't.

"Me too, baby."

My arms were around his neck as I rode him like a pony. His face was buried in my chest while his arms were around my hips.

We held each other tight as we came at the same time.

Chapter 2

Pebbles

After screaming my lungs out, I climbed off of Gabriel, back into my seat. I pulled out two feminine wipes. I used one on him and then me, tossing them both out the window.

Gabriel leaned the seat back up. "Damn, girl. You about to have a nicca sprung, for real."

That had me cheesing. "That's how you're supposed to be." I reached over as if I was cracking a whip at him.

He chuckled, pulling out of the parking space. "I think you're the one who's whipped. You practically ripped my clothes off and took the dick."

I laughed loudly. "Whatever. You liked it."

At the light, he leaned over pecking my lips. "Correction, I loved it. You can take it anytime you want."

I smiled again. This man had me so gone. I was digging everything about him.

He pulled up in front of the grocery store around the corner from his place in Hyde Park.

"You coming in?"

"Yeah." I checked my face right quick. "I gotta make sure these bitches stay in check."

He snickered. "You don't have nothing to worry about. I don't want anyone but you."

Everybody Got A Secret 2: A Drama Filled Romance

"Sounds nice." I still had my reservations about him. That feeling of him being a player lingered in the back of my mind.

Grabbing my hand, Gabriel led the way into the store. He grabbed a cart. "What do you want to eat?"

"I don't know. I'm sick of seafood, though."

"Let's do Italian then. With bread and salad and wash it down with a bottle of wine. How does that sound?"

"I'm cool with that. And who's cooking all this?" Because he had another thing coming if he thought I was slaving over a hot stove.

"I am," he answered confidently.

"I hope you can cook. I don't eat Cajun."

We both laughed.

"I can. I've been cooking since I was a little boy. My mother taught me."

"I hear you. Grab that whipped cream." I winked at him. "We can use that later."

He got it out the freezer. "Go get some chocolate syrup. We can use that too."

"Oh," I said, feeling horny all over again. "I like the way you think."

He smacked me on my butt as I walked away. "Don't take all day, sexy."

I wandered off to find where the syrup was at. It took me forever. This grocery store wasn't set up like a normal store. Shit was in all the wrong places. After nearly walking around the whole store, I found it by the freezer section with the ice cream. I was so mad I wanted to kick the whole display down.

I made my way back to where Gabriel last stood. He wasn't there anymore. He must've finished shopping. Strolling from aisle to aisle, I casually looked for him. He wasn't nowhere in sight.

Just as I was about to give up, I saw him checking out. I walked over to where he was as if I wasn't flustered, handing him the syrup. I thought he was about to say something slick when he handed me a dozen fresh red roses. "These are for you. Beautiful flowers for a beautiful woman."

"Thank you," I said, feeling warm and mushy inside. Gabriel definitely had me open. I hadn't felt this way since Chip.

He kissed my cheek. "I want to do a lot more for you."

I grinned while he paid for the groceries.

Gabriel carried the two bags to the car, opening the door for me, and putting the groceries in the backseat.

I sat in the car feeling like I could spend the rest of my life with this man. It was just something about him that made me feel so comfortable. I felt this way since we met. I denied it and tried to reduce our relationship to just sex. It was obvious that it was more than that. And I think he is feeling the same way. At least that's the vibe that I got.

"You ok, beautiful?" Gabriel asked me, rubbing my leg, snapping me out of my trance.

I gave him a half-hearted smile. "Um, yeah, I'm good. Why?"

"You looked like you had something on your mind."

I leaned over kissing his lips. "I was thinking about you."

Now, it was his turn to grin. "Well, in that case you can stare off into space as much as you like."

I popped his arm. "Don't get the big head."

He smiled. "Never that."

His place was nice. A spacious two bedroom on the second floor. Neat. Everything was in its place. Even his bed was made. That's one thing we didn't have in common. My place looked like a hurricane just went through it. Shit was everywhere. Being nosey I strolled into the other bedroom. I couldn't put my finger on it, but this room seemed to have a woman's touch.

"You live alone?" I asked, looking around.

"Yeah. Who else would be living here?" he asked me from the kitchen. He was taking the groceries out of the bag.

"I thought maybe you had a roommate."

"I did. A couple months ago."

That would explain the womanly touch. Standing in that room, I got a bad feeling, but I shook it off because I didn't want to think the worse of Gabriel. Besides, he doesn't seem that messy to have me here if he was living with another woman.

I walked into the kitchen. "Mmmm. Smells good in here."

"Thanks. I do a little something, something. Taste." He held the wooden spoon to my mouth.

I tasted the homemade tomato sauce. "That's good. I guess you can cook."

"I told you." He took a sip of wine. "Would you like a glass?"

"Yep. I wanna be nice too." He handed me a glass, pouring it full. "You smoke?"

"I used to smoke weed. Gave it up a year ago. I never smoked cigarettes. You?"

"Neither. I mean, I tried weed before but it ain't me. I'll be right back." I wanted to get more comfortable.

Prancing out of the kitchen, I went to his room and changed into a tank and booty shorts. I returned to the kitchen, sitting down at the table, watching him do his thing at the stove. Sipping on my wine, I checked him out. He had on a wife beater, shorts, and an apron. Doesn't sound sexy, but for some reason, it really turned me on.

After finishing my glass of wine, I was ready to fuck again. Coming up behind Gabriel, I put my arms around him. "You smell so good. He turned around, kissing my forehead.

There was two ways to a man's heart. Food and fucking. Some women wouldn't agree with me, but being a master of pussy whipping, I knew my power. And I planned on giving Gabriel so much that he wouldn't have no choice but to remember me and my good nana.

Dropping to my knees, I climbed under his apron, yanking his shorts down. His dick sprung forward, pointing right at my mouth. The fact that he didn't have no underwear on almost made me cream in my shorts.

"What are you—"

I wrapped my lips around his dick, jerking on it, sucking him slow.

"Shit! Let me cut the stove off before you have us both with third degree burns."

I heard pots and pans clanking as I kept on sucking. I guess Gabriel managed to get things situated without me having to stop. He took the apron off, grabbing a handful of my hair, thrusting himself between my jaws. I didn't mind. I was superb with my oral skills too.

"I'm about to cum," Gabriel said, trying to pull away.

Gripping his ass, I pulled him in and out of my mouth. That's what I wanted him to do.

"Aaaaaaah! Fuuuuccccck!" He practically screamed.

I continued to squeeze his ass as he deposited in my mouth. When I felt he was done, I stopped sucking and swallowed.

Gabriel looked down at me breathing hard. "What are you trying to do to me?"

I smiled, knowing that I accomplished what I set out to do. Make a lasting impression. "What? You can't hang? All that dick and you can't use it?"

Gabriel stared at me, stepping out of his shorts. Then, he pulled his wife beater over his head. "Baby, I'm an island boy. Fucking is in my blood."

He reached down, grabbing my hand, yanking me to my feet. Flipping me around, with my backside to him, he snatched my booty shorts off and pulled my shirt over my head. Without warning, he pushed me forward across the table, shoving his erection inside of me. His rugged thrusts set my whole body on fire.

"This is what you wanted right?"

"Oh my God! Yes!" I cried out, cumming instantly.

He grabbed my hips, jerking my body towards him. "I'm about to make this pussy leak."

"Damn, you hitting it right."

Gabriel responded by jerking my hips even harder.

"Ah! This dick is so good right now." I was supposed to be putting it down on him, but he was putting it down on me. Fucking my mind all up. Had me scratching at the table and shit.

Everybody Got A Secret 2: A Drama Filled Romance

"Oh! Oh! Oh!" I screamed, cumming again. My mouth hung open. My chest heaved. I took long hard breaths. The trembling started in my vagina and shot down to my toes, making them curl. I rose up and fell back against the table as my legs shook wildly. I was still shaking when Gabriel pulled out of me, flipping me onto my back. He opened my legs sucking on my clit. Then, he held my legs in the air with his lips around my pearl until I came.

"Can I hang?" he asked, entering me while I was still cumming. My eyes rolled into the back of my head. This man was writing his name all over my coochie.

"Can I?" he asked, gently grazing my g-spot as he grinded inside of me. "All this dick got you speechless?"

"Ah! Ah! Ah! Ah! Ah!"

"Say my name," he demanded, raising my legs in the air. Holding me by my ass, he forcefully jerked my pelvis to him. "Say it!"

I screamed, "Gabriel! Gabriel! Gabriel!"

Dropping my legs, he laid flat on top of me. Grabbing my hair, he French kissed me. "Say it again."

The lust I felt for this man. "Ssssssssssss. Gabriel!"

He pushed my legs back up, still kissing me. Tilting my hips upward gave him full access to my g-spot. "It's so damn good. I gotta nut."

"Yes! Oh my God! Yes, it is."

"I'm about to let loose."

"Oh my God! Oh my God! Me tooooooo!" I yelled out, coating his dick with sticky cum.

Gabriel moaned in my ear, cumming with me.

I know it must've been good because he started speaking another language. I have no idea what the hell he said, but it sounded sexy as fuck.

"Damn, girl, that was incredible," he whispered in my ear, still breathing heavy. He got up and helped me off the table. "Let's do another round in the shower."

"You already know, I'm down."

Princess Diamond

Gabriel and I played around in the shower throwing soap on each other before rinsing off. He lowered himself to his knees sucking my coochie with expertise until I came. Then he picked me up and carried me into the bedroom where we made love until we were both exhausted.

"I probably shouldn't tell you this, but I'm falling for you." He was spooning me. His cheek was on top of my cheek.

I started laughing.

"I pour my heart out to you and you laugh." He moved away from me.

"I wasn't laughing at you." I rolled over moving closer to him, laying my head on his chest. "I feel the same way."

He looked me in the eye. "I'm serious."

"Me too," I said honestly. "Why do you think I got so mad at you when we couldn't spend time together? I was feeling some kinda way then."

He smiled. "You know, I've never been in love. I guess, I never thought I'd meet someone that I could fall in love with." He caressed my cheek. "But you, you make me feel all that mushy stuff. You make me want to do all the weak shit that men do when they fall hard for a woman."

I laughed. This time he laughed too.

"Be mine." He rolled back on top of me, in between my legs, resting his head on my breasts.

"I'm already yours."

*****

Opening my eyes, I looked around, forgetting where I was. I was in such a peaceful sleep. Stretching, I wondered where Gabriel was. He wasn't in the bed next to me. As soon as I swung my feet over the bed, I had to pee. Rushing to the bathroom, I could have sworn I saw the front door open.

Jumping from foot to foot, I couldn't get to the toilet fast enough. "Aaaaaaaaah," I sighed. I was too happy to relieve my bladder. After washing my hands, I opened the door and I was greeted by some skank.

"Who the fuck are you?"

"Bitch, who the fuck are you?" I shot back at this tacky weave wearing trick.

"You about to find out," she said, swinging at me.

I ducked and slid underneath her arm, rushing into the bedroom, locking the door so I could put on my clothes.

"Open this door, bitch!" she screamed, banging on the door like a mad woman. "I'm going to make you wish you never met my man."

Her man? I was pissed. I wish Gabriel was here. Because after I whooped her ass, I would be whipping his.

"Open the damn door!" she yelled again.

After I was fully dressed, I opened the door, punching her right in the face. She fell back a little. I wasted no time punching her ass again, and again, and again. "I'm going to make you wish that you never tried me." She got ahold of my hair, but I kept on punching her until I knocked her ass out. This bitch was out cold in the hallway by the bathroom when I finished.

I looked around the apartment. No Gabriel. I'm not sure where his ass went, but I couldn't help but feel like he set me up. "I knew this muthafucka was a player," I said out loud while stuffing my things into my bag. "I fuckin knew it."

Storming towards the door, I tripped over ol girl's purse. I snatched it up on my way out. When I got downstairs, I realized that I didn't drive. Gabriel brought me here. Shit! Shit! Shit!

That meant I had to catch the damn bus home. I hated riding the fuckin bus. It was always a damn adventure. Making my way down to the bus stop, I passed by a bum. Here we go with the bullshit.

"Say, pretty lady, with the tight jeans on. I know you got some spare change, as fine as you look. Wit yo pretty little self."

I sat down on the bench next to an older woman and what looked like her grandchild.

Princess Diamond

"Pretty lady," The bum said, moving closer to me. "I'll hold your bag for you until the bus comes. I'll stand here." He showed me a balancing act. "Right here, next to you, and won't move for five dollars."

I refused to even acknowledge this muthafucka, but for some reason he kept on talking to me, trying to get my attention.

"Pretty lady—"

"Go on, now, shit." I wasn't trying to be mean but I didn't want to keep seeing his no teeth having ass in my face. And I didn't want to keep smelling his musty, funky ass either. Then it dawned on me, the bum is happier than I am, and he's homeless. I really needed to get my damn life. For real.

I didn't say anything else to the bum. I let him harass me until the bus came. Before I got on the bus, I reached in my pocket and gave him my last five dollars. That's all I had on me besides my bus fare. I left my debit card at home.

After I settled in my seat on the crowded bus, I went through ol girl's purse. The first thing I saw was a picture of her and Gabriel. All hugged up together. Damn. I guess she wasn't lying. He was her man.

Tears came to my eyes. I didn't even wipe them away. I let them fall. Out of all the guys that I met since Chip, Gabriel was the only one I was really feeling. He made me think I was special.

My phone vibrated. I looked at it. I had a text. I smacked my lips when I saw it was from Gabriel.

Gabriel: Baby, where are you? I've been looking everywhere for you. I left to go back to the store and I came back and you were gone.

His text was followed by a picture of the lovely dinner that he prepared accompanied by two glasses of wine. The whipped cream and chocolate syrup in the background made me tingly. I wanted to jump off the bus and run back to his apartment to be with him.

Why did you have to lie Gabriel? Why?

I wanted to text him back and tell him off. I wanted to kick myself for falling for an international player.

Everybody Got A Secret 2: A Drama Filled Romance

I sighed.

I should have left it as just sex.

I fucked up.

I thought about Gabriel for the rest of the bus ride

When I got off the bus, I threw that bitch's purse in the trash. I walked further down, making my way to my apartment. Once inside, I saw Juicy sleep on my expensive couch with her hand in a bag of flaming hot Cheetos. I wanted to put a few knots on her head for sleeping on my furniture with food. It took me six months to get this furniture set out of layaway.

My phone rang. This had better not be Gabriel. I promise, I won't hold back on telling his ass off. "Speak," I said with major attitude.

"Bitch! Don't be answering me like that. And why the fuck do you sound like you been crying?"

I laughed, wiping away my tears. "I thought you weren't going to say that no more."

"I never said that shit," Joss said, popping gum in my ear. "Bitch is my word. Anyway, you still going out with me?"

"Naw, I'ma have to pass."

"See, you bogus as hell, but that's ok. I know your ass better go next time or it's going to be a problem."

"Or what?" I joked.

"Bitch! Don't make me get stupid on your ass. Next time you going. Hold up. Hold up. Let me call you back."

As soon as I hung up with Joss, my phone rang again.

"Pebbles," my sister cried. She sounded awful.

"What's wrong, Vanity?"

All I heard was her sobbing uncontrollably. It was so bad that she couldn't even tell me what was wrong.

"Where you at?"

"H-home."

"Hold tight. I'm on my way."

Chapter 3

Vanity

The limousine pulled up for Marcel and them. Still no Ivan. The driver got out and began to load their luggage in the trunk.

"You know you can come with us," Marcel said with concern. He was worried because everyone else was gone. "I'll make sure you get home. You don't have to stand here waiting for a nicca."

As soon as the words left his mouth, Ivan turned the corner in his black BMW, driving all crazy. He sped up and then hit the brakes, jumping out of the car like a fool. "VANITY!" he yelled. "Bring your ass the fuck on."

Natalia and Karen were already in the limo. Cash was about to get in, but he paused when Ivan called out to me in a disrespectful manner. Cash closed the limousine door, walking back towards us, like he knew something was about to pop off.

A scowl came across Marcel's face as he stared at Ivan with hatred. Marcel kept on talking as if he didn't hear anything Ivan just said. "Get your shit. You're coming with me."

"No, Marcel. I'm already in enough trouble. I made my bed, now I have to lie in it. It is what it is."

Everybody Got A Secret 2: A Drama Filled Romance

Marcel twisted his face. "I don't fucking trust that nicca. Why don't you come with me right now? You can always see him once things have cooled down."

"It's cool. I'll be ok."

Ivan must've felt disrespected because nobody acknowledged him. He slammed the car door, strutting towards us on an ego trip. "Didn't you hear me fucking calling you?" he asked me before hocking up a nasty ass loogie, spitting it on the ground. "Let's muthafuckin roll. You can call this nicca on the phone."

Ivan always kept a slight attitude, but he was way out of character, acting like he didn't give a fuck about shit.

I grabbed my luggage, ready to haul ass when Marcel put his arm up stopping me, addressing Ivan. "Yo, that's how you talk to your wife? Fuck wrong with you, B?"

Ivan stepped closer to Marcel. "What concern is it of yours? I'm not talking to your wife like that."

Marcel stepped even closer, towering over Ivan. All in his face. "You better not talk to my wife like that, nicca. It'll be a muthafuckin problem. Believe that shit." Marcel was playing Ivan so close that their foreheads were almost touching.

"Fuck you care for?" Ivan asked, not backing down. "I'm not talking to your wife. I'm talking to my wife. And I'll talk to her any fuckin way I feel."

I was getting real nervous. Marcel looked like he was about to stomp a hole in Ivan's ass. And Ivan had this wild look in his eye that said he didn't give a fuck about nothing or nobody.

Cash approached them. "Cell, let that shit go, bro. He ain't worth it. You got too much to lose."

"Nah, fuck that, yo," Marcel spoke to Cash, never taking his eyes off Ivan. "I'm not about to see him disrespect Vanity like that. He talking so slick to a woman. I want him to talk that same shit to me." Marcel was still in Ivan's face, looking him dead in the eye. "Bitch ass nicca."

"But this ain't the time, though," Cash said, pointing his head in the direction of airport security.

WOOP! WOOP! "Move your vehicle or be towed," airport security said through a bullhorn. "Move your vehicle or be towed. This is a no parking zone. All vehicles must go."

They were giving out tickets a few terminals down. It was just a matter of minutes before they would be handing us one.

Marcel eyed Ivan, looking him up and down, like he wasn't shit. "Clown ass nicca. Vanity, you coming?"

Ivan took his eyes off Marcel, eyeing me. His expression told me I better not go with him. "You go with him and we're done. Don't bring your ass back home. Stay the fuck over there with him. Let him take care of your spoiled ass."

I knew Ivan was serious. Guilt was eating me up. I thought about how good he was to me. A time when we were madly in love. I wanted those times back. "Thanks, Marcel, but I'm going with my husband." I sure hope I made the right decision.

Ivan smiled at Marcel as if he already knew what I was going to say. "Like I said, homie, you handle your wife, and I'll handle mine." Ivan backed away from Marcel, still grinning. He looked at me. "Say your fuckin goodbyes and then bring your ass on." Ivan strutted back towards his car in a real cocky manner.

Marcel kept his eyes on Ivan. "I hope you know what you're doing. Because I don't trust his ass."

"Me either," Cash said with his eyes on Ivan too. "Nicca's a snake."

"I'm doing what I have to do," I said, still wondering if I was making the right decision.

"Fuck that. What you need to do is get your shit and be out. That nicca's crazy as fuck," Marcel said. "A fuckin sandwich short of a fuckin picnic."

"I can handle him," I lied. I looked calm, but on the real, I was about ready to piss on myself. Ivan was on twenty. I ain't never seen him act like this. He was capable of anything.

"Aight. Call me if you need me." Marcel sighed, hugging me. I could tell he was still heated. He probably wanted to crack Ivan's jaw.

"I will. Stop worrying."

Everybody Got A Secret 2: A Drama Filled Romance

"I can't help it. I'm getting a bad feeling about all this. Like this nicca about to get real stupid."

I hugged Cash, calling him by his government name. "Bye, Cash Dollar."

The look that Cash gave me sent chills down my spine. "Be easy, baby." His eyes darted from me to Ivan who was now sitting behind the wheel, looking like he wanted to run all three of us over.

"I'll see y'all later," I mumbled, wondering if I should follow after them.

They got in the limousine and I wheeled my luggage in the direction of my husband's BMW. When I walked up to the car, Ivan didn't even bother to get out and help me with my luggage. He just popped the trunk and watched me struggle with it. After nearly dropping the heavy bags, I finally got it in.

"Thanks for helping me put my stuff in the car," I said sarcastically, sliding into the passenger's seat.

Ivan pulled off, speeding pass Marcel and them, turning the corner at full speed. "How the fuck did you get it out the car when you went?"

"I took it out by myself, but it wasn't as heavy then. I came back with more stuff."

Ivan picked up speed, racing pass the line of cars about to get on the expressway. "Well, there you go. I see you left without my help. If you didn't need my help going, why the fuck do you need me to help you with it coming back? You wearing the pants, remember? You treat me like I'm your bitch. So, keep wearing the fuckin pants, and lift that heavy shit yourself."

"Fuck it," I mumbled.

Ivan reached into the glove compartment, tossing some papers into my lap.

"What's this?" I asked.

"All the transactions you made taking money out of our savings account on fertility drugs."

I got real quiet. There was no rebuttal for this. I was very aware of what I was doing when I took the money out.

23

"Did you see the total?"

"I saw it," I said, knowing he was about to talk crazy.

"Twelve muthafuckin thousand dollars on some bullshit."

A cop came out of nowhere. He swooped behind us with his sirens on.

"Aww, fuck." Ivan said, slowing down a little, getting into the right lane. "I'ma be pissed off if I get another ticket." He made his way onto the shoulder.

I looked out the rearview mirror as the cop swerved around us, taking off after someone else.

"I'm glad that muthafucka peeled out. Leave me the fuck alone and get another nicca." Ivan looked over his shoulder, hopping lanes

As we were cruising down the expressway, I saw Stoney pulled over. I turned around, straining my neck to get a better look. He was standing on the side of the road. Without thinking, I pulled out my phone, texting him. You good? We just rolled by you.

Stoney: Yeah, I'm straight. Are you ok? I miss you!

"What the fuck you breaking your neck to see?" Ivan glanced in the rearview mirror trying to figure out what I was looking at.

"Nothing," I said, texting Stoney back. I miss you too.

"Are you even listening to me? Gimme that damn phone," he said, snatching my phone out of my hand.

I tried to grab it back but Ivan was hell bent on looking at my text. "Give me my phone, Ivan. You always playing too much."

"Pebbles can wait." Ivan switched hands, driving with is right hand while looking at my phone with his left.

If he only knew. It wasn't Pebbles. I sighed, feeling a head-ache coming on. "You're an asshole."

After he stared at my texts for a moment, he replied. "And you're a whore."

My mouth hung open. I couldn't believe he just called me that. "Insensitive bastard."

Everybody Got A Secret 2: A Drama Filled Romance

Ivan put the pedal to the metal, switching lanes until he got in the far left lane. "I'm insensitive? You got a lot of fucking nerve when you're the one who cheated." He chuckled. "You must think I'm a pussy nicca. Don't you?"

I ignored him, looking out the window.

"Go ahead and deny the shit like you did in the Bahamas." I kept looking out the window ignoring him. "That's right. Keep quiet. Cuz you know I'm right. All that bullshit you said over text. Now, you ain't got nothing to say. Who the fuck was this nicca?"

"Disrespectful ass."

"I'm disrespectful, but you're texting this nicca while I'm in the car talking to you." Ivan stared at the next text message that came in. "That was the nicca on the side of the road that got pulled over?" Ivan was livid then, getting off at the nearest exit. "Fuck that, I'm turning around."

"NOOOOO!" I yelled. "Let's just go home so we can talk about this."

"Oh, now you want to talk." Ivan pressed the talk button, holding my phone to his ear. "Let's see how much you have to say when I call your man."

"Give me my phone!" I yelled, reaching over, trying to get it.

He held it out of my reach. "Naw, we about to call the man that you brought into our relationship."

"Ivan don't."

"Watch me. It's ringing." Ivan put it on speakerphone.

"Hey Bae!" Stoney said.

Ivan glanced at me. "Who the fuck is this?"

Thank goodness. I didn't have Stoney's name programed in my phone.

"Who the fuck is this?" Stoney hollered back.

"Her muthafuckin husband, nicca!"

I got nervous when I heard Stoney laugh. I mean, he cracked the fuck up. "Not for long. That sweet pussy belongs to me. Ask her how many times I made her cum? Ain't no way you can satisfy her after I put my dick down."

Ivan was flying through the streets. Barely turning corners. Almost running lights. Rolling through stop signs. "I ain't gotta ask her shit. I know my woman. She might have slipped up with you but she will always be loyal to my dick. My name is tatted on her pussy forever. Until death do us part, nicca."

"You wish. You getting my seconds, nicca. Ask her who hit it first."

"You still on the side of the road? I'm on my way to see you, punk muthafucka."

CLICK!

"I know this bitch nicca didn't just hang up on me." Ivan hit redial. Stoney's voicemail came on. "Scary ass." Pissed, he clicked my phone off and tossed it in the backseat. "And what the fuck is he talking about? He hit it first?"

"I-I don't know," I stammered, nervous as hell.

"You don't know, huh?"

I looked out the window to avoid his stare.

"I bet you knew when you opened your legs to that nicca."

Ivan rolled through the light driving further and further into an isolated area that I'd never seen before. It looked abandoned, like all the business packed up and left the area. He kept on driving until he found a really secluded spot that was camouflaged by four tall, empty buildings. It looked like mob bosses brought people here to torture them.

Tears came to my eyes.

"Fuck you crying for?" Ivan stopped the car between two buildings. He stared me down, shaking his head. "You're nothing but a fuckin cunt."

"I'm sorry," I said, realizing how stupid I sounded. It was a little too late to be apologizing. I'd been denying my infidelity the whole time. Arguing and flipping things around on him to make him think I was telling the truth. I even accused him of having an affair, just so I wouldn't look guilty. Ivan might be crazy, but he never cheated. I know that for a fact.

"Oh, you about to be real sorry."

Everybody Got A Secret 2: A Drama Filled Romance

I wondered what he was about to do.

Ivan unfastened his pants, pulling out his massive erection. "Suck it."

"No, Ivan, please," I begged. He knew I didn't like giving him head. I rarely did it so it would figure this would be his way of punishing me.

I sat there crying.

Ivan grabbed me by my neck pushing my face to his crotch. "Either you suck it or I really lose my cool."

My tears fell on his lap as I took his dick into my mouth. He grabbed my head, nearly choking me, thrusting his dick to the back of my throat. I gagged while Ivan moaned. He was taking pleasure in my agony. After what seemed like forever, Ivan released his seed in my mouth.

When he let my head go, I rose up, ready to spit that shit out.

"Swallow it," he said through gritted teeth.

I couldn't. I felt myself about to throw up when I opened the door, spitting his cum out.

"See, I tried to be nice to you. Get the fuck out." He kicked me with all his might. I fell out of the car into the gravel.

"Stop!" I screamed. "You know how much I don't like giving head."

"I don't give a fuck what you like." Ivan jumped out of the car, racing around to the other side, towering over me. "You smell just like that nicca too." He grabbed my foot dragging me a little. My shirt rose up, skinning up my back. "Take this shit off!" he yelled, snatching off my shoes.

I kicked at him, but he caught my feet. Stooping down, he yanked my shirt, ripping it. "Quit, Ivan! You play too much."

"I'm not playing. You coming out this shit." After tearing my delicate shirt to shreds, he began tugging at my skirt until I was left in my bra and panties.

I rolled onto my stomach, skinning up my knees. Standing to my feet, I started running, but I didn't get far without having my shoes on. The rocks were tearing my feet up.

Ivan was on my heels, grabbing me. He picked me up and tossed me across the hood of the hot car. I started crying even harder when he gripped my hair, yanking my head towards him.

"Shut the fuck up and take the rest of that shit off."

"Please, Ivan, I know I messed up, but baby, you're making everything worse."

Ivan huffed like a madman. "I said, "Shut the fuck up, and take the shit off, before I do it for you."

I knew that I pushed him to this point. More tears streamed down my face as I unhooked my bra, allowing it to fall on the hood of the car. I guess I wasn't moving fast enough for Ivan so he tore my panties off, throwing them in the air.

Flipping me onto my stomach, he pulled my legs until I was hanging off the side of the car with my ass exposed. I screamed when his heavy hand struck my bottom. I closed my eyes, trying not to concentrate on the sting from my backside.

"You deserve every one of these hits." Slap! Slap! Slap! "Whore." Slap! Slap! Slap! Slap! "Slut." Slap! Slap! Slap! Slap! "Dirty, nasty little cunt."

"Ivan, you're hurting me!" Slap! Slap! Slap! Slap!

"So, the fuck what! You didn't care if you were hurting me when you fucked another nicca. Did you?" Slap! Slap! Slap! Slap! Slap! "I bet you're real wet right now. Aren't you?" Rubbing between my legs, he felt a puddle. "A fuckin whore. Just like I said. Only a whore would be this wet after being forced across the hood of a car, getting her ass slapped. I guess you really do like it rough. You weren't playing when you asked me to do it harder, were you?"

Maybe Ivan was right. I didn't have a clue what was wrong with me. As guilty as I felt, I had no idea why all this abuse had me super turned on.

"Well, that's exactly what I'm going to give you," Ivan said, ramming into me. He yanked me by my hair, thrusting as fast as he could. "I can't believe you gave my pussy away. Do you know how many times I could have cheated on you?"

"Aaaah!" I moaned, loving how good Ivan felt.

28

Everybody Got A Secret 2: A Drama Filled Romance

"I'm pouring my heart out to you, and all you can do is moan? Fucking slut." He let go of my hair, gripping my hips as he thrust even harder. "This is what you like? That hardcore shit."

I sucked in a deep breath as I climaxed. "Aaaaaaaaah! Aaaaaaaaah! Aaaaaaaaah! Aaaaaaaaah!"

Ivan climaxed too. Low guttural groans as he deposited inside of me. I was shocked that he came in me. It's been years.

Ivan pulled out backing away from me. He tucked his dick away, picked up my skirt, tattered shirt, and bra, walking around the car. "I hope you got a way home."

I jumped off the car, racing around to the passenger's seat. "Where are you going?" I banged on the window. "Don't leave me."

Ivan threw the car in reverse, quickly backing away. "Tell that nicca you fucked to come and get you, since you were all on his dick just a minute ago.

I ran after the car as he pulled away, laughing at me. "Good luck getting home, bitch!"

When he drove out of my sight, I fell on my bare ass, crying my eyes out. Ivan has done some mean things to me, but this incident here has to be the worse. I should have left with Marcel like he asked me to. Now, I was somewhere unknown, naked, with no phone, and no way home. Besides, my feet were already hurting and probably cut up from running across the rocks.

The only thing I could do was pray. God, please help me. I know what I did was wrong, but I don't deserve to be naked and abandoned in the middle of nowhere.

I'm not sure how long I sat there in the cold. It felt like forever. As I was about to pray again, I heard a car approaching. When it came into view, I saw it was Ivan.

"Get your stupid ass in before I change my mind."

I hopped up from where I was running as fast as I could before he changed his mind. "Thank you, God," I said as I approached the car.

As I was about to get in, Ivan stopped me. He tossed my clothes out the window. It landed on the ground and I had to fetch it like a dog. "Put that shit on. You can't be riding around with me like that."

As soon as my ass hit the seat, Ivan started in on me again. "Did you call that nicca? Why he ain't come and get you?"

"I couldn't call him. My phone was in the car with you."

"Wrong muthafuckin answer." He handed me my phone. "Call that nicca now then. Ask him to come get your sloppy, cheating ass."

Ivan had really lost his mind. I was trying to give him a chance to get his frustration out because I was wrong, but this shit was ridiculous. "I'm not calling him."

"You better or you'll have your ass right back sitting in them damn rocks."

I huffed, dialing the number. I hoped that Stoney didn't answer.

"Put that shit on speaker." I did as he said. The phone rang until Stoney's voicemail came on.

"And this the nicca that you fucked around with? He won't even answer his phone for you. You could be dying right now. You throwing your marriage in the toilet for a muthafucka that don't give a fuck about you. You's a stupid ass chick. Get your damn mind right. This is why I talk to you the way I do. I'm starting to think you're real fuckin slow."

In the back of my mind, I was hoping that Ivan was wrong about Stoney. I fucked my marriage up and this nicca was ghost. He talked all that shit in the Bahamas about how he was going to be by my side and to call him at any time. Fuckin liar.

Ivan laughed at me like he just read my thoughts, pulling off towards the expressway again.

Any other time, I might have cussed his ass out, but he was right. I played myself. Drained physically and mentally, I pulled my knees up to my chest with my head facing the window, silently crying.

I barely breathed, thinking that at any moment, Ivan was going to put me out again, making me walk home. Meanwhile,

Everybody Got A Secret 2: A Drama Filled Romance

Ivan ignored me, cranking up the music, rapping the rest of the way home.

I let out a sigh of relief when he finally pulled into our driveway. Getting out of the car, I quietly followed him to the door.

I was about to go back to the car to get my luggage when Ivan grabbed me by the arm, yanking me towards the master bathroom. "I can still smell that nicca on you. Jump your ass in the shower before you really piss me off."

By this time, I had a serious headache from crying my eyes out. "Did you muthafuckin hear me?" Before I could respond, he was in my face, ripping my clothes off once again. "That vacation must've fucked up your hearing too. You came back special than a muthafucka."

"I heard you," I said in a low voice.

"Well, fucking act like it. Moving like you got all damn day. Get that nicca's scent off your ass!" Ivan stared me down. "You should be glad I'm still here. Any other nicca would have left your ass in an alley somewhere, fucked up."

"I'm grateful," I mumbled. I didn't want to set him off even more. I jumped into the shower, grabbing my sponge, lathering up. The sooner I got Stoney's scent off me, the sooner Ivan would calm down. Although, I wasn't so for sure about that either. He was pretty angry.

Ivan grabbed the hand-held scrub brush that I used to clean the bathroom. He poured liquid soap on it and walked in my direction. I thought he was going to clean the walls or something. It didn't make sense to me, but at this point, nothing he did made any sense.

"Ow! Ow! Ow! Ow! Ow!" I screamed when the bristles scarred my skin. It was the most intense burn I'd ever felt. Worse than sliding on the rocks. I reached out trying to grab the scrub brush from him and accidently socked him in the face.

Ivan paused, looking at me like he was about to really fuck me up.

"I'm sorry," I said quickly. "I was just trying to get the brush away from you. That's all."

I started crying even more when he dropped the brush, holding his jaw. "You've fucked up now, bitch," Ivan said, socking me in the eye. I fell back against the shower wall, slipping and falling back into the tub, hitting my head.

I sat there in a daze when Ivan reached into the tub, giving me three body blows.

I took all this shit in an attempt to make peace for what I did. I was starting to see that there was no peace. Ivan was going to keep at it until he hurt me really bad. I was afraid, but I knew I had to try and fight him back. The moment he leaned in to hit me again, I swung my arms and legs like a wild woman.

"Well, look who woke the fuck up from all that crying and shit. You think you can take me, bitch?" He gave me this crazed look.

Ivan had never called me a bitch before today. Now, every other word that came out his mouth was bitch. This let me know that I wasn't dealing with my husband anymore. This person talking to me was a complete stranger. "It takes a bitch to know a bitch," I said standing up in the tub.

Ivan slapped me so hard that I fell back into the tub. I swung at him too, connecting another punch with his jaw.

It was on and popping after that.

He reached for me and I pulled him into the tub, quickly jumping out. He must've fell hard because I had time to put on a T-shirt. Ivan was furious when he got out. He charged at me like one of his football buddies, knocking me back onto the bed, choking me.

"You gon die today, bitch. Your time is muthafuckin up."

I clawed at his fingers around my neck, unable to speak.

"I might as well get some more pussy before you check the fuck out."

It hurt when Ivan entered me. This was the first time his ten inches brought me so much pain.

Everybody Got A Secret 2: A Drama Filled Romance

"You're still wet. Even when someone is about to kill your ass, your pussy is still soaked. Now if that ain't a whore in action, I don't know what is. I bet you like being raped too."

I felt myself losing oxygen as Ivan thrust deep inside of me. He grunted and moaned like I was giving him the best sex of his life.

"Ah fuck! This shit is so good. I'm about to squirt in this tight, gushy pussy."

Ivan squeezed my neck as hard as he could when he came.

A single tear rolled down my cheek as I took my last breath.

Chapter 4

Keystone

It pained me to walk away from Vanity. I had a nagging feeling that something was about to pop off. It was one of those feelings that I just couldn't shake. I tried to think about something else. I even tried to push those bad thoughts to the back of my mind. Nothing seemed to work. I kept feeling like she was in danger.

Besides, I knew Ivan. That nicca wasn't playing with a full deck. As far as I was concerned, he never had one. That's why I was surprised that Vanity married him. I'm assuming that he never showed her his other side. Rumor had it that he flew off the handle quite often. He had all the characteristics of a psycho. Impatient, picky, egotistical, hot-headed, and a downright I don't give a fuck about you attitude.

Ivan should have been history. If I didn't have my own issues when we were younger, I'm sure she would have stayed with me. She would have been my wife. Not his. And she wouldn't have to deal with being unhappy because I would make sure she never wanted for anything. She knew I loved her. I made that very clear from day one.

I might have messed up back then, but I was about to make things right now. That's why I went to the Bahamas. To take her away from that crazy ass nicca and make her mine again. She didn't belong to him. She belonged to me. We just fit. No arguments. Compatible, extreme chemistry, and the sex was magnificent.

Just like I was her first, she was mine too. We might have been young but we were a couple of freaks. After she got comfortable with having sex, we got it in everywhere. Yeah, Ivan was still in the picture. Way in the background though. Temporarily, he forgot about Vanity while he was messing with a well-known slut named Lila. A chick that I wouldn't touch if I had a bulletproof dick. Everything about that hood rat was nasty. She looked like she had some shit. Even her walk was stank. A big wide ass gap.

Vanity, on the other hand, she had freak in her but she always remained classy. Her freak meter was controlled by me. For example, she didn't like giving head. I respected that. She turned me on so much that I didn't need her too. One look at her and my dick got rocked up anyway.

I bet Ivan would be jealous if he knew that I was the only man that Vanity enjoyed giving head to. I'm sure she didn't pleasure him like she pleasured me. He was probably begging for a little mouth action. I never had to. She always offered. Just like in the Bahamas, she willingly went down on me. I tried to get her to stop, but she wanted to stay sucking my dick. But that's how things have always been between us. Because I would do the same for her. Lick her whenever she wanted me too.

Ivan was going to be even more salty when he found out she was carrying my baby. I'm glad he didn't want kids with her. My aim was to get her pregnant during our vacation anyway. So, when she said she wanted a baby, I jumped at the opportunity to knock her up. That made things easier for me. Ain't no way she could stay married to him if she was pregnant by me.

I loved everything about Vanity except for one thing. Like a typical woman she liked playing mind games. She might not realize it, but it was manipulative. Back in the day, I just let her have her way. We're too grown for that now. I needed her to mean what she says and say what she means. I didn't have time to pick her brain like we're on a game show.

And this is why I smashed Pebbles. I knew that Vanity was telling me what she thought I wanted to hear. The thing is she never asked me. She just assumed. I'm nobody's puppet on a string. She can't just say or do things that might hurt me and keep it moving like I have no feelings whatsoever.

Do I regret being intimate with Pebbles? Just a little. I don't feel bad for sleeping with her. I feel bad because now I feel some kinda way about her. It's like Pandora's Box has been opened. When I set out to bone her, I never thought her pussy would be so sweet.

Don't get me wrong Vanity's pussy is just as sweet, but Vanity isn't uninhibited liked Pebbles. She makes no excuses for loving sex. And the way she acts in the bedroom is priceless. She fucks me like my dick belongs to her. She has no problem doing whatever feels good to her. And if that means she has to let it all hang out to get what she wants, she has no problem with that either. I liked a bold, aggressive woman in the bedroom who wanted to fuck me just as much as I wanted to fuck her. And Pebbles, she put it on me, making a brother feel addicted.

I laughed.

"What's so funny?" Kim asked, snapping me back to reality. Her name was Kimaya but I always called her Kim.

"Nothing," I replied, giving Vanity one last look before I made a U-turn. I'll be back for you, bae.

"Don't look like nothing to me," she said, rubbing my thigh, looking at my erection.

I pushed her hand off my leg. "It's nothing." I was horny as hell but I didn't want her. I wanted Vanity.

"Nothing sure looks like something to me."

"Well, it's not," I said, maneuvering into airport traffic.

Kim fell back in her seat with her arms crossed. "I bet if I was Vanity, it would be something."

Everybody Got A Secret 2: A Drama Filled Romance

She knew mentioning Vanity's name would get a rise out of me. "Yeah, well, you're not," I snapped. "So get the fuck over it."

"Baby, I don't get it. She doesn't love you like I do. I'll do anything for you. That's why I proposed to you. I can't see my life without you."

Everything that Kim said was true. I had no doubt that she loved me. I just didn't love her the same. I'm not sure why. Kim was real hot. I mean sizzling red hot. Sexy as fuck, hot. From her good looks to her bombshell body she could turn any man on.

Her mother was from Taiwan and her father was Black. Her father met her mother while he was in the service. They married a year before Kim was born. She was the oldest of four girls. Other than her jet black silky hair and slanted, round Asian eyes, she looked like any other Black chick with a cinnamon complexion.

Her pussy skills were tight. Her head game was legendary. Plump ass. Nice breasts. Tiny waist. Wide hips. She was all natural too. She stayed in the gym at least two hours a day to make sure her body stayed right. She cooked. She cleaned. She washed clothes. No man could ask for a better woman. Still, I wasn't in love with her.

"You're in love with another woman, but you're engaged to me." She sighed. "How is our marriage supposed to work when I'm the only one committed to us?"

"I don't know," I said, honestly.

I only accepted her proposal to piss Cash off. The look on his face was priceless. I had no intentions of marrying her. I just hadn't found the right time to break things off. I was having too much fun, poking at Cash about his failed relationship with her. I found the shit hilarious how she dumped him, but she was all on my dick. Cash tried to hide it, but he still wasn't over his breakup with Kim. He loved Karen with all his heart, but Kim was his first love. He fell hard for her. I find it so ironic that only days before she left him, he had the nerve to give me relationship advice.

I laughed again.

Kim sucked in air. "Am I a joke to you?"

"No, I wasn't laughing at you." I wiped the smile off my face. Regardless of my feelings for Vanity, Kim was still my woman. I cared about her, even though I wasn't in love with her. And I had no intentions of treating her badly just because my heart was elsewhere. "C'mere."

Kim took off her seatbelt, scooting closer to me. I gave her a passionate kiss while were we stalled in airport traffic.

"That's what I'm talking about, Daddy. Let me handle that big dick for you."

"No," I said, pushing her hand away again. "Sit back and put your seatbelt back on before I get a ticket."

Her hand landed back in my lap. This time she began unfastening my pants. "But I missed you. Let me show you how much." Her soft hands reached through my open zipper, pulling out my hardness, swallowing my penis whole.

"Fuck!" I closed my eyes with my head against the headrest, thinking about Vanity. Our passionate kisses. Naked images. How good her warm pussy felt.

Enjoying the feel of Kim's wet mouth, I almost forgot I was in traffic, nearly running into the back of this white Lexus. I let go of Kim's hair and swerved around it just in time.

"Drive faster, Daddy. You know I like it when you speed. That shit makes my pussy drip."

Dirty talk really did it for me. I liked the back and forth thing and when women played hard to get. My foot slammed down on the accelerator, pushing my Carrera over ninety miles an hour.

Kim's mouth felt wonderful. With one hand on the steering wheel and the other hand tangled up in her hair, I began to thrust upward, fucking her mouth. "Yeah, baby, suck it."

"Anything for you, Daddy," Kim said, taking a dick break before she went back to deep-throating.

Weeee-Errrrrrrrrr-Weeeeee-Errrrrrrrr-Weeeeee-Errrrrrrrr

Everybody Got A Secret 2: A Drama Filled Romance

I saw flashing red and blue lights. Quickly, my eyes watch the speedometer. I was doing ninety-five. The police car weaved in and out of cars until he got behind me.

"Suck harder," I told Kim. I was about to get a ticket anyway so I might as well bust a nut first.

Recklessly, I closed my eyes, fucking her mouth until I came. "Sssssssssss. Aaaaaaaaah! Fuuuuccccck!" I moaned, busting off in her mouth. Kim kept on sucking, swallowing every drop.

"What the hell?" she asked, finally looking up and seeing the officer flying down the highway behind us. "You could have said that the cops were behind us."

I smirked. "Oh, yeah, I wanted to tell you, but I was too busy enjoying myself. Be cool. Sit back and put your seatbelt on."

Shifting lanes, I made my way over to the shoulder and the police officer did too. I wasn't worried about no cop. However, this ticket was going to be nasty as fuck.

I waited patiently in the car while the officer, got out. He coolly walked towards my car with his standard uniform and dark shades.

I rolled down the window when he approached my vehicle. "Good day, officer."

"License and registration."

Pussy ass cop. I grabbed my wallet, pulling out my license. Kim handed me the registration. I was about to hand it to him when he busted out laughing. "Nicca, you was shook. Look at your face."

He took off his glasses. It was my cousin Angelino aka Angel. My Uncle Antonio's oldest child. "Fool, you almost made me wreck." I hopped out the car, showing him some love.

"Your ass was scared." He was still laughing at me. "Nicca, you was about to piss on yourself and shit."

"Nah. I was cool. I was like fuck it. I was speeding. Just give me my damn ticket so I can be on my way."

"You was driving like I used to back in the day when shit was hot."

We both laughed. Angel wasn't always on the right side of the law.

"Nah, I was getting my dick sucked, if you must know. Why the fuck are you on patrol harassing me? Ain't your ass FBI? Shouldn't you be FBI'ing some shit?"

Angel grinned. "Man, both of my captains, old and new, are best friends. So when Ecko and I got our asses handed to us for that last bullshit case, my new captain thought it would be cute for us to work patrol again. But enough about me. How was the Bahamas? Did you hit it? All that talking you did about her. Please tell me you fucked."

I pulled out my phone, showing him a picture of me and Vanity. "Does it look like I fucked?"

Angel put his fist up to his mouth and bit it before laughing aloud. "Damn, baby is bad. I know you wore her little pretty ass out. She got a sister?"

"You know I did. Yeah, I hit that too."

"Get the fuck outta here. I should have went on this trip. That's too much pussy for you. Let me see what her sister looks like."

I flipped through and showed him a picture of Pebbles when we were all spending the day at the beach. She was sexy in a string bikini.

"Shit!" Angel grabbed his dick. "I need some lotion."

I chuckled. "Your ass is a pervert."

"It's my dick. I'll beat the muthafucka if I want to."

I laughed even harder. "Why the hell are you still single anyway?"

Angel was a really good looking dude. He was my first cousin so we favored a lot, especially with the light eyes. He's dated some fly-ass chicks so if he was beating his dick, it was because he wanted to.

"I'm sick of banging hoes and thots. They fuck good, but they come with too much bullshit. The last one I was dealing with almost got me locked the fuck up. How the hell would that look? I'm in a cell with the same niccas I just put away. Fuck that. And you know Pops ain't going for them slip ups. I'm not trying to get mangled over no bitch. Besides, I'm ready to settle down. You feel sorry for me?" He gave me a fake-ass sad look.

"Muthafucka, I don't feel sorry for you. Not at all."

Angel cracked up. "You don't? Why not?" He laughed even more.

"Nicca, get the fuck on. You got pussy laying at your feet. Chicks love you. They practically knock me down to get to your ass."

"That's bullshit and you know it." Angel was still looking at my pictures from the vacation when Marcel's name flashed across the screen. "You got a call, bro."

I answered it on speaker phone. "What's good?"

"STONEY, I SWEAR, I ALMOST FUCKED THAT PUNK NICCA UP. HE MUTHAFUCKIN LUCKY THAT I CAN'T AFFORD NO BAD PRESS RIGHT NOW. YOU JUST DON'T KNOW HOW BAD I WANTED TO KNUCKLE UP."

I looked at Angel and he looked at me. Marcel never lost control like this. "Wait a minute. Now, what had happened?"

"NAH, FUCK THAT PUSSY NICCA."

"Aight, man, but you need to calm down. Where y'all at?"

Marcel let out a long, breath. "Stuck in fuckin airport traffic. We haven't even left this bitch yet."

I heard Cash in the background. "We just had a run in with Ivan's mental ass. That's why Marcel is heated. He wanted to put his hands on him."

"Word? What happened, though?"

"I wanted to murder this nicca. He had me tight, yo. You would have lost it if you were there too."

"Fuck him, Marcel," I heard Cash say. "He's not worth it. That broke nicca wishes he was you. Don't fuck up what you built over his dickhead ass. He's a back-biting, bottom-feeder."

Cash must've taken Marcel's phone because I heard Cash clearer and Marcel sounded further away. "Bro, look, Marcel and Ivan had words. A stand-off right at the airport. It was about to get ugly if I hadn't stopped Marcel. All of us would be in jail right now. He was about to pound this nicca's brains out."

"He didn't put his hands on him, did he?" I asked.

"Naw, he kept it cool, but I knew he wanted to. You know Marcel keeps his poker face. But I think that's why he is so angry. He wanted to react and he couldn't."

"This shit is wild." My eyes met Angel's again. "Well, I'm not too far away. I'm standing on the side of the road with Angel. He thought it was cute to pull me over."

"Oh, yeah? Tell him what up."

"What up, cuzzo," Angel said.

"I got you on speaker phone, Cash. Where was Vanity when all this went down? Is she ok?"

"She was there and then she left with that pussy. She could be cut up in little pieces by now. He had this crazy look in his eye. You know, the kind all the serial killers have right before they go postal."

I scratched my head. I knew I had a bad feeling about leaving her. "Don't let Marcel do nothing stupid. He's spazzin right now and I don't want him to risk his brand. I'll handle it."

"What are you going to do? I don't want you getting your hands dirty either. Ivan is scum. He'd be glad to drag you down to the pits of hell with him."

I was about to answer Cash when I saw Vanity drive pass in a black BMW. I assumed Ivan was driving. I stared at the car, memorizing the license plate as it went by. "Aye, Cash, let me get back at you. They just drove by."

"Who?"

"Ivan and Vanity."

"You sure? What kinda car was it?"

"A black BMW."

"Yeah, that was them. Be careful. I know I don't show it much, but I care about what happens to you, bro."

Me and Angel snickered. Sentimental ass. "Aight, nicca, nothing is going to happen to me."

Angel spoke into the mouthpiece. "Ain't shit going down, Cash. You know how we roll. This Ivan nicca bet not fuck with

Everybody Got A Secret 2: A Drama Filled Romance

Stoney. La Familia. He'll wish he never crossed my path. I'll skin his ass alive."

I was a tough nicca, but I cringed when Angel said that because I knew he meant it. My Uncle Antonio's kids were ruthless. Honestly, I think that's why Uncle Antonio had so many children. So that he knew who had his back in these streets. It was about thirty of them. Most of them were cold-blooded killers. That's how he raised them. Uncle Antonio personally trained them in weaponry. They were people you didn't want to fuck with. Being responsible for most of the missing person's cases and the most heinous crimes in Chicago. All of his kids were well-diverse in street affairs as well as high-society.

Uncle Antonio learned from the best—The Chicago Mafia. Started by my grandfather Chewy Gunz and his twin brother Richie Muscle. I guess violence was in our blood since we were part of the Chicago Crime Family also known as The First Family in these streets. My grandfather and great uncle were legends. They ran the largest crime organization in the United States and walked away from over fifty indictments. To this day, I still don't know how they beat those charges and walked free. The case got thrown out. Just like that.

The next day, Uncle Antonio took over. And just to make sure the streets were secure and people knew who was in control, he started his own gang called The Panthers. They were his muscle. Doing all the foul shit that was necessary to keep the drugs flowing smoothly.

My Uncles Domingo and Armando, on my mother's side, were my Uncle Antonio's connect. They got the purest coke from Peru, which was transported from the Dominican Republic to the United States. I don't know how me and my brothers escaped a life of crime, especially when crime surrounded us on both sides of our family.

After Cash hung up, I rattled off Ivan's license plate to Angel. He began searching information on him from his squad car.

"I'm not finding nothing except for a few tickets that were paid." He picked up his phone. "I'm going to text Amante. He'll be able to pull more info for you."

I'm sure it was in code. They had this made up language that I barely knew because I didn't major in organized crime like Angel and Amante did. Angel was a gang-related, drug-dealing, crooked cop. Amante was the leader of the Panther's Street Gang by night. A barber, landlord to one of the best buildings downtown, and a soon-to-be lawyer by day. Yes, my family believed in getting that money. Legal and illegal.

While Angel spoke to his younger brother, I decided to text Vanity. As soon as I was about to hit send, a text from her came through. I must've been on her mind like she was on mine. That unbreakable bond.

Vanity: You good? We just rolled by you.

Me: Yeah, I'm straight. Are you ok? I miss you.

Vanity: I miss you too.

It took her a moment to reply back. Now, I was worried for her safety. This nicca might be aware that she's texting me. I was relieved when she called me instead. "Hey, Bae!"

My jaw twitched when I heard Ivan's voice. "Who the fuck is this?"

"Who the fuck is this?" I hollered in that nicca's ear. I wanted to yank his ass through his phone.

"Her muthafuckin husband, nicca!" He had the nerve to say.

I laughed in his ear. He might have Vanity scared, but he sure as fuck didn't scare me. "Not for long. That sweet pussy belongs to me. Ask her how many times I made her cum? Ain't no way you can satisfy her after I put my dick down."

I didn't intend to go there, but Ivan had a way of pressing all the wrong buttons. I see why Marcel was livid. I was shitty off this brief conversation.

I heard the anger in Ivan's voice. "I ain't gotta ask her shit. I know my woman. She might have slipped up with you but she will always be loyal to me. My name is tatted on her pussy."

44

Everybody Got A Secret 2: A Drama Filled Romance

"You wish. You getting my seconds, nicca. Ask her who hit it first."

"You still on the side of the road? I'm on my way to see you, punk muthafucka."

CLICK!

I didn't have time to argue with this nicca. "Angel, I'ma have to roll out. Did you tell Amante what was up?"

"Yeah. He said he will text you in a bit."

"Aight. Cool. I'll catch you later."

"Call me if you need me. I'll get all in that nicca's ass. That way you don't have to get your hands dirty."

"Ok. I'm going to try and keep this peaceful, but I don't know. You might be getting a call."

"I'll be on the lookout."

We dapped it up and I got back in the car. "Wow!"

"Surprise, Daddy." Kim was completely naked. One foot on the dashboard, exposing her neatly trimmed pussy. She threw her head back, dipping two fingers inside. "Let me suck you off again. Show you how much I miss that big dick."

Shit. I jumped in the car just now realizing how cold it was outside. My hands were freezing. I left my gloves in the car. Cutting the heat on blast, I unzipped my pants, freeing my erection.

Kim stopped playing in her pussy, sliding over, leaning into my seat. She held my rigid pole in her hand stroking it up and down. "I just love giving you head, Daddy." While stroking me, she got on her knees in the seat with her ass in the air, giving my member tongue kisses.

My hand caressed her backside before sliding two fingers into her wet hole. She rocked back and forth against my fingers while her lips stayed wrapped around my stiffness.

This is what I liked about Kim. She was always in the mood and willing to please me anytime, anyplace.

"Your fingers feel so good, Daddy." She slobbed on my knob while twisting her hips on my fingers. "And your dick tastes even better. You ready to cum in my mouth again, Daddy?"

Damn, I loved the way she said, Daddy.

Chapter 5

Ivan

I was sitting on the bed next to Vanity's motionless body, smoking a square and thinking. My mind scanned over everything that happened from the time she walked out that door to go on vacation up until now.

I was so fuckin pissed off at Vanity. A part of me was hoping her stupid ass was dead. She threw away years on a quick fuck with some no-name nicca. If I had known that, I would have never gotten married. What made me even angrier was I passed up a lot of pussy being faithful to her spoiled ass.

I know, I spoiled her too, but I had no choice. Her fuckin father gave her the world so she expected me to do the same. What kind of husband would I be if I couldn't treat her as well as her own daddy, if not better?

What had me heated was, no matter what I did for her, it was never good enough. No matter how much I gave her, she needed more. She was never satisfied with simple things. She needed extravagant over the top shit. That's why I didn't want a baby. I couldn't afford to spoil her and the baby. That six-thousand square feet house that cost over $500,000 had me tapped out. Four bedrooms, five baths, a stunning patio, in-ground pool, and a landscape that was fit for royalty.

Princess Diamond

At this moment, I was glad I didn't have kids by her. I wasn't sure if I wanted to stay married to her. If she had kids, then divorcing her wouldn't be an option. I grew up in a two-parent household and my kids were going to have the same thing.

The more I kept thinking about Vanity and this nicca, the angrier I got.

A fit of rage came over me. I jumped off the bed, seething. Staring down at her, I began to imagine all the horrible things I wanted to do to her. Taking the cigarette in my hand, I began to burn her flesh with it. I wanted to hurt her. It would make me feel better by inflicting pain on her. I started at her foot and burned my way up to her breasts. The cigarette was only inches from her face when I stopped. The conversation replayed with that nicca in my mind.

Fuck it. She'll heal.

I began to put little burn holes on her face.

I looked down at Vanity's lifeless body again.

Was the bitch dead?

Now, I was starting to get nervous. Prancing out of the bedroom, into the bathroom, I retrieved one of her compact mirrors. Returning bedside, I put the mirror under her nose to see if she was still breathing. When I didn't see anything, panic set in, for real. I started pouring down sweat.

Did I really kill her?

Leaning down, I put my ear to her chest. She had a faint heartbeat. I took a deep breath. That's all I needed to know.

Damn, she looked good. The T-shirt was up around her waist, exposing her sweet vagina. Her harden nipples poked through the white shirt. She looked as if she was striking a sexy pose just for me.

My dick got hard instantly. I figured I better get one more fuck in. When she finally woke up, I know I wasn't going to get any for a while. Going for it, I yanked her legs open wide and shoving my dick into her hole. I wanted to put a hurting on her coochie the same way she put a hurting on my heart. Holding her lifeless body like a ragdoll, I wrapped her thighs around my arms, ramming her pussy up until I busted off a nice load.

After washing up and changing my clothes, I headed out to the weed spot. I hated coming to that muthafucka, but I needed a blunt badly. Usually, I called my boy Row and he would meet me somewhere. He always brought what I needed, whenever I needed it. However, I had been calling him half the day and he hadn't hit me back yet. This was an emergency. Vanity had my nerves on edge. If I didn't get a blunt soon, I was going to wild the fuck out.

Everyone knew the Panther's sold the best shit in the city. Hell, maybe even the Midwest. From what I heard, all of their products were bona fide. Everything they had was pure. The smoke smelled homegrown. Like the shit was fresh out someone's botanical garden. I wouldn't put it pass them if someone had a secret garden somewhere in South Shore, growing pot.

Sitting in the driveway, I scrolled through my downloads. I was about to get nice so I needed the right music. I came across Marcel's tracks. Delete! Fuck that piece of shit, faggot-looking muthafucka. I wasn't a fan. Vanity liked listening to his lame ass shit. He was overrated if you asked me. I could give two fucks if I ever heard or saw the nicca ever again.

I settled on Drake, peeling out of my driveway, headed to the Panther's block in Jackson Park. I have no damn idea why they called it The Block. They had the whole area on lock. That's why I hated the idea of coming over this way. The niccas in charge looked like highly-trained killing machines. And they didn't give no fucks about nothing. They made even the hardest muthafucka shit on themselves.

As soon as I pulled up on The Panther's Block, niccas with guns came out of nowhere, pointing the shit at my BMW. I even saw a few snipers on roofs. This is why I didn't like coming to this muthafucka. I wasn't a fuckin narc. All I wanted was a few blunts so I could smoke away my troubles.

"Get the fuck out the car," the gorilla looking nicca with a shotgun demanded. "Don't make me ask you twice."

I raised my hands in the air about to take my keys out of the ignition before I got out.

"Naw, homie, leave the muthafuckin keys. Who you here to see?" I took a look around me before I answered. Not only was I outnumbered but I wasn't strapped either. I couldn't even defend myself if I wanted to.

"Row," I said, shitty as a bitch.

"I don't know no muthafuckin Row, nicca. I should blow your fucking face off for wasting my damn time."

I cocked my head to the side. This some bullshit. "I cop from Row all the damn time. I know Row in this piece some- where. All I want is some blunts. Save this bullshit for the rats. I don't have time for the theatrics. I got enough bullshit going on in my life."

Gorilla nodded his head at someone but they were all fro- zen like chess pieces with their guns pointed at me.

"Call Row and tell him Ivan is here. He knows me. We grew up together. I—"

"Shut the fuck up!" Gorilla exclaimed, practically shoving the shotgun up my nose. "Don't say shit until I tell you, bitch, or your brains will be splattered all over the ground."

I got the hint loud and clear. Shutting the fuck up. I stood there looking unfazed. However, the angry mugs, fancy guns, and rolling up on a brother twenty-deep, had me feeling shook like a mug.

"He's good," I heard Row say behind me.

Gorilla didn't remove his shotgun from my face so I didn't bother turning around. I just stood there like a mummy.

Row approached Gorilla. "He good. Stand down."

Finally, Gorilla lowered his gun. It wasn't pointed at my face anymore. He lowered it to my legs.

"Look, Row, I didn't come here for all this. Can I just get my blunts? Y'all doing the most over here."

Row laughed. I didn't see a muthafuckin thing funny. "Joe, I got you." He turned around to the dude to my right who had a Tec-9 pointed at me. "Get me ten, Lil Glizzy."

Everybody Got A Secret 2: A Drama Filled Romance

The young soldier dropped his gun to his side, strolling down the block.

"What are you doing here?" Row asked me.

Shit, I was wondering why the fuck I came on The Block my damn self. If Vanity hadn't stressed me the fuck out, I would have just copped some bullshit weed around the way.

Row stared at me for a moment. "Next time, call me like you usually do. I'll bring it to you. Don't come back here again."

"Aight, that'll work." He didn't have that to worry about.

The young soldier came back with my blunts. I paid Row and eased my ass off the fucking Block. He didn't have to worry about me ever coming back again.

I was smart enough to avoid joining a gang. That didn't mean that I didn't have a few Panthers in my back pocket. They were the largest gang in Chicagoland. Though, they were the quietest and the smartest too. They moved in silence and they were quite sophisticated to be a street gang.

Once I was back in civilization, I decided to stop at the liquor store off Stoney Island and get a fifth of Hennessy to go with my freshly rolled blunts. It was beyond crowded in his joint. Something told me to go to one closer to the crib, but I said nah. I figured I was already here. Got a decent park out front. That almost never happens. My aim was to run in and get it right quick and roll out.

"What's happening, youngster," an older cat said, coming out as I was coming in. I had no idea who this drunk ass nicca was.

He held the door for me. "Nothing much, my brother. Thanks." As I was about to walk inside, this rude ass young dude rushed in front of me, stepping on my J's. "Excuse you. Watch where you're going. You just stepped on my kicks."

"Shit, you should have been walking faster."

"What the fuck you say?" I asked, stepping inside, letting the door close behind me. I heard his punk ass, but I just needed to make sure that's what he meant to say. He had a chance to switch his shit up and come correct, if he knew what was good for him.

"What you hard of hearing too? Man, get the fuck outta my fa—"

I stole on him before I knew it. Way too much had gone on today. I just wasn't in the mood for this dude's flip-ass mouth. I continue to hit this muthafucka until he landed on the floor, then I began to stomp his ass out. As usual someone called the police. They must've been nearby because I heard the sirens closing in. I stopped kicking dude, racing out of the liquor store to my car. I sped away without looking back. I still planned on getting my drink. I was going to my usual liquor stop, like I should have done in the first place.

After getting my Henny, I headed over to my brother Chip's crib. He always had a way of making me feel better. Although, he got on my damn nerves too. I'd just have to deal with it because I didn't plan on going home no time soon. Seeing Vanity's face right now might make me snap. I just couldn't get over the fact that she gave my pussy away. The shit was driving me insane.

I parked in his driveway, got out, and rang the doorbell. It was taking him forever to come to the door. I knew he was home. I parked right behind him and I heard the loud music blasting. After ringing his doorbell two more times, Chip finally let me in.

"It's about fuckin time."

"What's up, big bruh?"

"Vanity." I said, walking in, taking my shoes off. I went straight to the kitchen to grab a cup and some ice for my Henny.

"What about her? Did you two get into it again?"

"She really fucked up this time." I took a sip of my drink. "You got a lighter?" I set two blunts on the table. I didn't want to pull out the whole stash. Chip would smoke all my shit up. And these blunts nearly cost me my damn life. I wasn't about to share all of them.

Chip walked into the living room, got the lighter, and came back, sitting down at the table. "What she do?"

Everybody Got A Secret 2: A Drama Filled Romance

I lit the blunt and took a puff. "She gave my pussy away. That's what the fuck she did." I took another hard pull. The words might have rolled off my tongue, but I was real fucked up inside. "I know I accused her of cheating while she was in the Bahamas, but deep down inside, I really felt like she was just trying to make me jealous. I had no idea that it was really true."

Chip looked as if he didn't believe me. "I don't believe it."

"Well, believe it. Remember that picture on Pebbles' page? The one with that one dude licking on her."

Chip nodded his head yes.

"That was him."

Chip still didn't seem convinced. "But how do you know for sure? Cuz you jump to conclusions sometimes. Shit could be pink and you'll be swearing that it's blue."

I sighed and gave him a strange look. Is he fuckin questioning me on my shit? "Trust me. I know. Her ass was texting the muthafucka on our way back home."

Chip sat next to me, looking perplexed. "I still can't believe it, but then again, I told you this shit was going to happen."

"Don't start with that I told you so shit. I'm not in the mood." I poured more Hennessy into my cup. "I don't care how unhappy she was, she didn't have to fuck our marriage up. Why'd she marry me if she was going to cheat?"

Chip took the blunt from me, took a few hits before handing it back. "Panther's got the best shit, on everything." He blew out smoke rings. "It's no secret that you two have been going through something. It's clear that you both are unhappy. And for the record, you cheated on her up until y'all got married."

I sighed. "I'm not speaking on old shit. I'm talking about since being married. I didn't know she was this unhappy."

"So, what are you going to do? Divorce? Counseling? Stay?"

I gulped down my drink, enjoying the burn. "I'm going to set shit off. That's what the fuck I'm going to do."

"Don't you get tired of that?"

"Tired of what? I don't ever get tired of setting niccas straight."

"Let me hit that," Dino said, walking into the kitchen. I handed him the blunt. "Yeah, this that good shit. You must've hit up Row. What's up with the long faces?" he asked, handing me back the blunt. "Y'all should be laughing and shit off this good, baby-making weed."

Chip nodded his head at me. "Ivan found out Vanity was cheating."

Dino got a cup and poured himself some of my Henny. "Word? That's fucked up. With who though? Don't tell me you know the nicca?"

I was getting heated just thinking about this bastard. "Fuck no, I don't know him. If he was someone I knew, I'd be at this nicca's shit instead of chilling over here with y'all."

Dino sat in the seat to my left, across from Chip. "How did you find out? Did she tell you?" Dino sighed. "I can't believe this shit. I had high hopes for y'all."

"Fuck hope. That bitch don't have no love here." Smoke came out of my nose. "I want to beat her ass and shoot this cocky ass muthafucka"

"Wait." Chip exclaimed. "You said that like you had a run in with him or something."

I shrugged. "I wouldn't say it was a run in. We had words over the phone."

"For real, tho. What he say?"

I repeated exactly what happened in the car when we exchanged words.

Chip shook his head. "I know you're angry with dude, but this shit is really between you and Vanity. Either you want her or you don't. And if you still want her then you need to find a way to work things out. This is partially your fault too."

"I'm sick of hearing that shit!" I said, jumping up from the table, knocking over my chair. "I didn't fuck another bitch."

"I'm not saying that she doesn't share the blame too," Chip said, calmly. "But you've done a lot of things to push her away.

54

Everybody Got A Secret 2: A Drama Filled Romance

How many times have I called you and told you she was over here sitting on the couch crying over your ass?"

"Fuck that shit. She takes things out on me too."

"Yeah, man, but instead of you expressing how you feel, you just blow up. A marriage takes a lot of communication."

"Stop trying to tell me about my marriage when you can't even keep a fuckin girlfriend. When you can stay faithful long enough to get a wife, holler at me then."

"Oh, that was cold as fuck," Dino said, shaking his head.

"And that's the same shit you do to Vanity," Chip said, striking back at me. "When you hurt, you hurt the people you love most. Not cool, bruh."

Dino sighed. "So, where is Vanity now?"

"I'm not sure," I said. "She was laying across the bed after I choked her out."

"You did what?" Chip yelled. He pulled out his phone. I assumed he was texting Pebbles.

"That's right. Run tell your ex like you do with everything else."

"You damn right. Cuz you've lost your damn mind."

"You ain't seen nothing yet. Vanity and her lover about to wish they never fucked with me."

Chapter 6

Kimaya

As soon as I walked into Stoney's house, I began stripping out of my clothes. By the time he walked in with his luggage, I was completely naked. "I'm ready for some dick now. All that car action got me hot and horny."

Stoney looked me up and down and smiled. Vanity might have his heart, but I know I controlled his body. He found me irresistible, which gave me a little leverage.

Undressing him with passion, I kissed his body all over before getting on my knees, sucking him off again. I know I gave him two blowjobs before we got here, but you can never give your man too much head. Especially for a man like Stoney, who got hard with a blink of an eye. He enjoyed getting his dick sucked multiple times a day. His sex drive was through the roof. This man could literally fuck all night long. It was as if he couldn't get enough.

I stared him in the eye while slowly working his tool in and out of my mouth. Stoney took the pin out of my hair, allowing my long hair to flow freely down my back. "I'm ready to feel those walls," he said, helping me stand to my feet.

Holding hands, he led me upstairs to his bedroom. We kissed with fever from the hallway into the bedroom. Lifting me up in the air, my bottom landed on his dresser. I opened my legs wide receiving his big dick. Stoney pumped inside of me, grunting. I touched his beautiful face, kissing his sexy lips, and staring into his hypnotic eyes. Oh, how I loved this man. I couldn't wait to be this man's wife and have his baby. Stoney hardly ever fucked me raw so I was enjoying the feel of his meat. It was just something about skin on skin action that turned me on.

I locked my legs around his waist. "Oh, Daddy. Your dick feels so good."

Stoney's lips found mine again."Mmmm."

"I missed you. Did you miss me?"

"Mmmm," he moaned, gripping my thighs.

Stoney's loving was the best. Don't get me wrong, Cash sexed me good too, making me cum multiple times. But I didn't love him, which was the reason why I said Stoney was better. Every time, Stoney made love to me, it felt like he made love to my soul. My orgasms were always powerful and they lasted forever.

I held his tight ass cheeks, lifting my ass off the dresser, meeting his thrusts. "Daddy, you beating this pussy up."

I felt tingles in my vagina. I tried to suppress my orgasm, holding on a little longer, but I couldn't. Stoney was working his magic like he usually did, making me cum quick. "Damn, Daddy, I'm about to cum on your dick."

Stoney picked me up as I was cumming, making my orgasm even sweeter. I wrapped my arms around his neck and my legs around his hips. I screamed over and over again, enjoying the perfect feel of his hardness. "I fuuuuckin looooove yooooou!"

Stoney reached behind me, grabbing something off the dresser before he carried me over to the bed, laying me down on my back.

Pulling out of me, he opened the Magnum condom. As he was about to slip it on, I grabbed his wrist. "Why do we need this? We're engaged. I like the feel of you being inside of me with no protection."

Stoney eyed me. "Kim, you know I can't."

He tried to put the condom on again and I snatched it out his hand, tossing it on the floor. "What the fuck is your problem? I like feeling you. Damn, you act like I got something."

He sighed. "I know you ain't got nothing. We get tested every three months together. I know you're disease free. It's not that."

"What is it then?" It just dawned on me that he doesn't want me to get pregnant. "You're afraid that I might get knocked up. You already know I want your baby."

"Yeah, that's the thing." He backed away from me, reaching for another condom on the nightstand. "I'm not ready for all that." He slipped the condom on, entering me.

I turned my head when he tried to kiss me. "I bet you fucked Vanity raw. I bet if she asked you to get her pregnant, you'd do it."

"Shhhhhh," he whispered, thrusting deeper inside of me. "I'm about to cum."

"Let me up." I tried to raise up when he pinned me down.

"Chill. You're fucking up my vibe."

"I'm not horny anymore." Tears started to flow. I pushed him. "Get off of me. I don't want you inside of me with a condom on."

He laughed. "Girl, you're giving me this pussy or I'm going to take it."

I looked at him like he was crazy. "You're not taking nothing. If I don't want it, you need to respect that."

Stoney gave me a nasty look. Angrily, he pulled out, rolling off of me. He landed on his back, lying beside me.

I regretted talking sideways now. All I wanted was for him to want me like he wanted Vanity. "Did you fuck her raw? Yes or no?"

"Kim, I'm not playing these games with you."

"What games? I'm pissed off that we're going to be married soon, and you can't even give me your dick."

"What are you talking about? I give you as much dick as you want."

Everybody Got A Secret 2: A Drama Filled Romance

"You know what the fuck I mean. I want skin on skin action," I said, making the sound of a booty clapping with my hands.

"I don't have time for this shit." He got off the bed, ripping the condom off. "I'd rather jerk my dick than to deal with your nagging ass."

As mad as I was with him, he was still sexy as hell walking away from me in to the master bathroom. I wanted to kick myself. My jealousy was going to drive him right into Vanity's arms. That's not what I was trying to do. I just wanted my husband-to-be to treat me the way he treats her. I saw how he held her at the airport. He never held me like that. And I watched him take a second look at her as we drove away. Then, he looked at me like he wished she was in the car instead of me.

I entered the bathroom willing to do whatever I had to do so that I wouldn't lose him. I knew he was pissed off with me, and rightfully so. Getting in the shower, I did what I did best; I got on my knees. I tried to put his erection in my mouth and he moved away from me. I really fucked up this time. He never resisted my head game. No matter how mad he was with me.

"I'm sorry," I said, still on my knees as water ran down my hair, face, and body.

He continued to wash, ignoring me. Then he got out of the shower, leaving me on my knees in the tub. I stood, grabbed a towel, and chased after him. "Stoney, please, I'm sorry."

He still didn't acknowledge me, standing before me, naked, drying himself off. Humph. Humph. Humph. Stoney knows he is fine, from head to toe. God truly blessed this man. Letting my towel fall to the floor, I walked up behind him and took his towel out of his hands, drying him off. I expected him to stop me. When he didn't, I moved even closer, kissing him. "Baby, I'm so sorry."

To make things perfectly clear, I grabbed another condom off the dresser, putting it in my mouth. I stooped down, eye level with his penis, using my mouth to slide the condom on. I worked his tool in my mouth, and then jerked it while sucking his balls.

"Let me take care of you. Lay on your back for me, Daddy."

Stoney laid in the bed with his dick standing at attention. I climbed in bed with him, straddling his lap. Just as I was about to slide down on his pole, he stopped me.

"I can't," he said. "I'm just not into it. Vanity is heavy on my mind."

I wasn't even surprised. I knew she was on his mind. Recently, she stayed on his mind. This is one of the reasons why we were having problems. I knew that I could be with another man, but I didn't want another man. I wanted Stoney. And if I didn't have sex with him multiple times a day, then he would get it from someone else—like Vanity. So, I did what I had to do to keep my fiancé and his dick with me.

All of a sudden, an idea popped in my head. "Close your eyes."

"I'm not feeling it, Kim."

"Baby, just close your eyes."

Stoney reluctantly closed his eyes with a sexy frown on his face. He might be confused about getting it on, but his penis wasn't. It was still standing strong.

Sliding down on his hardness, I leaned forward, arching my back. Slowly rocking back and forth on his erection, I whispered in his ear. "Let's role play. Pretend that I'm her."

I felt him stiffen inside of me. "I can't let you do that."

His eyes were still closed when I kissed his lips. "I want to. Let me be your Vanity," I whispered in his ear, knowing her name turned him on. "Tell me how she is in bed."

"Slow and sensual. She likes for me to be in control, putting in that work."

"Submissive?" That wasn't me at all, but I'd do anything for Stoney.

"Sort of. Submissive but very much into it at the same time."

"Kinda wild but you're in control?"

Everybody Got A Secret 2: A Drama Filled Romance

"Something like that. You sure you want to go there? You don't have to," he said, thrusting upward. He seemed to be totally into it since I mentioned Vanity.

Oh, I was going there, without a doubt. "Yep. Now, fuck me like you fucked her, so we can cum."

A breathy moan escaped from his lips. I could only imagine what his thoughts had drifted back to. I'm sure he was thinking about how he made love to her on the beach.

Using the remote, I dimmed the lights and closed the blinds so that we could barely see each other. I wanted to create the full effect. "We've just gotten back from the beach. You've been thinking about how wet my pussy was all day."

"Ok," he said, rocking his hips with mine.

"I removed my tiny bikini. Now, I'm in your room naked and asking you to make love to me. I need to feel you inside of me."

Stoney really seemed to come to life. He flipped me onto my stomach. "You feel this dick now," he said, pumping me hard and fast.

I could get used to being Vanity. She got platinum dick. The shit was so good I was literally stuttering. I've never felt his dick this deep inside of me. All I could do was moan. "Aaaaaaah. Aaaaaaah. Aaaaaaah." I wanted to cuss so bad, but I didn't know if Vanity cussed or not. I didn't want to do nothing to fuck up the good dick that he was giving me.

I felt myself about to cum. As I reached under me to rub my clit, I felt him gently move my hand out of the way, rubbing my clit for me. "Yeeeeeesssss, Daddy! Give it to me. Yeeeeessss. Your diiiiiick is sooooo goooood."

"Aaaaaaah. Ssssssss. Aaaaaaah." Stoney moaned, humping me faster and faster until he came. He got up, taking the condom off, dropping it on the floor.

He made his way back to the shower. I was tired but I wanted to join him so we could talk. Easing in with him, I began washing his back. "I can be her as much as you like. I don't mind."

"Nah, I want you to be you."

"But I know you would rather be with her." The pain of saying those words really ate me up inside.

"I can't lie to you, I do want her. I love that woman with every part of my being. I'd give anything to be with her."

I wasn't a crybaby, but hearing him say that so freely instantly brought tears to my eyes. "What about me?"

He stared at me as if my tears were a shock to him. "I appreciate everything that you do."

I just stared at him with teary eyes. "But I want you to love me the way you love her."

"That'll never happen so you need to stop sweating me about my feelings for Vanity. You knew what it was when we met. Accept that I love another woman. What she and I share is not what you and I share. But at the same time, I like you, I respect your hustle, and we have our own thing. Let it be what it is. You're so busy worrying about her that you can't even enjoy when I'm with you. Learn to be in the moment."

I lowered my eyes. "I got it." I sniffed. "I won't question your love for her anymore."

"Good. You're focused on the wrong L-word."

I was beyond disgusted. "And what L-word should I be focused on?"

"Loyalty."

He pecked my lips.

I was too hurt to kiss him back. At this point, I just wanted to get out of the shower. There was no need to do anything extra. I knew where I stood. "Do you even find me attractive? Or am I just a pawn in your little scheme to get back at Cash?"

"I find you very attractive." He pulled me into his arms, making me look at him. Water cascaded down his body, making him look like a Greek God. My heart fluttered. This time when he kissed my lips, I kissed him back. I just couldn't resist. The sensual kiss got me wet all over again. I was surprised when his fingers caressed my peach.

I moved his hand away. "You don't have too. I know how you feel about me," I said with a fresh set of tears.

Everybody Got A Secret 2: A Drama Filled Romance

"I want to."

We stood under the water staring at each other.

"Let me taste you," he said, kneeling down. "Show you how much I appreciate you being my everything. Holding me down."

I was surprised. I gave Stoney oral constantly. He never licked me. The sex was still off the hook so I never complained. I shuddered when his lips touched mine. It's been a long time since my kitty was kissed. Naturally, my hands gripped his head as his fingers spread my lower lips. His tongue slithered against my pearl, making me gasp. "Ssssssss. Oh, Daddy, your tongue feels so good."

He picked me up wearing my pussy over his mouth like a mask. The shit felt incredible. With my back against the wall, he licked up and down my wet slit. I lost complete control when his lips wrapped around my pearl, sucking and licking at the same time. Orgasmic tremors tore through my body. Stoney continued to suck while I screamed my lungs out.

As soon as he sat me down, my knees nearly buckled. "Hold up, baby, I need to get this call." He dashed out of the bathroom naked to get his phone. "Hello. Yeah. I can do that. I'm on my way."

I sighed. I was hoping he would lick me like that again and then dick me down once more.

He came back into the bathroom. "Baby, I need to make a run. Why are you standing there like you can't get out?"

I giggled. Because I couldn't. I was too weak. He must've realized that I needed help out of the bathtub. Picking me up, he carried me into the bedroom, sitting me down on the bed, handing me a towel. His phone rang again and he walked out of the bedroom.

I was heated until I looked down at the floor. My frown turned into a smile when I saw what Stoney left behind. I rushed over quickly picking it up.

"Baby!" Stoney yelled.

"Yes!"

"This is important. I'm going to drop you off at home, ok?"

"Ok!" I yelled back, masking my hurt. Hell no, it wasn't ok. He's been gone for several days. His first day back I expect him to spend it with me. Not chase down someone else. I dressed and grabbed my things. As I rushed downstairs with an attitude, Stoney came running down behind me.

"Are we still on for dinner tonight?"

He looked at me like he totally forgot. "Aw, baby, can I get a rain check? Something's—"

I blew out hot air. "Yeah, yeah, yeah, I know. Something's come up." I was pissed. Before he could finish the rest of his sentence, I spoke up again. "And you'll make it up to me."

Oblivious to my true feelings, Stoney kissed me on the cheek. "I knew you'd understand." He smiled, ushering me out of the house to the car.

Stoney and I didn't say two words to each other the whole ride to my house. The moment the car stopped, I jumped out, storming towards the door.

"I'll call you later," he said before he pulled off.

He didn't even make sure I got inside like he normally did. I didn't want to believe it but I'm sure his urgency had something to do with Vanity. Ever since he found her again, he hasn't been the same attentive fiancé that he used to be.

Rushing inside, I couldn't help but wonder if I made a mistake leaving Cash for Stoney. He was so good to me. I took it all for granted. The issues that I have with Stoney, I never had with Cash. I guess I got caught up in Stoney's sex appeal instead of focusing on Cash's love for me. I grew up with money, but I was still a chick from the hood. Thugged out dudes turned me on. Stoney wasn't so much thugged out as he was confident, sexy, and sometimes he just didn't give a fuck. His nonchalant attitude turned me on.

Cash was just the opposite. He had hood in him but he was more refined. The loving type when he was in a relationship. Although, he tried put up a front like he wasn't in love. His jokes masked his real feelings. Truth is, he was a hopeless romantic. The more time I spent with Cash, the mushier he got.

Everybody Got A Secret 2: A Drama Filled Romance

Listening to the wrong women, people who I thought were my friends, I mistook Cash's love for me as a sign of weakness when he was only showing me how a real woman should be treated. Due to all the bullshit that Stoney put me through, I finally understood what a great man I had in Cash. At this point, I'd trade in all my love for Stoney to have Cash's love back. With Cash, I was never a runner up.

I sat my stuff down, and put my special find in the fridge, before texting Cash. Hey, I know I'm the last person you probably want to hear from. I need to talk to you. Can we meet somewhere?

I wasn't sure if he was going to respond, but I had to reach. I'd been thinking about him off and on for a while.

My phone vibrated.

It was a text from Cash. Where?

I texted back. My home. I texted him my new address.

Cash: Be there in an hour.

I was so excited that he agreed to see me. I decided to take a fresh shower and put on something sexy.

An hour later, Cash showed up looking handsome as ever. He had on brown designer baggy jeans, a black and brown T-shirt, and black Jordans.

"Hey," I said, running up to him, hugging him tight as if there was no static between us. When he didn't hug me back, I stepped away from him. Ah, he smelled so good.

I could tell he was still feeling me by the way he stared. "What's up? What did you want to talk about?" He was still standing by the door as if he was about to leave at any given moment.

"Come in." I gestured. "Have a seat. Can I get you anything?"

Cash laughed like I was a joke. "This ain't a social visit. What do you want?"

"I saw you earlier and I felt like we needed closure."

His eyes scanned my satin robe. "Put some clothes on and I'll think about having a seat."

Princess Diamond

I see Cash wasn't going to make things easy for me. He was different from when we were together. Karen must've helped him find his balls. "I have on clothes," I said, opening my robe, revealing a fitted tank that showed off my flat stomach and booty shorts.

I could tell that what I had on made him uncomfortable. "Alright, let's get this over with." He took a seat on the couch.

I let my robe fall to the floor and purposely walked past him putting my ass all in his face. When I sat down, his eyes were all over me. "I missed you, Cash."

He let out a nervous chuckle. "I'm not doing this with you," he said, standing to his feet.

I grabbed his hand. "I'm serious."

He snatched his hand away. "Stop playing games."

"I'm not!" I shouted. "I regret that I left you for Stoney."

"That's too damn bad."

"I know you probably hate me."

"I do."

"Well, you'll be happy to know that as much as I love Stoney, I can't deny that you were very good to me. And if I stayed with you, I would be your pregnant wife right now." I didn't intend to get so emotional, allowing tears to fall. "Cash, I messed up. I'm sorry."

I knew without a doubt that Cash genuinely loved me. Now, I finally realized how he felt when I left him. I broke his heart just like Stoney was breaking mine.

Cash paused, sitting back down, looking at me. "I was really good to you and you fucked it up." He glanced at me like he wanted to slap the taste out of my mouth.

"You're right. I did. I'm sorry. I wish I could go back in time. I would have stayed and understood that you weren't cheating all those late nights. That you were trying to build something for us. I was so stupid," I said, wiping my tears.

"Too late. That shit was years ago. I've moved on. You've moved on. Why are you doing this now?"

"Because I know I hurt you."

Everybody Got A Secret 2: A Drama Filled Romance

"I could sit here and be tough about this, but the truth is I don't have to. Yes, you hurt me back then, but you leaving was the best thing that ever happened to me. I would have never met Karen if you stayed."

"But does Karen make you happy? Because you were very happy with me."

"Karen is nothing short of amazing. I couldn't have married a better woman. She is my happiness."

"So, you don't miss me?"

"Nope."

My eyes dropped to his erection that he was trying to hide. I know I still had an effect on Cash. Even if he didn't want to admit it. "So, you don't still love me?"

Cash cleared his throat. "I'm out."

I sprung up from the couch, running to the door, beating him there. I used my body as leverage so that he'd have to touch me in order to get out. I struck a sexy pose in front of him. My shorts were looking more like panties and my shirt was barely covering my breasts. "We're finishing this conversation, Cash."

He sucked his teeth. "No, we're not."

"You not fooling nobody. I see the way you look at me. You still want me. I want you too."

"Girl, get the hell on with all that. I told you, I'm happily married. I'm not thinking about you. Get over yourself."

"Does Karen know where you are?"

"Of course. We don't have any secrets. I told her the moment you texted. What you thought? I was triflin and snuck over here? Nah, I'm not that type of dude."

"I know what type of man you are." I stared him down. "I could have you back if I wanted you. I'm just trying to make things right with you before I get married to Stoney."

Cash laughed in my face. "I hate to bust your bubble, but he's not going to marry you."

He had a lot of nerve. "That's what you think."

"That's what I know." He chuckled even more. "Stoney doesn't love you."

"You underestimate me. You always have. Stoney will be mine."

"Keep dreaming." Cash moved me to the side, about to open the door.

I came up behind him. He tensed up. I wrapped my arms around his firm body, loving the way he felt. I always found Cash very attractive. He was just as sexy as Stoney. I was just too blind to see it until now. My hands caressed his chest, sliding down his hard abs, until I reached his erection.

"Mmmmmm. I missed this fat dick."

He grabbed my hands, moving out of my hold. "You left me for Stoney, now deal with it. Stupidity costs. Later, Kim." He opened the door and walked out.

He actually walked away from me. This was a first. I stood in the doorway watching him leave. I was messed up. I fell in love with the wrong brother. Now, I'm paying for it.

Cash stopped when he got to his Infiniti truck. "I want to thank you for not fucking up my life. Good luck with Stoney. You're going to need it. He's going to break your heart just like you broke mine." He blew me a kiss and got in his truck and pulled off.

I shed a few tears when he left.

I fucked up when I let him go, but I wasn't out the game yet. I had another trick up my sleeve. I went to the fridge and pulled out the condom full of sperm that Stoney left on the bedroom floor. Normally, Stoney flushed his condoms down the toilet. He slipped up this time. Being in such a hurry, he forgot all about it.

I smiled at the semen. He nutted a hefty load. "I'm going to get my baby after all."

Quickly, I dressed. I was on my way to see my friend who was a fertility doctor.

Chapter 7

Cash

I kept it together while in Kimaya's presence, but that shit still hurt. I wanted that apology for the longest. It felt good to hear her finally say that I was the better man. I knew I was. It's still so much sweeter when the person who hurt you admits it. I didn't think I needed that closure. I guess I did. I loved Kimaya and I think I always will. Back then, I saw myself with her and only her. I never thought I would get over her either. I mean, I had women before her that I liked a lot, but I'd never been in love until I met her.

Not only did I give her a ring, I was in the process of coming into all this money. That's why I was working so hard. Late nights and early mornings, grinding. Doing what a man was supposed to do to provide for the woman he loved.

Like most women, she thought I was cheating on her. If she would've waited six more months, shit would have been set. She wouldn't ever have to work again. I now know things weren't meant to be. I'm glad I didn't set her up lovely. Any woman who is bold enough to leave me for my brother is a fake ass bitch.

I would never go back to her. I wasn't stupid enough to think with my dick, like most dudes. As attracted as I am to her, I would never disrespect Karen nor would I ruin my marriage by cheating on her with another woman. No matter how I felt about Kimaya, she was the past. Karen was my future. She held the key to my heart now.

Princess Diamond

When I pulled up in front of my home, I saw Karen waddle out, getting into her truck holding a bat. I couldn't do nothing but laugh. My baby was so gangsta. She threw her Infiniti truck in reverse, speeding backwards out of the driveway. Her foot slammed on the brakes when she saw me standing on the sidewalk looking at her.

She rolled down the window. "I was on my way to that bitch's house. You were taking too long."

"Park the truck so I can tell you about it."

Karen sped back into her parking spot and got out of the truck, still holding the bat.

I cracked up. "What were you going to do with that?"

"Beat that bitch with a bat. She's fucking with the wrong woman."

I took the bat out of her hand, putting my arms around her. "You don't have nothing to worry about."

"I know she tried something, Cash." She sniffed my shirt. "You smell just like that hoe."

"It's not what you think. Let's go inside and I'll tell you all about it." It was freezing. I didn't want her or my baby to get sick. I escorted my wife into the house, helping her out of her coat.

"So what happened?" She said flopping down on the couch. "If I hear anything out of pocket, I'm fucking her up. It's just that simple."

I sat down next to her, taking her feet into my lap, massaging them. They stayed swollen. "She called me over to apologize. I guess Stoney's bullshit finally got to her."

"And what else?"

"She went on to say that she should have never left me. She regrets it."

"And what the fuck did you say?"

"I told her that I was happily married to you, and that I wouldn't mess up my marriage for her."

"Ok, so how did her scent get all over you?"

"She hugged me."

Everybody Got A Secret 2: A Drama Filled Romance

"She was trying to fuck you. Come out and say it, Cash. I already know that's why she called you over."

"Yeah, she tried. I checked her ass and left."

"That's all."

"Everything."

"Did you kiss her? Or touch her? Or anything else that I should know about?"

I pulled Karen into my lap. "Baby, nothing else."

Karen shook her head fighting back tears. "I know she broke your heart, but I refuse to compete with her."

I stared deep into her eyes. "And you don't have to. All I wanted was closure to that whole situation. And I got it. She finally admitted that she was wrong. I didn't want anything more." I kissed Karen's tears. "Don't cry. She's not worth your tears."

"You know I'm not jealous, Cash. But Kimaya is the only woman that could take you away from me. I fear that if she wants you back that you might entertain it just because your feelings ran so deep for her."

"Karen, that won't happen. Yes, I loved her, but I'm never leaving you. Every time I see Kim, I think about how she's fucking my brother." I groaned. "I don't know how I feel about any of this. But what I do know is, I love you very much. And you'll never have to worry about me cheating. I'm committed to us. For better or worse."

Karen stopped crying, smiling. "Even if I get fat? What if I gain two-hundred pounds?"

I laughed. "You better not get fat. I'm taking your ass to the gym as soon as the doctor says it's ok."

She laughed. "I'm going to sit on this couch and feed my fat face all day long."

"Like hell you are."

She really cracked up then.

I was just glad my wife was smiling. I hated to see her cry. I rubbed her stomach. "You're making me hot, bouncing around in my lap. Unless you're going to give it up, you gotta get off of me."

"It ain't nothing to it, but to do it." She stood, quickly taking off her clothes. Turning around, she bent over with her ass in my face.

"I was just joking. I know you said you were hurting down there. We don't have to. I can wait." I never pressured her for sex. We haven't had sex in about three days because Karen hasn't felt up to it.

"I'm not in pain anymore. Just don't beat it up like you usually do. Take it easy on me. I'm handicapped for the next two months."

The only time she asks me to ease up is when she's in her last trimester. "I won't put a hurting on this pretty pussy."

I found Karen ultimately attractive. It didn't matter if she was pregnant or not. Sex was always unbelievable between us. I like how she moved, how she felt, and the way she handled me in the bedroom. The love that we have for each other complemented our sex life.

I took my pants and shirt off. "I feel neglected. You haven't told me that you loved me."

Karen yanked my boxers off me like I was her bitch. "I love it," she said, holding my dick hostage.

"That's all you love? You ain't shit."

She laughed, straddling my lap, pushing my stiffness deep inside of her. "Oh my God, I missed this dick." She worked her hips slow. "You know, I love you."

I kissed her, slowly grinding inside of her. "I love you too. I'm so backed up. I promise, if you weren't already pregnant, you would be today."

"Mmmmmm. You gonna let me see it? I love it when you cum a lot. That's sexy."

I laughed. "Freak."

"Yep. Now, shut up, and let me have my way with my dick."

Chapter 8

Keystone

Amante sent me a text while I was with Kimaya. He said to meet him ASAP. He had the information I requested. I know Kim was upset with me for abandoning her when I just got back from vacation. Too bad. She'll have to understand. Nobody told her to get her feelings involved.

When we met, I didn't even know she was with Cash, but she knew who I was. She used me as a rebound to make Cash mad. I met Kim at a club. I was invited to a celebrity birthday party. We were both chilling in VIP. I knew she looked familiar. However, I couldn't remember where I saw her previously.

I'd been drinking, partying, and clowning with my boys. The turn up was real that night. So, when she approached me, all I saw was a beautiful sexy woman who wanted to get her freak on. I left the club with her, we checked into a hotel, and fucked for three days straight. Her energy was wild and out of control. I loved every bit of it.

I didn't find out she was with Cash until I invited her over for dinner. Before I could explain, Cash attacked me. Later, I found out they had been going through some major problems. Cash and I weren't speaking at the time so I had no idea. We hadn't been cool for years. Only tolerating each other and being cordial in front of family.

Princess Diamond

That day we got into a horrible fight. I mean, it was so bad that we both drew blood. Both of us needed stitches. Cash still had the mark on his neck where I tried to slit his throat with a knife. And I still have the scar on my arm where he sliced me with a piece of broken glass. Both marks were small, but everyone that was there and witnessed the fight, could see our war wounds clear as day. We literally tried to kill each other. And if Uncle Carlo hadn't fired his gun, we might have succeeded.

The right thing to do would have been to stop seeing Kimaya, but just because Cash got all out of pocket and attacked me, I continued to fuck her. She was my sweet revenge. I didn't think we were nothing more than a casual fuck relationship. That is until she proposed to me.

If it wasn't in front of my whole family, I probably would have told her ass no. Cash was there with sad eyes, therefore, I had to say yes. I even put the icing on the cake by grabbing her, slobbing her down, and announcing to everyone who didn't hear that we were officially engaged. We've been together for five years now, engaged for two.

I'm starting to feel the pressure to marry her. I probably would have considered it if I hadn't found out Karen was Vanity's cousin. That through a monkey wrench in my wedding plans. Now, all I can think about is Vanity and how I can finally get my second chance with her. I thought she was gone forever. The fact that she is having marital issues only means that I'm a contender. I plan on doing everything that Ivan won't do. Being the man of her dreams and treating her like the precious queen that she is.

"How may I help you, sir?"

"I'm here to see Amante Giuliani," I said to the front desk clerk.

"Just a moment, please." She picked up the phone, dialing his extension, telling him I was in the lobby. "He'll be right with you, sir. Can I get you anything? Something to drink maybe?"

I glanced around the office. It looked nice before, but the renovations were definitely next level. An expensive French décor. I spotted new paintings, tile, and a fresh paint job. My Uncle

Everybody Got A Secret 2: A Drama Filled Romance

Antonio had to be getting some serious paper. Zander Guiliani Law Firm looked like something straight out of a magazine. "No, thank you. I'm just fine."

"Yes, you are," she mumbled.

I pretended like I didn't hear her. More pussy was the last thing I was thinking of.

"Maybe I can offer you a pastry? Or water?"

I chuckled. She was trying way too hard. "No, I'm good," I said, still looking around, not even acknowledging her thirsty ass.

Just as she was about to see if I wanted anything else, Amante came strutting down the hall, looking like a billion dollars wearing Salvatore Ferragamo from head to toe. His suit and shoes were killer. He always dressed nice. Even when he was about to hit The Block, he was still fresh.

Family and friends called him Mante or Tey-Tey. Panthers knew him as Chief. He was 5'9", twenty years old, and finishing up his MBA in Criminal Justice. Following in his father's footsteps, he was soon to be a high-powered attorney. Quite frankly, the man was a genius. His IQ was so damn high that they couldn't even determine it.

When he wasn't an intern at the law firm, he ran Kut It Up Barbershop, which was adjacent to his sister Ko-Ko's Kutie Pie Beauty Shop. Both businesses were put in someone else's name because they fronted for illegal use.

Amante favored Uncle Antonio a lot. They had the same piercing golden-brown eyes. He got his slanted eye shape from his Asian mother. Women always complimented him on his physique. He was muscled up. Not too bulky like a body builder. Just enough muscle to show off. He had curly hair, light skin, and he kept a permanent frown on his face. He hardly ever smiled. Even when he did, it still looked like he was frowning to me.

He spoke seven different languages—English, Italian, Spanish, French, Chinese, Vietnamese and his primary language Japanese.

Princess Diamond

Out of all of Uncle Antonio's kids, he had to be the most deadly one, living a double life. By day, he was Amante, the lawyer, barber, landlord, and businessman. By night, he ran the most brutal gang in the city. His illegal activity consisted of everything from contract killings to torture to overseeing drug operations and washing money. He was definitely one nicca that could put the fear of God in anyone.

We've had our issues in the past. We've even fist fought. Hands down, by far, he was still one of my favorite cousins. We were pretty close despite his lifestyle. Blood is thicker than water in my family, always. The only time loyalty was questioned was when people from both sides of my family got involved. The Guiliani's and the Diaz-Santana's always seemed to intermingle. That's when things got super complicated.

This is why Amante and I fought in the first place. He has a baby by my twenty-two year old cousin Neyeli Diaz-Santana on my mother's side. We called her NeNe for short. These two were like dynamite together. One minute they were fucking. The next minute they were fighting. Their relationship kept both sides of the family at odds. The only reason why my uncles hadn't snatched Amante up yet is because of their relationship with my Uncle Antonio. They were getting too much money together to get involved in their love spats.

"What up, Tey-Tey?" I chuckled.

He snarled at me as he handed two folders to the receptionist. "These need to be mailed out tonight. They are very important. Make sure you overnight them."

"Yes, sir," the thirsty clerk said, standing to her feet right away. She jumped up so fast that I thought her seat was on fire. "I'll get right to it, sir. Is there anything else that you need, sir?"

"Oh, I'm going to be gone for the rest of the day. I have two important calls coming through. One on the Fitz case and the other one on the Billup case. I told them to press 0 and speak to you."

"Yes, sir. Anything else, sir?"

"No. That'll be all. Have a good day."

"You too, sir."

Everybody Got A Secret 2: A Drama Filled Romance

I followed Amante through the gold plaza doors into the blowing wind.

"Why'd you give me the evil eye?" I knew he didn't like to be called Tey-Tey. It was a habit. I'd been calling him that since a kid.

"You know the fuck why."

I cracked up.

"Your ass is stupid. Where you park? In my spot?"

"Yeah. Where's your car?"

"Ko-Ko dropped me off."

Ko-Ko was his sister who was a year younger than him. She was his only full-blooded sister, sharing the same mother and father. All his other brothers and sisters shared the same father, Uncle Antonio, but different mothers.

If Ko-Ko wasn't my cousin, I'd definitely wife her. She was my type. In a way, Kim reminded me of Ko-Ko. I guess with them both being half Asian, they had similar features, long, silky jet black hair, and the same body type.

Amante walked around to the driver's side. "Let me get the keys."

I tossed them to him. He caught them with one hand, hitting the unlock button on the fob. This is what most people couldn't handle about Amante. He was always the boss, commanding your attention. Either you played along and did things his way, or you didn't get his help at all. I needed his help so I had no problem sitting my ass in the passenger's seat of my own damn vehicle, letting him drive.

He cut on my stereo and plugged up his iPhone. Loud trap music blasted out of my Bose sound system as Amante made his way out of the parking garage. He sped into traffic whipping through the streets of downtown Chicago as if he were the mayor of the city.

"You going to Hyde Park?" I asked. He had an apartment overlooking Lake Shore Drive.

"Nah, downtown. Off State Street."

"I can't wait to see it. I heard it's on fleek."

"Yeah, it's pretty neat."

Amante owned Grand Plaza Luxury Apartments. He lived in a penthouse within the building. Marcel and Cash had penthouses there too.

It felt like we literally drove around the corner, down the street from Clark to State into another car garage.

Amante whipped my car into a spot and hopped out. "Let me give you a tour right quick."

I jumped out, following behind him into this luxurious plaza. Not many things amazed me. I grew up with money and fine things, but I'd never seen anything like this. Out back, there was a huge barbeque area, a golf course, pool, a track, and an outdoor eating area. On the lower level, there was a fitness center, basketball and tennis court, a club house, a party room, a library, a grocery store, a cyber café with Starbucks, and a business center that was equipped with a copier, scanner, fax, computers and printers.

The carpet felt like I was walking on air. "Wow! This is living."

Amante grinned as we stepped on the elevator. "I'm on the tenth floor. Ko-Ko's staying with me while she's waiting on her place. I know how close you two are. Stop by and see her sometime. I'm positive she's not here right now though."

"Ko-Ko is my heart. Of course, I'll come by to see her. What floor is Marcel on? I need to holler at him right quick."

"Fifteen. Don't take too long. I got other things to do."

He was always demanding too. "It'll only be a moment."

Amante didn't even address me, strutting off of the elevator when we got to his floor. I didn't pay him no mind, riding up to fifteen. Marcel's apartment took up the whole damn floor. It was five apartments in one. This is what long money looks like. I rang the doorbell. I assumed the camera looking down at me gave Marcel access to see who was standing at his door. After waiting in silence for a few seconds, the platinum-looking door opened. Standing in front of me was Marcel and the twins.

"Uncle Stoooooney!" Celina jumped into my arms wearing a blue Disney Cinderella costume dress with matching shoes and jewelry. I scooped her right up, kissing her chubby cheeks. We rubbed noses like we always did.

She hugged me tight. "You're my favorite, Uncle."

"No, you're my favorite, niece."

"Wait a minute," Marcel said, pretending like he was jealous. "What about me?" he asked Celina. "I thought I was your favorite." Marcel pretended to frown with a sad face. "You forgot about your Daddy already?"

"Oh no." She gasped, dramatically putting her hands to her face. "I'm sorry, Daddy. You're my favorite too." She leaned back, kissing Marcel on the cheek. Then she wrapped her arms around my neck, resting her head on my chest. "I missed you while you were gone, uncle. I never want you to leave me again."

I kissed her forehead. "I missed you too, my little buttercup."

Marcel just looked at us, shaking his head. "You know you got her spoiled rotten. You're the reason why she thinks she can get away with murder."

"That's because she's my little lady. Ain't that right, booboo?"

She raised her head, looking me in the face. We rubbed noses again. "I want my date, uncle. You promised."

"I got you, sweet pea. I didn't forget. I just need a little more time. If that's alright with you?"

She put her hand on her hip. "I guess I can wait. Not too long though."

I always made time to take Celina out. I let her pick out the restaurant or wherever we went. It was my way of helping her realize how special she was so that she understood how a man was supposed to treat her. I took on the responsibility because people always said she looked like my daughter. Maybe because she had green eyes too. I don't know. But Marcel has been extra generous to me. Helping him out with his kids was the least I could do.

Marcel pretended to barf. "Y'all so lame. She was in time-out before you came."

"What'd she do?"

"Talking back to her nanny. You know, I don't allow disrespect." He waved his belt at her and she held onto me tighter.

"Is that true, Celina?"

She looked at me with teary eyes. "Yes." She looked over at Marcel and then back at me. "I'm so sorry. I not do it again."

Marcel wasn't fazed by her cuteness like I was. "Stop putting on a show. I'm going to let you slide so you can quit faking it and get rid of the tears."

She wiped her tears with the back of her hand, nodding her head at Marcel. "Yes, Daddy."

"Dramatic just like your mother," Marcel said, waving his belt at her again. "Next time, I'm going to spank your bottom. I've told you one too many times and you keep doing it."

I stared at her cute little face. She was melting my heart. "You can't be talking back to your nanny, Celina. That's not right. You wouldn't want someone to treat you like that. Would you?"

She shook her head no, wiping away more tears.

The tears were breaking my heart. "I think you should go apologize."

"Oh-kay. I'ma do better, Uncle Stoney. Please don't be mad a me," she said with crocodile tears.

"Go right now," Marcel said, taking her out of my arms, putting her down on the floor. She took off running back into the penthouse. "That girl got you wrapped around her finger. Wait until you have a daughter. I'm going to spoil her rotten. She's getting a Ferrari for her first birthday."

I laughed. "Oh that's real foul."

We both cracked up laughing.

"What it do, Uncle Stoney?" Marcelius looked up at me, grinning. This boy was dressed like he just stepped out of a 90's Hip Hop video. The headphones on his ears were bigger than his head.

Everybody Got A Secret 2: A Drama Filled Romance

I gave him a fist bump. "DJ Cellie Cell. I can't call it, baby. Where you about to go?"

"Daddy is going to let me DJ in the party room downstairs."

"Oooooh. Sounds like you're about to get it poppin."

"You already know," he said, striking a B-boy pose. "That's what I do."

Marcel laughed. "Come on in, man. Messing with these kids, you'll be standing in the doorway until tomorrow."

I walked in and saw Harlem and Bronx in the playpen with their toys. Markel aka Rio was laid out on the floor sleep.

"Where's Natalia?" I asked.

"She's in the room. She was watching TV. I'm sure she's sleep now. Oh, you know what I wanted to tell you."

"What's that?"

"I was just about to text you. I got a call from the producer. They picked up the reality show."

"Are you serious?" I smiled. "That's what's up. I know it's not about you and the kids."

"Nah. Nothing like that. It's going to be about my quest to find talent. I want to go all out and get busy like Diddy did when he put together Making The Band."

"Now that's going to be dope."

Marcel got hyped. "It's about to be major. You know, I want you, Dash, and the rest of the crew to come through. It'll be a singing and dancing competition. Nothing about your personal life."

"You know I'm down. Whatever you need. When are they going to start filming?"

"Well, we're still negotiating right now. After that's final, I told them that I wouldn't even think about making a move until Brooklyn was born. I would say at least a year before we went into production."

"Aight. Just let me know. I'm there." I gave him a pound. Aye, let me holler at you for a minute." I walked away from the kids so they weren't in earshot. "You good? Cuz earlier, you were pretty upset. You had me a little worried."

Marcel chuckled. "Yo, that Ivan dude is greasy. He'll make the most sane nicca snap."

"Well, just so you know, I'm handling that. That's why I'm here. Amante's got some info to give me."

Marcel nodded. He understood exactly what I meant. He knew how Amante got down.

"Speaking of him, let me get back before I piss him off, and I don't end up with shit. You know how he gets about his time. Super impatient."

"Dude's got a few screws loose too. I mean, he's always been cool with me, but I know he ain't wrapped too tight."

I laughed because Marcel was telling the truth. Amante was a cold piece of work. "I'll text you later." I gave Marcel some dap and left.

I heard yelling coming from Amante's apartment as soon as I got near the door. I sighed. I already knew what time it was. Bring on the bullshit. This is what I didn't have time for. I just wanted to get the damn information and roll out. I tapped on the door.

My cousin NeNe opened it. "Oh good, maybe you can talk some sense into your damn cousin. He's tripping as usual."

"I'm not tripping," Amante said with an attitude. "You're in my shit talking to me like you running things. Not up in here." He walked up on her, pointing his finger in her face. "Never that."

"What's yours is mine, remember?"

"Why are you here?"

"I'm dropping off your son. You claim I never let you see him. So, I brought him over here so you could spend time with him. Ungrateful ass muthafucka."

"That's it. Get the fuck out. I don't give a shit where you go, but you have to bounce up outta here."

I stepped inside, moving past them arguing, on my way to the living room. I picked up their son Domiere aka Dom, taking him with me. He didn't need to see his parents arguing. Although, I'm sure he was used to it. While they were going back and forth, he was sitting on the floor nearby playing his Nintendo 3DS. I can only imagine the bullshit this child has seen. But then again, my parents were much worse than them and I turned out ok.

I pulled my earbuds out of my pocket, plugging it into my phone. After cutting on a kid approved playlist, I put the buds into Dom's ears. He was such a good kid. He sat on the floor next to me still playing his game. Not moving or saying a word.

"Stoney, you need to get your damn cousin, before I fuck him up."

Amante stared me down, daring me to jump in.

"I'm not in it. Leave me out of your mess," I said. The last time I helped NeNe out I ended up with a broken nose and a busted lip. They were going at it so bad that I got clocked twice. Trying to get at each other, they ended up hurting me.

The time before that, I jumped in, and me and Amante got into a huge brawl. It was real nasty too. I literally thought we were going to kill each other. I banged him up pretty bad, but he whooped my ass. I'm a great fighter, but Amante is a trained black belt. He's skilled in some other type of martial arts too. I can beat the average nicca, but not his ass. That bullshit landed us both in the hospital. Never again.

Even though I didn't win that fight, I gained Amante's respect. He didn't test me too much afterwards. Even to this day, he still knows that if he jumps bad, I'm going to jump bad too. I might have gotten my ass kicked, but I'm not scared of nobody. I'd fight his ass again in a heartbeat. Bitch don't run through my blood.

"Stop asking for help," Amante told her. "You so big and bad."

NeNe raised her hand trying to hit him. He grabbed her hand, twirling her around. He opened the door about to toss her out when she grabbed a hold of him. "I bet you'd let me stay if I was Tanika's busted ass. I don't see why you fuck with her anyway. She ain't shit. She don't hold you down like I do. You just gonna say fuck me, huh?"

"NeNe, you're wearing thin on my patience. Get the fuck out before I have you thrown out."

"Throw me out, muthafucka."

He yanked her by her shirt and it ripped.

"Oh, that's how you like it? Rough, huh?" As if he asked her to strip, she started taking off her clothes. "This is what you like. Stripper bitches. Cuz that's what Tanika's hoe ass is. A two-dollar trick."

He stopped her from stripping. "Tanika was a virgin when I met her."

"Oh and I wasn't? I had your baby and look how you treat me? Like I'm nothing to you. What happened to us?"

Amante's face was red with anger. "I don't give a fuck. Get out!"

He opened the door, trying to push her out. She held onto him, tight again. "You used to want me."

"Girl, if you don't get the hell out, I'm going to call security and have you thrown out."

NeNe started taking her clothes off again. "When's the last time you hit this? It's been awhile. I know you want it. That wannabe gangsta bitch can't fuck you like I can."

"That's it. I'm done with you."

Amante opened the door, tossing NeNe out in her bra and panties. She landed on her ass in the hallway. "Fuck you, Mante! Fuck you!"

"I'm sure that's exactly what you want me to do. Fuck you," he said, tossing her clothes out into the hallway with her. He picked up her purse, throwing it out too. "Stay the fuck out of my life."

"I'm never going anywhere as long as I have your son."

He slammed the door so hard I almost jumped. "If she wasn't your cousin, I promise I'd slit her fuckin throat."

There was banging on the door. "Mante, let me in. I just want you to take me back. Please."

Amante turned towards the door. "Get off my door, bitch!"

Everybody Got A Secret 2: A Drama Filled Romance

"I'm not going no fuckin where. If you want me gone, remove me yourself. You can't do it, can you?"

"That's exactly what I'm going to do." He opened the keypad by the door, punching in a few numbers.

Within minutes, there was a scuffle on the other side of the door. I assumed it was security. I heard what sounded like someone kicking the door a few times before it was completely quiet.

"I hate that bitch," Amante said, pounding his fist into his hand. "Everyone was right when they tried to keep us apart. I should have listened. I should have never fucked with her lunatic ass."

These muthafuckas made my nerves bad. This is the young love that I didn't have time for. I promised myself I wouldn't say anything and before I knew it, I'd opened my mouth. "You still love her, man."

Amante looked at me like I was the enemy. "You see the shit she pulls. She drives me fuckin crazy. Dealing with her, I'll be a damn crack head. Smoking that shit."

I snickered, but stopped abruptly when I saw how angry he was. I didn't want him pissed at me. "Yeah, but I bet you're still hitting it, though. That's why she's acting the way she is. She still wants you. Don't bite my head off, but I think you still want her too."

Amante stared at me for a long time. He looked like he wanted to ring my neck. After looking at me for a few more seconds, he walked over to Dom, stooping down next to him. He took the earbuds out. "Hey, buddy, did you eat?"

"No," Dom said, politely, looking up from his game.

They spoke in Spanish for a little bit. Amante asked him how was his day at school and Dom told him all the things he did. I sat there thinking I'm so glad I learned Spanish. Unlike Emerald and Cash, they didn't know a lick of it. Maybe they understood some because my mother spoke Spanish, but they couldn't speak it well. There's no way I could fuck with Uncle Antonio or his kids and I didn't know Spanish. Besides, my father knew Spanish. You couldn't live in my house and not know how to speak it.

"C'mon, let's go to the back." Amante held Dom's hand, walking towards his home office.

I got up off the couch, following behind them. Amante was a neat freak so I made sure I didn't touch shit. Everything seemed to be in its place. It looked like there wasn't a speck of dirt in the entire apartment. His office was like a cozy studio apartment. Amante sat Dom on the couch, cutting the TV on so he could watch cartoons. I sat on the couch next to Dom while Amante sat in the office chair behind the computer.

All this shit that just happened swirled around in my head. "What did happen between you and NeNe? Y'all used to be so in love. I remember when you two would sneak off, hiding your relationship." They were so determined to be a couple. After what I witnessed today, I can see why both sides of the family wanted to keep them apart.

Amante got up from the computer, totally ignoring me. "I'm going to change right quick. It'll be just a moment for the information to download."

"Avoid my question if you want to. I know you still love her. I'm just trying to figure out why you two are at odds."

"Just drop it, ok."

I let out a long sigh. "Fine."

My phone rang. I looked at the number. I didn't recognize it. Normally, I would let it roll to voicemail. Now, that I'm dealing with this Ivan shit, I was on high alert. This call could be Vanity. "Who is this?" I answered.

My heart dropped when I heard crying and sniffling. "Vanity?" I felt my temper rising. If Ivan put his hands on her, I was going to see his ass with my guns.

"No," the voice said. "It's NeNe."

What the fuck? "Oh, ok, what's up?" I glanced at Amante who was staring right in my face as he changed out of his suit into street clothes. I looked at the huge Panther tattoo he had across his lower back while NeNe spoke.

86

Everybody Got A Secret 2: A Drama Filled Romance

"Stoney, I know you don't want to get involved but I'm in the parking garage with no clothes. Can you please come down?"

"I-I don't know, NeNe." She was trying to fuck my shit up. Have Amante salty with me. Then, I wouldn't get one damn word on Ivan.

"Please," she cried loudly. A gut-wrenching cry that I couldn't ignore. "Please, Stoney, please. Security stripped me of everything. I'm using someone else's phone right now." She cried some more.

"Ok, I'm on my way down." I hung up the phone and stood to my feet.

"Who was that?" Amante asked, dressed in Marcel's apparel. He looked at himself in the full-length mirror. "Harlem Wear ain't that bad. I thought Marcel's clothing line was going to be fucked up. You know how Black people's shit can be sometimes. He stepped his game up with this." He checked himself out some more.

"Man, that was NeNe. She's in the parking garage naked."

Amante snickered as he laced up his Harlem Wear shoes.

"That's not funny. You had them do that to her."

"So what if I did. What the fuck are you going to do about it?"

I snatched one of his shirts out of his closet. "I'm going down there."

"I didn't say you couldn't."

"How could you be so damn cold? She's still the mother of your child." We stared each other down "Oh, I will be back. And you better let me in."

He looked me right in the eye. "Niccas come up missing for making threats."

I didn't back down. I wasn't nobody's punk. "You act like I give a fuck." I started walking towards the door. "Like I said, I'll be back and you better let me in."

I stormed out of Amante's place, getting on the elevator, headed down to the parking garage. When I stepped off, nothing could prepare me for what I saw. My cousin was stooped down in the corner trying to hide herself. I know she told me she was completely naked. I heard her, but I just couldn't believe she didn't have on a stitch of clothing. I came over to her. She stood up, revealing her womanly curves. I turned my head, sticking my arm out, handing her Amante's expensive dress shirt.

"Why do you still fuck with him? He's made it very clear that he don't give a fuck about you. Something has to be wrong with you to go through this type of treatment."

"I love him, Stoney." She sniffled. "I love him from the bottom of my heart. And I think I'm pregnant again."

"See, that's the problem. All y'all do is fuck and fight." For the life of me, I didn't understand that shit. I didn't like fighting. All I wanted to do was fuck. Angry sex wasn't my thing. Once and a while was cool. Not all the time though.

"I'm going back upstairs."

"For what?"

"For us. For love."

This girl was bananas. Ain't no way Amante was trying to hear what she's talking about. She's about to reason with the same nicca that had her stripped naked in a parking garage.

"You're stupid," I told her. "And don't drag me into your shit when he leaves your ass outside in the cold again."

Amante was waiting for us as soon as we got off the elevator. Standing in the doorway with a smug look on his face. "She can't come in here with my shirt on."

"Well, what the fuck is she supposed to wear?" I asked, getting involved, once again. One day I will learn.

"Nothing," Amante said, like that response was normal.

I looked at him like he was nuts. "I don't want to see that shit."

"But I do," he said, smiling.

"This shit has gone way too damn far." I sighed. I was going to need blood pressure medication after fucking with these two.

88

Everybody Got A Secret 2: A Drama Filled Romance

"Look Stoney, my house, my rules. Either you deal with it or leave. I don't have a gun to your head. The choice is yours. That's the rule if NeNe wants to come back in here."

"It's ok, Stoney. I appreciate your help." NeNe looked at Amante, taking off his shirt. "Here you go." She handed it to him, standing there proud in her birthday suit.

He grinned. "That's much better. Come on in."

"What about Dom?" I asked.

"He's in his room playing. He's not coming out."

As soon as NeNe and I came in there was a tap on the door. Amante opened it. Security was standing there. They eyed NeNe for a moment before speaking. "Is everything alright, sir?"

"Yes, just fine. Thank you. Can you please bring me Ms. Diaz-Santana's things? Also, I need a Happy Meal."

"As you wish, sir."

Amante closed the door, looking back at NeNe. "Take a shower. You smell like filth."

NeNe quickly walked toward the bathroom.

I stared at Amante, rubbing my temples. "You know what, I'm out. I can't deal with this shit."

Amante laughed at me. "You're weak."

"I don't give a fuck what you call me. This shit makes my nerves bad. I can't. I'll get Ivan's ass on my own."

"I keep telling you, if you don't put bitches in their places, they will run all over you. Mark my words. You'll see things my way very soon."

What he said caught my attention. "What the hell are you talking about?"

"Nicca, I was you. In love and shit. Mr. Chivalry. Treating these women right. I got my heart stepped on, kicked, and broken. You asked what happened to our love? She cheated on me with some no name nicca. This random bastard didn't even have a fuckin car. She's driving my shit to pick this bum nicca up."

"Wow." That's all I could say. "I had no idea."

"Yeah, you wouldn't. I'm always the bad guy. NeNe is a master manipulator. And the only way to get through to bitches like her is break her ass down. You see she acting like she got some damn sense now."

Damn. I hated to admit it, but in a way he had a point.

"I'm not a monster, Stoney, but I can be. I'll be the worse muthafuckin nightmare ever created if someone fucks with me."

"Yeah, but still, you doing way too much right now."

"Let's see how you feel when Vanity breaks your heart."

He had a lot of nerve. "That won't happen."

"That's what you say. I'll be right there to tell you I told you so when she does. Things are peachy while you're chasing Vanity. Being her side dude. You're rescuing her from her husband. But have you ever thought that maybe she liked being with him? Why hasn't she left before now? And if you do take her away from him, will she go back?"

I rubbed my temples again. "Let me get this information so I can leave. Is it finished downloading?"

"Look who can't handle the truth," he chuckled for a hot minute. "Yeah. I'm sure it's done."

I followed Amante back to his office. While the information was printing, NeNe stepped into the doorway wearing a towel. "You want me to cook?"

"If you want to," he replied. They were speaking to each other as if all that craziness didn't just happen.

"Have you eaten?" she asked him.

"No, but I'm about to leave in a minute."

"Oh." She sighed. "I'll leave you two alone."

The doorbell rang.

Amante yelled, "Get the door. That's security with your stuff and Dom's food."

"Ok," she yelled on her way to the door.

Lawd, these two were dysfunctional as hell. I still can't say they were the worse that I've seen though. Like I said, they were a replica of my parents. They fought like cats and dogs and then fucked right in front of us. I should be used to this type of behavior by now.

"Here you go." Amante handed me the printout of Ivan's whole life story. It was everything from his mother's social security number to his first doctor's visit to his family member's addresses. "You should have everything you need there. If there's anything else, I'll get that too."

"Thanks, dawg. You always come through."

"Not so fast." Amante twirled around in his chair, facing me. "I need a favor."

Oh, lawd, this could be anything. "What's up?"

"Can you take Dom to my father's house? Since you live right around the corner."

"I can do that."

Amante stared at me. He always looked at me like he was looking right through me. "Just so you know, I help you out a lot because of Keno."

I cut my eyes at the ceiling. I hated hearing Keno's fucking name. It would figure that Keno is Amante's hero.

"Be easy for a hot minute," Amante said, still looking through me. "I know how you feel about your father. You have a good right to feel the way you feel. However, your relationship with your father has nothing to do with my relationship with him. Just like I have my issues with my father and you have a good relationship with him. Same difference. My point is Keno was always so good to me. I mean, all the shit that I got myself into, he came to my defense each and every time. Some of this stuff that I know how to do today was all because of Keno. He was smart as a whip and one hellva business man."

I didn't really give a fuck. "There's a lot of truth to that, but all I can think of is what he did to me. He fucked my life up. Me and E almost died cuz of his bullshit ego."

Amante nodded. "Point taken."

Chapter 9

Keystone

"Hey, Dad," my nine-year old son Eternal said, hopping in the front seat.

"What up, E? How was school?"

"Straight. You know I got the best grades in all of my classes. They not ready." He laughed.

I laughed too. "Put it right here," I said, holding my fist out.

E bumped knuckles and then made it explode. He crooked his neck looking in the backseat. "Hey Dom."

Dom gave E a head nod, all into his game. This little boy was a trip. He was two-years old going on twenty-two. At his age, he should be barely talking, carrying a sippy cup. I could tell he was going to be a genius just like his father. I just hope he didn't choose a life of crime like him too. NeNe was smart as well. Although she enjoyed acting like a thot. I have no idea why. I guess she knew it got Amante's attention.

E tossed his backpack in the seat next to Dom. "Can I have pizza for dinner?"

"I just put an order in. We can pick it up after you change."

"Awwwww." E frowned. "I want it now."

"What did I tell you about being whiny?"

E quickly straightened up his face.

Everybody Got A Secret 2: A Drama Filled Romance

"Besides, don't you want to eat dinner with your Uncle Dash?"

E sighed. "Yeah, I guess."

"You say it like you're too good to spend time with your Uncle Dash. What you don't love him anymore? He doesn't have much time and he tries to spend as much of it as he can with you."

"I know. I didn't mean it like that. I love all my uncles. Uncle Emerald, Uncle Cash, and Uncle Dan. I'm just hungry. That's all. That little school lunch does nothing for my appetite."

I laughed. This boy right here. "Your appetite, huh?"

He smiled. "Yeah, I'm getting older, Dad. I think I saw some hair on my chin, just like you."

"Let me see," I said while we waited at the light. "Oh, ok, I think I see something too." I didn't see shit, but I wasn't about to tell my son that and bust his bubble.

E pulled down the visor, checking his chin out in the mirror. "I knew it! I saw something when I was getting ready for school this morning."

I couldn't help but laugh. This boy had jokes. "We're going to your Papi Carlo's house so you can freshen up."

"That's cool. I want to get out of this uniform anyway."

E lived with my parents. Well, let me rephrase that, my other parents. My biological mother and my uncle Carlo.

"I wish I could have met my Papi Keno," E said with a sad face.

"What did you say?" I nearly swerved into the next lane. The car honked at me and I honked back. "You wish you could have what?"

"Met my Papi Keno," he said so innocently.

I was livid. "Where'd you get that from? Did someone tell you to say that?"

E picked up on my anger. "Did I say something wrong?"

I took a few deep breaths. I remained cool on the outside, but I was fuming on the inside. Carlo's fuckin ass put that shit in his head. Carlo knows how I feel about my father. I loved him

93

because that's how I'm supposed to feel. The man gave me life, but I couldn't stand his guts. Yes, even in the afterlife, I still despised him. The things he did to me, Dash, and Dan were unforgivable. Each one of us had the mental and physical scars to prove it. Dan still had nightmares to this day. Dash avoids everything. He stays in deep denial, avoiding things. Because Dash and I are only months apart, Karen stopped paying him attention when I was born. Keno never paid him any attention. Only adding to his abandonment, trust, and commitment issues. And me, I cope the best way I can. Some days are better than others. My temper has gotten the best of me on several occasions. I just black the fuck out. I've never hit a woman and I never will, but I'll fuck a dude up. I have zero tolerance for bullshit.

"I'm sorry, Dad." E was staring at me as if he was in trouble.

"No, son, you didn't do anything wrong. It's just that my relationship with your Papi Keno was really complicated."

"Like your relationship with my mom?"

I felt like I was going to hyperventilate. I was so glad we were around the corner from my parent's house. "Did your Papi Carlo tell you about her too?"

"No," E said with a sad face. "But I want to know."

"You're not old enough," I said stalling. "Give it a little more time, ok?"

E looked at me like he wanted to cuss. "Ok," he said, looking away, out the window. The same thing I did when I was shitty as hell.

Truth is, I wasn't ready to reveal who his mother was. I didn't want to answer all the questions that came with it. My heart ached for my son. If I could have gone back in time, I would have. I feel like my parent's death was all my fault. As bad as my parents were, I wished that I could go back in time and give them life again.

I saw Cash's truck in the driveway when I pulled up to my parent's house. E broke out of car like lightening running towards the house. Dom looked like he wanted to do the same, but he was confined by a car seat. He was squirming around when I got out of the car.

"Ok, Dom, I'm getting you out," I said, unfastening him.

As soon as I put him on the ground, he took off running too. I picked up E's book bag, carrying it into the house. Cash's wife Karen balled up her fists as soon as she saw me, like she wanted to steal on my ass. "What I do?"

She rolled her eyes, hard. "It ain't you. It's that Kimaya bitch that you're engaged to. I'm going to beat that bitches ass. Believe that."

I'm sure I looked perplexed. "Damn, I just dropped her off at home not that long ago. What the hell did she do that fast?"

"She called my damn husband over to her house to talk."

"And he went?" I asked. I couldn't see Cash talking to Kim. He hated her.

"Hell yeah, he went. She claimed she wanted to apologize, but I know what the bitch really wanted. The scheming bitch wanted to fuck my husband."

"Cash said that."

"Yes, he did."

I shrugged. "I don't know what you want me to do about it, Karen."

"I want you to keep your triflin ass fiancée away from my husband BEFORE I BEAT THE BRAKES OFF THAT HOE!"

"Ok. Ok," I said, putting my arms around her, hushing her up. I rocked her back and forth, calming her down. She was getting loud. I didn't come here to pick a fight with her. My bone to pick was with my parents.

I gently rubbed her back. "Don't let Kim stress you out. I might have my differences with Cash, but one thing about him, he is loyal. He's never going to betray you." Holding her for a moment seemed to calm her down.

"I'm still going to beat her ass."

"If you beat her ass, that's her problem. I don't care and I don't want to know about it. That's between you and her. Real talk, she should have stayed in her place."

"That's what I'm saying."

"And I feel you."

Cash and Karen's son Bash ran over to me. His real name was Cash Dollar like his father. We just called him Bash as a nickname.

"Hi!" he said, waving his hand at me. "Candy?"

He offered me a sucker that had clearly been eating on for quite some time. "Thanks, Bash," I said, pretending to lick it. Ain't no way I would take a lick off this sucker. It was all slobbed out. "Mmmm. That was good."

"More?" Bash said, holding the nasty looking sucker in my face.

"Noooooo. I don't want a tummy ache. But thank you for sharing."

"Ok." Bash smiled at me and stuck the yucky sucker back in his mouth.

"What's up, bro?" Cash said, walking into the living room eating a sandwich.

"Nothing. What's good with you?"

"I saw Kimaya."

The look on Karen's face when he mentioned her name.

I wasn't sticking around for this shit. "Well, that's my cue to exit."

I made a beeline for Carlo's home office. I needed to check his ass right quick. I knocked on the cracked door.

"Come in," my uncle said.

I stepped inside, leaving the door wide open.

"Oh, hey, Stoney." He stood from his desk, removing his reading glasses, giving me a one-arm hug. "What brings you by? Do you need help with something? How's business going?"

"Business is good," I said, unenthused.

He smiled at me, nodding his head. "That's good to hear. You know, you look more and more like your father every time I see you."

I felt my temper rising again. "See, that's what brings me by. I wish you would stop saying that. And stop bringing Keno up to E. He has enough issues. He doesn't need you shoving your brother down his throat too."

"Son, I didn't—"

"Oh, yeah, and add that to the list too. I'm not your son. I'm your nephew."

"I know exactly who you are. I was there the day you were born. And you are my son. All five of you boys are mine. I'm your father since your father is no longer here. That's what Keno would want."

"Stop doing that."

"What?"

"That! Each time I see you, you make sure I relive that Keno is no longer here."

"I can't forget. I miss him every day."

"I know. You tell me every time I see you."

"What I don't understand is how you can forget. If I killed my father, I would think about that every day for the rest of my life."

"Well, that's the difference between me and you, Carlo. We're nothing alike."

"Unless you did it on purpose."

"What is all this yelling?" My mother walked into the office, dressed in the same tired sweats and house shoes. Her hair was pulled back in a ponytail. She was a thick, pretty woman who dressed super sloppy. I rarely saw her fixed up. "What are you two fighting about now?"

Carlo stared at me and I stared right back at his ass.

"You got something you want to say to me?" I asked Carlo.

Not backing down, Carlo walked from behind the desk. "I said it. Did you kill Keno on purpose? It's no secret that you were fucking Karen."

"Wow." I couldn't believe he was coming at me like this. I was a damn kid. Karen and Keno are both responsible for their own actions. I looked at my mother. "This is all your fault. You made a baby with a coke head, woman beater." Then I looked at Carlo. "And you forced her hand to give me away to a child molesting freak. So, if you need to be mad at anyone for Keno's death, you need to fault yourself. If you were handling your business at home, your wife wouldn't have stepped out on you and fucked your twin brother."

Carlo charged at me, but my mother stepped in his path. "Oh no! Carlo, don't!"

I wasn't worried about Carlo or his pussy ass feelings. "Nah, let that nicca go. This has been a long time coming. He keeps coming at me about things out of my control. Keno shot me first. Somehow you forgot that detail. I'm lucky to be alive. And then he tried to kill my son."

Carlo looked like he wanted to put two slugs in me. The same way his brother did. Fuck him and Keno. My father was a troubled man who took his demons out on us. We walked around on eggshells growing up. Afraid that Keno would flip out and beat us or worse kill us.

Then, there was Karen. The woman who I thought was my mother until I was sixteen. My mother's first cousin. My second cousin. I still can't wrap my head around the whole situation. Karen was E's mother. That's why I didn't want to tell him who his mother really was. I was too ashamed.

I was totally blind to what was really going on until it was too late. Since I was the baby, I was always catered to. Karen gave me extra special attention. She breast-fed me until I was five. Some say that she just didn't want me to grow up. Now, I know otherwise. She took baths with me until I went into puberty. I slept in the bed with her until the same age. She would cuddle with me and hold me close all night long, rubbing against me. Then, there were the stares. I thought it was admiration. How was I supposed to know that the woman I thought was my mother was in lust with me?

When I was fifteen, Karen came into my room in the middle of the night. I thought she was Vanity. I hadn't seen Vanity since I transferred from Morgan Park to CVS High school. I was supposed to leave the back door open so she could sneak up the back steps to my room. Normally, she climbed through my window.

Everybody Got A Secret 2: A Drama Filled Romance

This particular night it was raining badly. Vanity called me. She said that she was going to try and get her cousin to drop her off. If she did come, it would be kinda late. I told her cool because Dan could bring her back home. I didn't have my license yet so technically I wasn't supposed to drive. Although, I'd dropped her off at her cousins house a couple of times.

It was getting later and later. I fell asleep naked waiting for Vanity to come. I was fast asleep when Karen entered my room. So, when Karen got under the covers with me, I thought it was Vanity. Karen was the same size and height. In the dark, there was no way I would have known the difference. Although, I did notice that Vanity seemed to be a bit aggressive and more experienced. Those thoughts quickly faded when she started riding me. This was Vanity's favorite position back then so I didn't think nothing of it.

I didn't even know it wasn't Vanity until I listened to my voicemail the next day. She left me a message saying she wasn't coming. I had no idea that it was Karen until she confessed. She said she wanted to be with me for a long time. It didn't help that Keno hadn't slept with her in months. So, she picked the next best thing, me. At the time, I didn't know I wasn't her son. The whole incident made me sick to my stomach. I hated that I wasn't more aware that night. Maybe I could have stopped all this from occurring. I tried to forget the whole incident by avoiding Karen.

I didn't know she was pregnant until I saw her small protruding belly. That's when she confessed that the baby was mine. I'm not sure how she managed to keep her pregnancy from Keno for nine months, but somehow she did. Between sniffing coke and the other woman in his life, Keno didn't pay much attention to Karen anyway.

The day of my sixteenth birthday party is when all hell broke loose. Vanity said she was coming to my party, but never made it. She was on punishment and couldn't sneak out. I had the bomb house party. A radio personality from WGCI was there hosting. The block was closed off so that my guests could chill outside.

The food was phenomenal. Catered by a bunch of local restaurants, including Harold's and Home of the Hoagie. There were contests and prizes. I got a brand new Mercedes Benz as a birthday present from Keno. Karen gave me a weekend getaway for four. The rest of my family gave over ten-thousand dollars in my birthday wishing well. I was the man that day. I was getting so much love until I didn't think anything could ruin the night.

After all my guests left, it was just me and Dan cleaning up. Dash ditched us for a girl. He cut out right after the party ended. Something he always did. Dash was always laid up in some pussy. Keno came into the kitchen asking me if I loved my present. I told him yes and thanked him. He hugged me and kissed me on my cheek, telling me how much he loved me. That I was his favorite son. He made no secret about that. He's told me I was his favorite since I was born. I'm assuming because I look identical to him.

Things turned tragic when Karen came downstairs, holding her stomach, announcing that she was in labor. Dash and Dan knew everything that happened. Keno was the only one in the dark. The smile on Keno's face turned to rage. In a blink of an eye, he was across the room, beating the shit out of Karen. Punching her like a man. Dan and I came to her defense. I wasn't about to let him kill my son. He stopped beating Karen, pulling out his glock, and shot her in the chest. Dan and I both froze when her body hit the floor.

Keno stared at me with hurt, disgust, and betrayal. I tried to explain to him what happened, but he wasn't trying to hear it. He pulled out his gun and started shooting as we ran to my room. Before I could close the door, Keno pushed his way in, firing four shots. Two hit me, one in the chest and one in the stomach. At the time, I didn't even know that I had been hit.

I reached under my bed, got my gun, and shot back at him. One killer shot to the dome. I'll never forget the dying look Keno gave me. He stared at me as if he couldn't believe that I killed him. Falling backwards, he landed face up with his fingers still wrapped around his gun. His eyes were wide open in shock. It's uncanny how Carlo stares at me the exact same way.

We rushed back downstairs when we heard Karen screaming. Blood was everywhere. I wasn't even sure how she was still alive with a huge hole in her chest. She was pushing the baby out. I kneeled down just in time to see my son's head crowning. I pulled him out and he cried immediately. It was a bittersweet moment because Karen took her last breath at the same time. Dan and I both stood there in shock once again. We just lost our father and now our mother was gone too.

My son's cries brought us both back to reality. We didn't have time to mourn. I told Dan to get me some scissors, a blanket, and one of Karen's hair tie. Dan rushed to get the items that I asked him for. As soon as he came back, I put the hair tie on the umbilical cord and then cut it.

"Hand me the gun," Dan said.

I didn't realize that I still had the gun in my hand. "What for?"

"Because you're a father now. I can't let you go to jail."

Now, I was feeling weak. I had come down off my adrenaline high. "Jail is the last thing on my mind. I'm not sure if I'm going to make it beyond tonight." I was bleeding so bad that blood was all on the wall, all on the floor, and all over the baby. "Promise me, you'll look after my son if something happens to me."

"Nothing's going to happen to you, Stoney," Dan said with tears in his eyes. "I can't lose you too. I already called 911."

I'm not sure how much time passed. I was in and out of consciousness when the ambulance and the police arrived. The last thing I remember was someone taking my baby out of my arms. "His name is Eternal," I mumbled.

"Don't speak," the female EMT said as she put me on the stretcher.

"Please. Make sure they know his name is Eternal. It's important. He has to live."

"Ok," she assured me. "Just don't say another word."

Princess Diamond

That was the last words I heard before I blacked out.

After spending seven months in the hospital and three more in rehab, I found out that my Aunt Emilia and my Uncle Carlo had adopted my son. Because I was a minor, they became legally responsible for me, which made them responsible for E too.

Also, I found out that Dan took the rap for me. He was sentenced to six years in jail for first-degree murder. Thanks to Uncle Antonio, he only ended up doing three. Uncle Antonio kept appealing his case until the appeal went through. That's when he was able to convince the court that it was self-defense.

Nearly a year later, I was able to come home. Not to my home, but to Carlo's house. Eternal was ten months. I was so excited to see him. The fact that he was alive was a miracle. He is the only reason why I fought so hard to get well. That's why I named him Eternal. I was claiming life for my son. I wasn't sure if my baby would recognize me when he saw me, but he did. That made me the happiest person alive when my son reached out for me, knowing that I was his father.

Shortly afterwards, I found out the truth. Emilia was my real mother.

"Stoney, baby, are you ok?" my mother said, snapping me back to reality.

I blinked a few times, realizing that I was stretched out in E's bed, holding his favorite teddy bear.

My mother scooted closer to me. "Talk to me, Stoney. Don't keep this bottled up inside."

"Don't touch me," I exclaimed. Every time I reflected on the past, I felt icky and I didn't liked to be touched.

"You have to talk about it. If you won't talk to me, then maybe you'll speak to a therapist. It might be a great idea if we go as a family. It might help us."

"I'm not talking to no shrink."

"I'm worried about you."

"Well, don't be," I said putting the teddy down, sitting on the side of E's bed.

"I love you so much," my mother said, touching my arm.

Everybody Got A Secret 2: A Drama Filled Romance

I jumped. "I told you not to touch me." I had to hold myself just to keep from shaking.

She scooted away from me a little. "I want to tell you something. Maybe this will help you." She got up and closed the bedroom door and then came back and sat next to me. "You weren't a mistake. I know you think you were, but you weren't. Keno and I planned to get pregnant. We were in love." She touched me again. This time I didn't tremble. "I was so happy when I was pregnant with you. I bet you always wondered why your father thought you were so special. It wasn't because you looked like him. It was because you were our love child."

Huh? I frowned. "Wait. What?"

She lovingly touched my face. "I can't tell you why we did what we did. Why we fell in love or why we cheated on our spouses. All I can tell you is, we both loved you very much. I just figured if you knew the truth, maybe that would set you free some kind of way."

What she said helped a little bit. "I really appreciate you telling me that. For nine years, I've always thought I was the abortion that lived. Like I'm an outsider and that everything is all my fault. Like I ruined both families."

"No. That wasn't the case. At all. There's so much more that went on. If anyone is to blame, it's Carlo."

Did she just say that? "What does that mean?"

"One step at a time. Let's start with you and I. Maybe we can finally form a real relationship."

I sighed again. "Maybe."

Tears came to my mother's eyes. "I know you hate me."

"Oh, I don't hate you. Emerald hates you. I just don't understand you. Sometimes I don't like you. And I don't feel that I can trust you."

She started weeping. "Well, maybe now that I made the first move opening up to you, we can start to bond."

I looked at her. All I could see was those frumpy clothes. "Maybe," I repeated. I know she was trying, but it's been nine years.

"It would mean the world to me."

E opened the room door, wearing a towel around his waist. "Oh, am I interrupting something?" He looked at us. "Let me get my clothes. I can dress in Papi's room."

"Nah, E. This is your room. Your grandmother was just leaving." I looked over at her. "Right?"

"Right. I need to check on dinner anyway." She leaned over, trying to kiss me and I deflected, turning my head so far away that she kissed the air. Disappointment washed over her face as she patted my leg. "One day."

"One day," I repeated. I was just feeling some kinda way. She needed to understand that.

I looked away while E put on his briefs. "C'mere," I said, checking him out for bruises. "Has anyone touched you?"

"No." E stared at me like I was crazy because I was turning him in every direction trying to make sure.

"Are you sure?" I asked him, getting all in his face. I'm sure my behavior was a bit erratic.

"You said if somebody touched me to beat they ass and then tell you."

I busted out laughing. That's exactly what I said too. I let go of E. "Ok, I guess you got it covered. Remember our talk, though."

"I will," he said walking back over to his closet, thumbing through is clothes. "Can you take me shopping? A lot of these clothes don't fit no more."

"What those grades look like?"

He looked back at me with a cocky smirk on his face. "Good like always."

"I heard you earlier, but I need to pull them up online."

"Go ahead. My grades are good. I got all A's and one B."

"I'll be the judge of that."

He smiled at me. "You'll see."

"Don't think I forgot about you cussing either. You better not say ass again."

"Yes, sir."

Everybody Got A Secret 2: A Drama Filled Romance

I loved my son. He was my heart. I didn't sign up to be a teen dad, but I wouldn't trade my seed for nothing. I glanced around his room. It was spotless like I told him. The last time I came, he had shit everywhere. I could hardly get in here. I stood up and walked over to one of the many drawings that decorated E's room. "When'd you do this one?"

"While you were gone," he said like it was no big deal.

"This is real nice." It was a painting of me holding him when he was a baby. "I'm taking this one with me."

He shrugged while putting back all the clothes that he dug through to find the right outfit. "You can have it. I'll just draw another one."

"I see you get your gift of drawing from me. And—" I almost slipped up and said his Papi Keno. It was a habit. Keno—that's who I got my gift of drawing from. "What do you want to be when you grow up?"

E flopped down next to me. "An entertainer like you and Uncle Marcel."

That's not what I expected him to say. "Have you thought about being an architect?"

He frowned. "Not really."

"You can still be like me. You know I'm an architect too."

E looked at all the drawings around his room as if he just noticed them for the first time. "Maybe."

"Did you know that drawing was a form of entertainment too?"

His eyes lit up. "No, I didn't know that."

I had his attention now. "I'll tell you what, if you keep up those A's, I'll let you put on an art show. Then you can show off your work. It would be similar to having a performance but a little classier. What do you say?"

E smiled bright. "That'll be real cool. My grades about to be on fleek."

E and I walked downstairs to the kitchen. Dom was sitting at the table eating and swinging his feet. "You just ate. You still hungry?"

He looked at me and nodded his head.

"I'm getting ready to leave. You going with me?"

Dom ignored me, chowing down on my mother's enchiladas, beans, and rice.

"Aight, Dom. Last call before I leave."

I cracked up laughing when Dom chucked me the deuces.

I told my mother bye. I hugged her and kissed her on the cheek to make up for the shade I threw earlier. That gesture seemed to make her smile.

As soon as I got in the car, I texted Amante to let him know where Dom was.

Me: Aye, your son sold me out for some food. He's at Carlo's.

Amante: That's how that little nicca do. I forgot to tell you, he'll sell anybody out for some food.

Me: CTFU. I see. Traitor.

Amante: He get that shit from his mama lol

Me: SMH But you slept with her though. What that make you?

Amante: Right. I should have strapped up. Both times. Cuz Tanika is pregnant too.

Me: Damn. You got that.

Amante: Fuck that. I hope you got one on the way too. In fact, I hope you have twins lol

Me: See, that's that bullshit. Later.

Amante: Peace.

As soon as I pulled off, Kimaya text me some bullshit about how much she missed me. I wasn't trying to hear nothing she had to say. She was up in Cash's face not that long ago. Her ass could wait.

"What do you think about Kimaya?" I asked E. "You like her?"

"Not really. She's pretty with a big booty, though."

Playfully, I punched him in the chest. "Don't be checking my girl out."

He grinned. "Well, you asked."

Everybody Got A Secret 2: A Drama Filled Romance

I picked up my phone and scrolled though until I came across a picture of Vanity. It was a beautiful picture of us on the Welcome Cruise. "What you think of her?"

I know E hadn't met her, but he was pretty good at assessing people. I wanted to know what his first thoughts were. He took the phone out of my hand, staring at it. "Who is she?"

"Her name is Vanity."

"Is she your new girlfriend?"

"No. We're friends for now. I knew her before you were born and we reconnected while on vacation."

He stared at the picture again. "I like her."

"What do you like about her?"

"Her smile. It's genuine." He handed me back my phone. "You look nice in that picture, Dad. I wished that I looked like you."

I didn't like that comment. Not one bit. "You don't like how you look?"

E shrugged. "I like how you look."

I had to nip this shit right now. Ain't no way I was going to allow my son to have a complex. I pulled into Meijer's parking lot off 92nd and Western. "What's this all about? There's nothing wrong with the way you look. You're handsome."

"But I don't look like you."

"No, but you look like your uncles."

"True, but I want to look like you. I'm your son and we look nothing alike. I want people to know that you're my father when they see us."

He tugged at my emotions when I saw him holding back tears. "Look at me." E turned his sad face towards me. "Everyone knows that you're my son. I'm proud of you. Just because you live at Papi Carlo's house doesn't mean that you're a secret. I'm happy to be your father. I couldn't have asked for a better son."

E leaped into my arms. "I love you, Dad."

This little nicca was about to make me cry. "I love you too, son," I said, hugging him tight. I didn't care if this made me look like a punk. I gave my son hugs and kisses all the time. I wanted him to hear and see how much I loved him at all times.

We embraced for quite a while. I didn't stop holding him until he let me go first.

"You're right, Dad. Besides, all the girls at school think I'm cute."

"Cuz you're fly. Just like me. Now, let's go get this pizza."

I pulled off on my way to Italian Fiesta Pizzeria in South Shore when I got a call from Pebbles.

"HE DID WHAT?" She was talking so fast, I could barely understand what she was saying. "Calm down, I'm on my way." I hung up the phone. "E, that pizza has to wait. Something came up."

The urgency in Pebbles' voice indicated that I needed to come right now. Vanity lived in Chatham. I was practically around the corner. It took me about eight minutes to get there. I parked in front of a really nice house off 89th place.

Pebbles came to the door, looking beautiful as ever. Rocking white thigh-high boots, fitted jeans that rested on her hips, a huge name belt accented in rhinestones, a long sleeve body-suit lace shirt, and a short-waist white fur jacket. She hugged me, wrapping her arms around my neck. My hands rested in the crook of her back. I took one whiff of her perfume and my dick got hard as a brick.

She stepped away from me with lustful eyes. It was obvious that she was feeling some kind of way about me. Just like, I was feeling some kinda way about her. I promise, if I could tap it just one more time, I'd make sure she knew I was the best she ever had.

"Thanks for coming, Stoney. This shit is insane. I'm ready to fuck Ivan's ass up myself."

"Now, what happened?" I asked Pebbles, walking inside. I couldn't believe this, but I had a bad feeling about Ivan picking her up. "And where's this nicca at?"

"He's at Chip's—" Pebbles stopped mid-sentence, staring at me. "Who is that?"

Everybody Got A Secret 2: A Drama Filled Romance

I was so concerned with Vanity's well-being that I forgot all about E. Damn. I didn't want to introduce him like this, but he's here now. "My son, Eternal. E this is Miss Pebbles. Say hi."

The stupid grin on his face told me that he really liked Pebbles. "Hi, Miss Pebbles," he said in the deepest voice he could muster. I could tell he was trying to impress her.

Pebbles shook her head. "I should have known you had a baby."

"You didn't know nothing. Where's Vanity?"

"I'm right here," she said slowly walking into the living room. Damn, he fucked her up something terrible. Her eye was black and blue, her lips were bruised and swollen, and she had marks all over her face and neck. On top of that, she was walking like she had a few broken bones.

"E, have a seat while I talk to Mrs. Vanity." Thank goodness he had his backpack. "Do your homework."

I whispered to Vanity. "Let me holler at you in the back." Vanity led me to their bedroom. "Now, what the fuck happened?" I asked examining all her bruises.

I sat on the bed and she sat in my lap, crying as she told me all the horrible things that Ivan did. Basically, this punk went in on her, trying to prove his manhood.

Then she took of her robe and showed me the bruises all over her body. Instead of this punk bitch stepping to me like a real man, he decided to torture her. I couldn't believe he choked her out.

What a sick bastard. "I got something for his ass," I said, fuming. I wanted to see how much of a big shit he was when I stepped to him, locked and loaded. Was he going to whip my ass like he did her? Something told me he was a coward. Most women beaters were. He liked intimidating women but he wasn't man enough to fuck with another nicca. I was about to pull his muthafuckin card, though.

I stormed out of the bedroom back into the living room. "Watch my son," I said to Pebbles, who was sitting down helping E with his homework. "Harm comes to him, that's your ass."

I meant that shit. If one hair was harmed on E's head, I was going to paint this whole city red. I hated that I was impulsive and drove over here. I should have dropped E off first.

"Calm down, Papa Bear. Ain't nothing going to happen to your cub. If somebody drops by, I'll just say he's my little cousin. Besides, he's cuter than you anyway."

That put a huge smile on E's face. He was sitting so close to Pebbles, he was practically in her lap. His eyes kept darting to her cleavage.

Vanity was right on my heels. "Wait, you have a son?" She looked at E with shock. "How come I'm just now finding out about this?"

"I don't let just anyone meet my son." Before Vanity could ask me anymore questions I shut her down. We weren't going to have this conversation in front of E. That's not how I rolled. "That's not why I'm here. Besides, you can get to know him while I'm gone."

"Where you going? I know you not going over to Chip's?"

"Why the fuck wouldn't I?"

Vanity stared at me with concern. "I'm afraid for your safety."

I chuckled. "You need to be afraid for that nicca's safety. Fear ain't in my vocabulary."

Pebbles laughed too. "Shit, you should be glad Stoney is stepping to his ass," she told Vanity. "He could leave you by yourself to deal with this bullshit."

"That's not how I meant it." Vanity still looked worried. "I just don't want nobody to get hurt."

"Too late for that shit. I'll be back."

She held onto me with tears in her eyes. "Be careful, Stoney. Ivan is crazy."

I gently pulled away from her. "I'm about to fix this shit." I was going to see Ivan's ass anyway. He just sped things up, acting a damn fool.

I stepped out of Vanity's house checking out my surroundings. I can never be too careful. For all I know, this wack nicca could be lurking around outside the crib.

Everybody Got A Secret 2: A Drama Filled Romance

I got in the car and went into my special compartment, pulling out my HK P2000 SK 9mm handgun. I loved this joint specifically for times like this. Living in Chicago was dangerous. Things got ugly real quick and I wanted to be prepared for anything.

I didn't tell Pebbles, but I already knew where Chip lived. It was included in the information that Amante gave me. According to the address, he only lived a few blocks over. I put on my holster under my jacket before tucking my gun away.

Chapter 10

Ivan

I was on Chip's porch, chilling. It was cool outside, but I was still heated about my wife's infidelity. Between the liquor, and being high as a kite, the cold air didn't even faze me. I was on the steps. Chip was sitting on the ledge to my right with his feet dangling over and Dino was on the ledge to my left.

While we sat there shooting the shit, I was texting the fuck out of Vanity. I called her every no-good ass, whore, bitch I could come up with. As long as I was hurt, she didn't deserve any peace. I wanted her to feel how the fuck I felt. I was in a shitty place. She needed to be in one too. This whole circumstance had me so gone that I didn't even have the urge to fuck. Normally, when I smoked and drank, I craved pussy. Right now, the only thing that could get my dick hard was retaliation.

Although, I was participating in the conversation with Chip and Dino, I was thinking of my next move. I felt like going back home and beating Vanity's ass again.

"You talk to Pebbles?" I asked Chip.

"Yeah, she wants to fuck you up for putting your hands on her sister."

I frowned at Chip. "She better stay the fuck out of this if she knows what's good for her."

Everybody Got A Secret 2: A Drama Filled Romance

"Look, I don't condone you putting your hands on Vanity. I think that is a punk move but—"

I loved my little brother, but I'd fuck him up too, if need be. "Keep your ass out of my marriage. This is between me and my bitch."

Chip gave me a hard stare. "I was just about to say, I'm out of it. But I'm warning you, if you put your hands on Vanity again or if you even think about doing anything to Pebbles, it's going to be a problem. You know how I feel about women beaters. You already crossed the line. The only reason why I haven't beat your ass myself, is because you're my brother. Trust me, none of this is sitting well with me."

He was blowing my high. "Yeah. Yeah. Yeah. You're entitled to your opinion. Just keep that shit way over there and let me handle my business with my wife."

"All this shit is going to backfire on you. Watch. You're pushing her right into the arms of that other nicca. I'm telling you—"

"Fuck that nicca. He can suck my big black dick. If she even thinks about leaving me for that muthafucka, she might as well sign her own death certificate. Cuz if I don't kill her ass, I'm going to make her wish she was dead until she comes back to me."

Dino laughed. "You finna kill a muthafucka over some pussy? Couldn't be me. I wouldn't give a shit if she was my wife, I'd let that bitch go and find me another bitch. Ain't no bitch worth my freedom."

"That's what I'm saying," Chip cosigned. "He losing his damn mind like Vanity is the last piece of pussy on earth. Either you going to work it out and save your marriage or divorce her and move on. Men outnumber women twenty to one."

"Both of y'all shut the fuck up! That's why both of you dickheads are single."

Chip leaned over taking the blunt from me. "The way you make marriage sound, I might need to stay single."

Dino cracked the fuck up. "Your brother is pussy whipped."

Both of these high muthafuckas cracked the fuck up. "Y'all can kiss my black ass. I didn't ask for your permission and I don't give a fuck what you think. Vanity is going to pay for this shit, believe that."

"Whatever," Chip said. "I still think you're wrong."

"And I said, I don't give a fuck what you think."

As we were going back and forth over how I handled my wife, a silver Mercedes CLS550 with mirror tint parked right behind my BMW, in front of Chip's house.

We were on guard immediately.

"Who the fuck is that?" Chip asked me. "You expecting somebody?"

"Nicca, I don't know. This is your fuckin house. I was about to ask you who the fuck this was."

Chip looked over at Dino. "You know who that is?"

Dino stared at the ride. "Naw, but I got a feeling we're about to find out real quick."

We all watched the car carefully as the door opened and a Gucci sneaker hit the ground.

"I hope this ain't no salesman," I said. "I'm not in the fuckin mood. Easily, this nicca will be cussed the fuck out."

Dino laughed. "They can be pushy bastards."

The mystery dude got out of his whip like he was auditioning for a video or some shit. I could have sworn I heard a director yell cut.

I started laughing. "Look at this corny muthafucka. I bet he thinks he's hot shit rocking Gucci from head to toe."

"Actually, it's kinda fly," Chip said. "This nicca got on all Gucci everything. Jacket, pants, shoes, shirt, belt, and watch. He's rocking at least four stacks, easily."

I looked at his ass sideways. Sometimes, Chip rubbed me the wrong fuckin way by the shit he said. I made a mental note to watch what I said around him from now on. He hasn't been very supportive lately. I wouldn't be surprised if he told Pebbles everything that I said about Vanity. They were close like that. Plus, he was real fond of Vanity, like a sister.

This dude looked familiar, I thought as he walked right up, towering over me while I sat on the steps. I stood up so that we would be face to face. He was still a few inches taller than me. It was clear that this nicca came here to speak to me. "Fuck you want?" I asked, laughing. Pretty boy, muthafucka.

"You know what the fuck I want," he said with venom in his voice.

"Oh, shit," Dino said. "What's up, Stoney? I want you to know I'm not in this. No parts whatsoever." Was Dino's voice trembling?

So, this is Stoney. This green-eyed bitch never took his eyes off me. "Aight, Dino. Fall back if you know what's good."

Dino's scary ass had the nerve to retreat further back on the porch, doing exactly what this muthafucka said.

"Stoney," Chip repeated, jumping off the porch standing next to me. "You got a lot of fuckin nerve coming over here."

"I got this," I told Chip. I didn't need him fighting my battles. "So, you're the punk muthafucka."

"No, you're the punk muthafucka. Any man that puts his hands on his wife is definitely a pussy. I'm going to tell you one time and one time only, if you ever put your hands on Vanity again, I'm going to crush your fuckin skull."

"So, you think because she let you fuck that you all big and bad? Obviously, you don't know who you're fuckin with."

"I see exactly who the fuck you are, fake ass nicca."

He talked a lot of shit, but I could talk just as much shit. "Well, know this, I will beat her ass as much as I feel like it. That's my bitch and I will put my hands, dick, or feet on my bitch if I want to." He laughed in my face. The same way he did on the phone. It caught me off guard. "What the fuck is so funny?"

"You think that this is the first time, don't you? Nah. I've been fucking Vanity since high school. Did you know that? You never had a chance. She only married your selfish, egotistical, wannabe ass because she couldn't find me. But now that I'm back in the picture, she can drop you."

I was on ten, opening and closing my fists. He was trying to play mind games with me. It's cool because now this nicca was on my shit list right with Vanity. I knew something wasn't right. I questioned why Vanity fucked around on me so easily. "You not getting my wife. Now, I don't know what you thought coming over here would prove. I suggest you get back in your toy car, and get the fuck out of my face, before shit goes left real quick."

In a cocky manner, this muthafucka had the nerve to say, "You can suck my dick! I'm not going nowhere until things are clear."

I just lost it, cracking his ass in the jaw. My fist was stinging and this nicca didn't even flinch. "I'ma let you have that pussy ass punch. That's the least I can give you since I beat Vanity's pussy up real good in the Bahamas. But be very clear, that's your only pass."

I walked up on Stoney about to swing on him again. He pulled out a 9mm, putting it right to my forehead. Ready to pull the trigger. Shit, this is the second time today I had a pistol in my damn face. "You gonna shoot me now? I dare you," I said, calling his bluff. I sounded hard, but I was shaking like a leaf on the inside.

"I wish he muthafuckin would," Chip said, walking up, pointing his Ruger at Stoney. "You put a bullet in my brother, I put a bullet in your ass."

Stoney raised his other hand, holding another 9mm, right at Chip. "Bust off then."

This was a tense situation. No matter what went down, I was a dead nicca. He had his gun pressed so hard against my forehead it felt like it was going to leave an imprint. I thought to myself, if I live through this situation, I was going to get me a gun ASAP.

I had no idea this nicca was coming over here on some gangsta shit. He certainly didn't look like that type. I underestimated him, big time. He had a lot more heart than I thought. From the pictures that Pebbles posted, he looked real booty.

"Oh, shit. Oh, shit. Oh, shit," Dino rambled in the background. "What did you do that for? You just started a war. We all about to die!"

What the fuck is he talking about? Dino needed to take his chicken shit ass in the house. He was getting on my nerves almost as bad as this nicca.

"Apologize to this man, Ivan," Dino's chicken shit ass said. This nicca was behind me, pacing back and forth, acting like he needed meds and shit.

Chip looked confused, probably wondering why Dino was bugging the fuck out. I knew my brother. We had our differences, but Chip wasn't going to let this no nicca harm me. Definitely not in his presence.

"Don't retaliate," Dino cried out. "Y'all muthafuckas better start begging too. Do you know who his family is? No, I'm sure you don't because if you did, you'd smooth shit out with this man and let him go."

Just to humor Dino, I asked, "Who?"

"Remember we went to school with them. They crazy as fuck. It's like a thousand of them. They got a few different last names. Diaz, Giuliani, Santana, and like one more. I know y'all heard the stories. All that shit is true. I don't want no trouble because y'all fucked with one of them."

"Go in the house, Dino," Stoney said, like this was his house instead of my brother's. I hated this nicca with a passion.

Chip kept darting his eyes over at me, even though, he never took his gun off Stoney. I could tell that Dino had gotten to him.

"What do you want?" I asked Stoney. I was going to play nice because I didn't want my face blown off.

"Keep your hands off Vanity. If you ever touch her again, I'm going to kill you."

"You act like I'm supposed to be scared."

"You should be. I put a bullet in my father's dome, killing him dead. What the fuck do you think I feel about your life? You're useless to me. I don't give two shits if you live or die. The choice is yours."

"The shit is t-t-true," Dino stuttered, standing inside of the screen door. "It made the news and everything. You can look it up. It happened nine years ago."

Damn, this nicca is crazy. "Aight. Lower your gun then."

Stoney smiled, pressing his gun harder against my forehead. "I'm not that damn stupid." He looked at Chip. "Hand me your gun."

Chip looked over at me like I lost my mind. "What the hell are you thinking? This man is about to shoot us both?"

"Stop fuckin talking to me and give this nicca your gun." Did he not see this gun pointed to my head ready to go off? What the fuck was wrong with his ass?

Chip looked like he wanted to fuck me up. "I hope you know what you're doing."

"I do," I said spit flying everywhere.

Stoney tucked his gun back inside his jacket and took Chip's gun out of his hand, pointing it at his chest. Chip smacked his lips, giving me the side eye. "I'm done with all this shit. Don't expect me to help you out next time. You're on your own."

"Did you see Vanity's face?" Stoney asked Chip.

Chip just stared at Stoney as if he had the audacity to even speak to him.

Stoney repeated himself. "Did you see pictures of Vanity's face?" he said with more of an attitude.

"No," Chip finally said as if he was wondering what was the point of Stoney's question. He might have been wondering, but I knew where he was getting at because I did it.

"Well, your brother beat her until her eye was black and blue, swollen shut. She has handprints on her neck from him choking her out. Cigarette burns are all over her body, including her face, that have blistered into tiny sores."

Everybody Got A Secret 2: A Drama Filled Romance

Chip's eyes darted over to me. "No, I didn't know all that. Is it true?" Chip had the fuckin nerve to ask me.

I remained quiet. I could tell Stoney's empathetic speech affected him. Chip's whole demeanor changed. He was turning on me right in front of my face.

"Of course, it's true. Isn't it Ivan?" he asked, tapping the gun against my head as he spoke. I still remained quiet. "Silence is golden," Stoney said to me before he went back to turning Chip against me. "Pebbles told me that you and Vanity were close. Well, Ivan almost killed her. Is that what you want? To get a call one day that Vanity is dead because your brother lost his temper."

"Why should I believe you?"

"Ask Pebbles. She'll confirm that I'm telling the truth. Your brother is a monster." Stoney laid his eyes back on me. "Nothing should make you spazz out the way you did, especially not on your wife. You have a fuckin problem."

I promise, I wanted to spit in this nicca's face.

We heard the police sirens in the distance. I was hoping someone called the cops. I hate them too, but I was glad to hear that familiar sound.

"I don't have no problem with you," Stoney said to Chip. Then, he looked back at me. "Keep my muthafuckin name out your mouth."

Stoney slowly backed away with both guns still drawn on us. When he got inside of his car, he tossed Chip's gun out on the lawn as he peeled away from the curb.

I ran up to the curb as fast as I could, picking up Chip's gun, letting off five shots as he turned the corner. I wasn't sure if I'd hit his car or not, but he was going to feel my fury. That nicca would pay. The little stunt he just pulled was going to cost him. I was going to take away something that he loved.

He seemed like a stand up type of guy. I wasn't. I was a dirty muthafucka. He brought this shit to my front door. Now, I was going to make him eat shit pie for breakfast, lunch, and dinner for a long as he was fucking around with my wife. When I got done, he was going to wish he never came for me.

Chip walked up to me, snatching his gun back. "You started this shit. We all about to get shot the fuck up because you lost your fuckin' temper. I told you Vanity wasn't happy months ago. You could have fixed that shit then, but you didn't. You kept on and on until she ran to the arms of the next nicca."

"You sound like you want her to be with that nicca."

"Look, I don't give a fuck about Stoney's ass. I'm just saying, if you loved Vanity so much, you would have quit acting a gawd damn fool, and been the husband that you used to be."

"So, you expect me to just sit back and let this nicca take my wife. Cuz that's what this is really about."

"No, I expect you to step up and be a man. Stop putting your hands on women and communicate with your wife. Tell her why you're upset instead of lashing out at her. Like I said, all this shit could have been avoided if you would have checked your pride months ago."

I didn't care what Chip said, it sounded like he was taking up for Stoney. As if he was on his side instead of mine. "So, I'm supposed to forget that Vanity cheated, right? And forget that her lover just came over here and put a gun in my face? Fuck is wrong with you? Obviously, you been smoking on more than just blunts."

"You hit the nicca. I would have pulled a gun on your ass too."

"What the fuck you trying to say?" I asked him, walking up in his face. "You'd put a gun to my head, just like that nicca did?"

"You act like you weren't born and raised here. Muthafuckas stay strapped. All day. If you jump bad, you gotta be willing to deal with the consequences." I was trying to speak and Chip over talked me. "You don't get it. This nicca ain't playing with you or me. And I'll be damned if I get shot over your stupid ass bullshit."

"This nicca came over here. I didn't go to him."

Everybody Got A Secret 2: A Drama Filled Romance

"Ivan, I know you. You probably had words with this dude earlier. You just didn't tell me. Cuz he came over here specifically to get in your ass."

I kept quiet. There was no getting through to Chip when he had his mind made up.

"You brought all this shit on yourself." Chip walked in the house, slamming the door behind him.

When I saw the cops cruising down the street, I hauled my ass in the house right behind him.

Chapter 11

Vanity

I was in the process of cleaning up. Ivan didn't clean shit while I was gone. The house looked like a train wreck. I needed to do something to keep my mind off of my current situation. I still couldn't believe Ivan put his hands on me. My face was fucked up. I looked like I'd been jumped.

"Can I do anything to help, Miss Vanity?" E asked me. He was standing there with a broom already in his hand.

"Did you finish your homework, like your father asked you too?"

"Yes, ma'am, I did."

He walked a little closer to me, waiting for my direction. I couldn't help but stare. Looking at him, all I saw was my baby that I aborted. She would have been the same age. It was apparent that Stoney was very active in his son's life. He spoke very highly of his father.

E was a handsome young man too. I could tell he was going to be a real heartbreaker in a few years. However, I didn't see any traces of Stoney in him. He favored Stoney's brothers. I assumed E's mother was Hispanic because he looked Hispanic. He might not have looked like Stoney, but he acted just like him. His mannerisms, his voice, even the way he looked at me with concern.

Everybody Got A Secret 2: A Drama Filled Romance

I'll admit I was in pure shock when Stoney said this was his son. I got the impression by the way he was in the Bahamas that he was kid-free. All that time we spent together. He never mentioned that he was a father, but then again, I didn't ask. Maybe that's what he was trying to build up to when we were having our romantic picnic on the beach. That's my fault for leaving. He probably would have told me had I stayed and got to know him better like he wanted.

"You can help me wash the dishes."

E put the broom in the hall closet, standing next to me. "Miss Vanity, you don't use your dishwasher?" he asked, looking inside of it to see if it was broken.

I laughed. "Well, I would, but these dishes have been here for quite a few days and they are disgusting. I don't think the dishwasher would get them clean."

"Oh," he said. "I understand. How about you wash and I'll dry."

"I'd like that," I said, enjoying his company.

He was a breath of fresh air. Apart of me wanted to be mad that I was babysitting Stoney's love child, but I just couldn't. He was too adorable. Besides, Stoney didn't have to come. I interrupted his time with his son. He could have bitched about it, but that's not how Stoney was.

So much was on my mind. I felt torn. I wanted to hate Ivan, but I couldn't. I still loved him, deeply. Things were progressing so quickly between me and Stoney too. And now that I met E, I'm sure things would be moving even faster.

E looked at me when I sighed. He didn't say anything. Unlike most nine-year olds, he didn't talk a lot. He spoke when necessary or when spoken too. Very well-behaved. I couldn't stand an unruly child. That shit drove me crazy.

"Is it just you and your father at home? Or do you live with your mother?"

E picked up the dishes I just sat down, drying them off. "I live with my Papi Carlo. My mother died when I was born."

Living with his grandparents would make sense. Stoney had him really young. Besides, Stoney is gone with Marcel all the time. E wouldn't have a stable environment.

"I saw pictures of you and my dad on vacation."

"Is that right?" I smiled.

"Do you love him?"

Did Stoney put his son up to this? Just as I was about to answer, Pebbles walked in. "Hey, I was cleaning up the bathroom and I came across these. Can I have them?"

I walked away from the sink, closer to Pebbles to look at what she was asking for. "Girl, what are you going to do with these?"

Pebbles cut her eyes at me. "Use them. What the hell do you think I'm going to do with birth control? Duh. Can I have them or what?"

I glanced at the pills again before I pulled her away from the kitchen so E wouldn't hear our conversation. "Those aren't birth control, silly. They're fertility pills."

Pebbles' eyes nearly bucked out of her head. She went into a coughing fit. "Water. Please," she mumbled.

I slowly walked back into the kitchen, grabbing her a cup of water. I couldn't run. My legs hurt too bad. "Here," I said, handing it to her. "Why'd you react like that?"

Pebbles took a few gulps of water. "I've been taking these for nearly a month. I thought they were birth control."

"WHAT! Why would you do something stupid like that?"

"Cuz I ran out of mine. I figured since me and you take the same ones, I could take a pack of yours. You had four packs so I took one. I didn't feel like going to the doctor paying my copay and then paying for the prescription too."

If I wasn't so sore, I would have fucked Pebbles up. Those fertility meds were expensive. "I had them in my birth control pouch so that Ivan wouldn't know. I was trying to get pregnant, remember?"

Pebbles fell back against the wall. "OMG! Vanity." Tears came to her eyes. "I've been taking that shit trying to prevent getting pregnant. Damn. I could scream right now. I don't want no fucking baby. I can't fuckin believe this is happening to me."

I hugged her. "Calm down. I've taken them off and on for almost a year now. They haven't worked yet. Personally, I think they are garbage. I got them really cheap and it shows. You'll be just fine. I'm just pissed that I wasted my money."

Pebbles wiped away a few tears. "You better be right. Getting pregnant is not on my agenda right now. I want to be married first. Besides, I did my thing in the Bahamas." Fresh tears formed again.

"You're overreacting."

"That's easy for you to say. You want a baby. I don't."

"Well, maybe you'll keep your ass out of my cabinet," I said, leaving Pebbles in the hallway. There was nothing more I could say to comfort her. If she wasn't meddling, she wouldn't have this problem to deal with.

When I walked back into the kitchen, the dishes were washed, dried, and put up. I looked in the cabinet just to be sure. "Thank you, E. You didn't have to do them. I was coming back."

"It's no problem." E was sitting down on the couch with a pencil and paper. It looked like he was drawing.

I was about to ask him what it was when the doorbell rang. After peeking out the curtain to make sure it wasn't Ivan, I opened the door. "How did things go?"

Stoney rushed in. "Can I talk to you in private?" He grabbed me by my hand, leading me to the back once again. On our way, Stoney bumped into Pebbles.

"Excuse you," she said with a nasty attitude. "Look where the hell you're going."

Stoney stopped racing towards the back, taking a good look at Pebbles. "What's wrong with you?"

"Nothing," she said, walking away sulking.

He stared at her as she walked away before directing his attention back to me. We walked into my bedroom. He closed the door behind us. "Did E give you any problems?"

"No. He was really good. What happened at Chip's?"

Stoney lowered his voice. "Some shit went down. Things got messy."

"What does that even mean? Is Ivan hurt?"

Stoney frowned. "Is Ivan hurt?" Anger washed over his face. "That's the fucking problem. You need to make a decision. It's going to be me or him. You can't have us both."

"I can't make that decision right now. I need time. It's not like Ivan is my boyfriend. He's my husband. You knew that I was married when we started screwing around. It wasn't a problem then."

"Well, it's a problem now. Ivan and I have some serious beef. There is no creeping around or pretending like we're free to do what we want like we did in the Bahamas. This nicca knows about you and me. And he's ready to set shit off."

"Did he say that?"

"Vanity!" He looked like he wanted to shake some sense into me. "Are you listening to me? This nicca is going to be on a rampage."

I stood there trying to process what he just said.

"Pack your shit. You're coming with me. It's not safe for you here."

"I'm not leaving my home, Stoney."

"Fuck that." He yanked me by the arm.

"Ouch! You're hurting me."

He didn't let my arm go until I reached the closet. "Get your ass in there, throw some shit in a suitcase, and put on some clothes. I'm not asking you, I'm telling you."

I heard the seriousness in his voice. Going against his orders would cause more problems. I didn't feel like battling him too. I was too sore from dealing with Ivan earlier. "Ok," I said.

"I'll be right back." Stoney left out of my bedroom, walking back into the living room. I heard him tell E to gather his stuff. Then, he told Pebbles that she was coming with him too. Pebbles must've been distraught because she didn't even protest. That wasn't like her. She didn't like nobody telling her what to do.

Everybody Got A Secret 2: A Drama Filled Romance

Stoney came back into the room, easing up behind me. "You're not mad at me, are you?"

"No. If you think I'm not safe here, and I need to be with you, then that's what I'm going to do."

Stoney kissed my shoulder and smiled. "Trust me. I'm right. That muthafucka is half-cocked. I fear that if you stay here he's going to come back and kill you."

"C'mon, I realize you two have your differences, but Ivan would never do that."

"Are you that naïve? This man has a few screws loose."

I guess I wasn't packing fast enough because Stoney took a handful of clothes and tossed them in the half empty suitcase. "Fuck it. Whatever you don't have, I'll buy."

I took off my gown and Stoney popped me on the ass. "Ouch! Quit it. I'm still hurting."

He grinned. "I couldn't help it."

Quickly, I slipped on my pink velour jogging suit. After pulling the hood over my messy hair, I slipped on my pink wedge sneakers. "Ok, I'm ready."

Stoney grabbed my suitcase while I grabbed a few personals tossing them into my shoulder bag. Pebbles and E were sitting on the couch, ready.

"Let's get out of here," Stoney said, directing us all towards the front door. "Wait," he said, stopping E from opening the door. He peeked out first. "Ok, the coast is clear."

"You act like Ivan is going to jump out of some bushes or something." I laughed.

He didn't. Quickly, Stoney ushered us all into his car, throwing the bags in the trunk.

At full speed, Stoney drove off of my block like he was being chased by the police.

Chapter 12

Keystone

"I'm glad we did leave when we did," Pebbles said, from the backseat. "Chip said that Ivan just pulled up at the house and he's going crazy. He also said that y'all drew guns."

"Yeah, something like that," I replied, calmly, racing through streets back to Beverly. "Things definitely got out of hand. That's for sure."

"Are you ok?" Pebbles and Vanity asked at the same time.

I grinned "I'm good, ladies." I rubbed Vanity's leg, letting her know everything was all good.

I was definitely feeling myself at that moment. I had my two favorite ladies in the car with me. If only things could stay this way. I'd have them both. I loved Vanity, but I was really digging Pebbles more and more. The chemistry between us was off the hook. It was definitely more than the lustful arrangement that we started off with.

My eyes met with Pebbles' eyes in the rearview mirror. I reached in the backseat and she put her hand in mine. I squeezed it lightly, giving the same sense of comfort I just gave her sister. What they didn't know was I was on top of things. That's why I went to Chip's house with both of my guns. I was prepared for anything, including death if it came to that.

Everybody Got A Secret 2: A Drama Filled Romance

I was almost at my parent's house when my phone started ringing. I already knew who it was. "You heard?"

"You already know," Amante said. "I'm about to handle it."

News traveled fast. This is what I was trying to avoid.

"Nah, cuzzo, I got it." Killing Ivan wasn't going to help me win Vanity over. Once Amante got involved, Ivan, Chip, and Dino might all come up missing.

"That's not what I hear. You know, Rah lives across the street. He said that shit looked real disrespectful. I'm going to send those niccas a message."

"Nah, I got it."

"Ok, it's your call. I think you need to be proactive. This nicca is about to be a pain in the ass. Oh, and Row told me that Ivan was on The Block earlier today. You wouldn't even have this problem if they would've shot his stupid ass. If my phone wasn't cut off while I was in class, I would have given the order."

I glanced over at Vanity. "Let me holler at you later, I got the girls in the car."

"Oh, word? Vanity's with you?"

I chuckled. "Don't sound so surprised. I told you that I got this. Now, maybe you'll believe me."

"Aight then. I see what you're on. You sure you're good?"

"Positive."

"Is Dom still at Carlo's?"

"Yeah, but I'm probably going to take him with me cuz I'm going to have E tonight too. I'll take them both to school in the morning."

"That'll work. I need to make a quick stop. Then go home and change. After that, I'll be by to bring you his clothes."

"Cool."

After hanging up the phone, I went back to pushing my whip to Beverly Hills.

"Wow, these homes are nice," Pebbles said admiring the view as we rode pass. "Especially that one right there. I would love to have a home like that one day."

"That's my grandfather's house."

People from miles around enjoyed riding pass the Italian villa design with the huge circular driveway and water fountain.

Pebbles continue to stare in amazement. "Your grandfather, the mob boss?"

I chuckled. "So they say." She must've gotten that from Chip. "E, text your Uncle Dash and tell him to meet me at home."

"Ok." E pulled out his phone texting right away.

Most people didn't realize that Chicago had a Beverly Hills too, called Beverly for short. This was the affluent neighborhood where I grew up. Majority of my family lived here too. Nearly every house from 99th to 107th and from California to Hale was occupied by a member of my family. I lived off 103rd and Seeley. My Uncle Antonio lived in West Beverly off 105th and Talman. My Uncle Carlo lived a few blocks over from me on 105th and Hamilton.

"This is your parent's house?" Pebbles asked. "Shiiiiit. Y'all balling out of control. I need a hook up or something. A cousin, brother, uncle or somebody."

I cracked up at her crazy ass. "Chill, gold digger in training."

She smacked her lips. "Now, see, you wrong for that."

"How long is this going to take?" Vanity asked, yawning.

"Not too long. I just need to get my cousin's baby and E some clothes."

E ran up to the door first and rang the doorbell. My mother came to the door and greeted everyone. She gasped when she saw Vanity's face. She went off cussing me out in Spanish. I had to calm her down and tell her that I didn't do that to her. My mother was wildin out. I don't know what made her think I would do something like that. I didn't hit women. E darted upstairs to get his stuff while Pebbles and Vanity took a seat in the living room.

Everybody Got A Secret 2: A Drama Filled Romance

"Where's Dom?" I asked my mother.

"He's in the family room with Carlo."

"I'm taking him back with me. E's spending the night so I might as well keep Dom too."

"Ok," my mother said "Let me get him out of the room."

"Can I get you ladies anything?" I asked Pebbles and Vanity.

Pebbles said no. Vanity looked like her eye was bothering her. I asked my mother if she had something for her eye. She turned around. Instead of going to get Dom, she went to the kitchen and came back with an ice pack for her.

"Mijo, go in the cabinet," my mother told me. "Get her some vitamin C out of my room. And when you leave here, go to the store and get her some pineapples and papayas for the healing."

Going into my mother's room was a mistake. It was pitched black when I came in so I didn't know Emiyah was in there sleep. Had I known that, I would have passed. The last thing I needed was to be stuck with her. Rushing to my mother's medicine cabinet, I grabbed the vitamin C and left out. The door slammed behind me as I made my way back to the living room, handing the vitamin C to Vanity.

"Daddee," I heard Emiyah say, standing behind me. We called her MiMi for short. She was walking into the living room towards me, rubbing her sleepy eyes.

"Why did you have me go into your room when you knew MiMi was here?"

"Stoney, don't start no mess. I'm concerned about Vanity's eye." My mother was still examining Vanity's face as if she was a doctor.

I cut my eyes at MiMi who was standing right in front of me now, begging for me to pick her up. "I'm not picking you up and you're not going with me."

"Peeeeese, Daddee. Pick up. Peeeeese."

"Uncle. I'm not your father. Say, uncle."

MiMi started jumping up and down whining, begging for me to pick her up. "Daddee. Daddee. Daddee."

I looked at my mother. "Where's Emerald? He always does this to me. I'm sick of getting stuck with his baby." I texted Emerald, letting him know that I didn't appreciate MiMi being put off on me all the time. This nicca owed me. Big time.

"Taylin dropped her off. I haven't seen Emerald at all today." My mother stood up, walking past me, going back into the kitchen. She came back and handed Vanity another ice pack. "You'll need both of these."

E came downstairs, dragging a huge suitcase.

"I said grab a few things, not bring your whole damn closet." The damn thing couldn't even close. He was holding it together as he dragged it downstairs. "You act like you're never coming back."

I started walking towards E to help him when MiMi screamed at the top of her lungs. "Ma, get her."

My mother picked her up and she started fighting my mother, trying to get back to me. "Daddee. Daddee. I want Daddee. Peeeeese."

My mother walked over to me, handing me MiMi. "Take her with you."

"No way. Taylin should have kept her."

My mother straightened MiMi's clothes while she was in my arms. "I'm not going to get any sense out of her now that she's seen you. I'll go get her stuff."

"Where's Dom? That's the baby that I came here to get, not her. Can you get him, please?"

"Peeeeese," MiMi said, imitating me.

"You hush," I told her, shifting her to my hip. I was trying to get some action tonight, not babysit. Dom and E were cool. As soon as we start watching a movie, they'll be knocked out. MiMi on the other hand, she is a cock-blocker. It's like she knows she's about to miss something. She needs a job with the CIA.

Everybody Got A Secret 2: A Drama Filled Romance

My mother retreated to the back of the house while I held MiMi's crybaby ass in my arms, sorting through E's heap of clothes.

"Aww, she looks just like you." Vanity said, getting off the couch, coming over to us. "She is too cute. Look at her pretty green eyes like her, Daddee."

"Don't say that. MiMi is confused enough. She don't need no help."

"Can I hold her?" Vanity reached out for MiMi and surprisingly, she went to her. This baby didn't like going with nobody. MiMi rested her head on Vanity's shoulder. "Awww, Stoney, I want a baby girl that looks just like her." She rocked her back and forth in her arms. MiMi seemed to love the attention.

I leaned over whispering in her ear, rubbing her butt. "I'ma give it to you too."

She smiled, playfully pushing me away, sticking out her tongue. "Stop it, I was just playing."

I came right back, giving her a kiss on the cheek "No, you weren't. We gonna work on that though."

"Why don't you just finish helping E so we can get out of here."

"You're right," I said, looking at the mess E created on the steps, sifting through clothes.

I sat on the steps next to him going through everything, helping him decide what to bring. It took a hot minute because he tossed every item he could find into the suitcase. Finally, I narrowed it down to four pairs of jeans with the matching shirts and three pairs of shoes. That was more than enough. I lived practically around the corner. I'd come back and get him more clothes or buy him some if need be. He didn't need any undergarments because I had them in his room at my house.

My mother finally came back holding Dom's hand and MiMi's Barbie suitcase.

"I think we're ready," I said, looking around at everyone. I felt like we were missing something. "You got MiMi and her suitcase," I said to Vanity.

She nodded.

"I got Dom." He was in my arms." I looked to my left. E was standing next to me with his suitcase. "I don't know why I feel like we're missing something," I said, standing at the door ready to walk out.

"Miss Pebbles," E said, pointing at her. She was laid out in Carlo's Laz-E Boy, sleep.

I walked over nudging her. "Get up, gold digger. It's time to go."

"I'ma beat your ass, Stoney." She stretched. "It took y'all long enough." She stretched again, getting up. "Damn, we got a whole daycare, don't we? Where did she come from? You got another baby? You're potent like a mug."

I laughed. "Stop playing. I only have one kid. That's Emerald's daughter."

"Oh, she might as well be yours then."

"You better bring your ass on before you get left."

Everyone shuffled towards the door.

"Ma!" I yelled. "We're gone!"

My mother came rushing out the kitchen. "I'll get the door, mijo." She hugged Vanity and Pebbles and kissed all the kids bye as if she was never going to see them again.

Everyone filed into the car. I put Dom in the back in his car seat. I didn't have one for MiMi. She wasn't going to sit in it anyway. Vanity held her. All this preparation just to drive four blocks away.

Emerald texted me back when I got in the car. He thanked me. He said something unexpected came up and that he got me. Whatever I needed.

I turned on my block and didn't see my brother Kardash. Dash for short. I was about to call his ass and go off when he came flying down the street, whipping around me, pulling into the driveway seconds before I did. He stopped abruptly, jumping out of his silver Benz that looked just like mine, eating a donut.

"What up, little brother? You got a whole gang of folks."

I got out of the car. "That's why I called you. Can you get the kid's stuff out the trunk?"

Everybody Got A Secret 2: A Drama Filled Romance

"I got you." He bent down looking at Vanity and then at Pebbles. "Hi, ladies." He smiled at me, winking. "Nice," he said, referring to them. I think Dash was the only one who had sex on his mind more than me. Literally, pussy was all he thought about.

"It's not what you think. I had a situation today."

"Oh, word?" Dash said, taking the suitcases out the trunk. "Something serious?"

"It might be. I'll fill you in on all the details later."

"Aight." He laid eyes on Pebbles when she got out of the car. He licked his lips. "Damn, she's sexy. I promise I would tear that pussy up."

"She's off limits."

That didn't stop Dash. He was determined to get at one of them. "What about the other one?"

"She's off limits too, bro."

He laughed. "That's bullshit. You ain't fucking them both."

I gave him a look that said, yes I am.

"Ok, let me rephrase that. Which one is your girl? Cuz you always got a girl."

"Yeah unlike your commitment-phobe ass. The one in the pink."

"Good because I wanted the one in the white anyway. Baby is bad. I plan on playing in that pussy all night long."

"She's off limits," I said again.

"Stop being selfish," he said, carrying the kid's stuff in the house. "I'm smashing that."

I grabbed Vanity's bag, following behind him. "Dash, I'm serious. Don't touch her. Why aren't you listening to me?"

That was Dash's thing. He liked being the side dude. Most of his women were married or in long-term relationships.

"I heard you," he said. "I just want to hit it for a minute. Then, you can have her back. Don't act like we've never shared before. Besides, she's not even your girl. If she was your girl, I would back off. And how are you fucking sisters anyway? That's just wrong."

135

Dash was messing up my fantasy. I wanted them both. It was a stretch, but a brother can dream, can't he? I figured as long as Vanity was confused about Ivan, I was going to be confused about Pebbles too.

Dash opened the fridge. "Ain't shit in this piece. What are we eating? I'm hungry as a mug."

"I placed an order at Italian Fiesta Pizzeria. I was on my way to pick up the food when this shit popped off. Oh, and we're going to need more food. Sal texted me and said just let him know when I was ready to pick it up. Can you do it? You see my hands full here."

"Ok, I got it covered. I'll place another order and get someone to drop it off."

I introduced Dash to Vanity and Pebbles. Then, I showed Pebbles her room and bathroom. Then, I escorted Vanity to my room. E and Dom already knew the routine. They went to E's room to clean up.

"I don't have any night clothes." Pebbles said. "Give me a T-shirt or something."

Dash slid pass me, putting his arm around Pebbles' waist. "Let me help you get settled in, pretty." He winked at me walking away with Pebbles.

I carried MiMi into my bedroom. Vanity was looking in the mirror when I entered. "I look horrible." She touched her face with tears in her eyes. "I'm never going to be the same."

"You're still beautiful to me," I said, honestly. "C'mon, let me run you some bath water. I'm sure you'll feel better after that. It'll take some of the stress away."

I ran her water and helped her undress, kissing her all over. I wanted to go further, but MiMi was in the bathroom with us.

"Ouch. Ouch. Ouch. Ouch," she said, sliding down into the water. I could only imagine how sore her body was. Tears came to her eyes again. She closed her eyes and let them fall. "I'm so messed up."

"Don't go blaming yourself for what Ivan did."

Everybody Got A Secret 2: A Drama Filled Romance

She opened her eyes. "That's not what I mean. I took a vow. I stepped outside of my marriage. I deserve what he did to me."

"Wait. Hold up. Are you justifying him beating your ass and doing all this crazy stuff to you? No woman deserves that. I don't care if she cheated or not."

She shrugged her shoulders. "He had every right to be mad."

"No, he didn't. He had no right putting his hands on you. I'm letting you know straight up, you can't be with this nicca and be with me too." I was getting angry as fuck. "Him and I are two totally different dudes. There is no damn excuse that he can use to justify hurting you the way he did just because you cheated. And I'm not just saying that because I want to be with you. If you can't see that this muthafucka is a psycho, then maybe I made a mistake by trying to build something with you."

I got up off the floor, grabbed MiMi who was playing with her toys next to me, and left Vanity in the bathroom alone. I couldn't look at her face another minute.

Me and MiMi went to check on the boys. Walking into E's room, Dom and E were on the bed, playing video games. They were cleaned up. E had on his pajamas. Dom had on one of E's shirt. It was swallowing him whole. I told them that the food was on the way. Things were so hectic that I hadn't even fed E. Being the good kid that he was, he didn't even complain.

MiMi wanted some juice so I headed downstairs. Dash was in the kitchen eating a bag of Fritos, watching old re-runs of Martin, cracking up. "Uncle Joey is bringing the food."

"Did he say when?"

"He just texted me. He'll be here in a minute."

I reached into the fridge to get MiMi some juice. As soon as I put it in her sippy cup my phone vibrated back to back with texts. I couldn't believe what I was reading.

"Here take her," I said, handing MiMi to Dash.

She started crying the moment Dash held her. "Who was that?"

"Angel. He said we need to come right away. Some shit is going down right now. I'm about to get the girls. Can you watch the boys?"

"Yeah, I got things covered here. You go handle that."

Chapter 13

Ivan

"I hate that muthafucka!" I yelled, kicking in Chip's flat screen TV.

I went through that bitch like the Tasmanian Devil, tearing up everything in sight. Televisions, stereos, couches, pictures, tables, and anything else in my path was destroyed. I tried to tear his muthafuckin house down.

Dino's scary ass went in his room and packed his shit. He said he wasn't coming back to this house until I had settled things with the family.

"Fuck that family, nicca. I'll take each one of them down, one by one if I have too. That nicca Stoney about to get his, believe that shit."

Dino didn't pay me no mind, hauling ass out the front door with two huge suitcases. "Chip, man, call me when the beef is over."

"Ain't no beef, nicca. This shit is war!" I spat.

"Aight, man," Chip said, walking his boy out.

It took forever to calm me down. Chip was trying to reason with me, but there was no reasoning. I wanted payback and I wasn't going to rest until I got it.

The doorbell rang.

I picked up one of the legs of the table that I broke. "That better not be this nicca coming back."

"Chill," Chip said, walking back to the door. "And your ass is paying for all the shit you broke too. Money don't grow on trees. I worked hard to decorate my crib."

I pulled out a wad of money, throwing hundreds at him. "Money ain't a thing, nicca. That should cover your damages."

Chip scowled at me before answering the door. "Ain't nobody but Stacks," he said, stepping to the side so I could see him.

Seeing Stacks put a smile on my face. I forgot I called him. "You got my package?"

"You got my money?" he answered with a chuckle, staring at all the bills on the floor.

"You already know. Let's get down to business."

Stacks stepped inside with two gift-wrapped boxes, handing them to me. In return, I gave him six-hundred.

"Nice doing business with you." He pocketed the money and walked out the door just as fast as he came in.

"Is that something for Vanity?" Chip asked. He had no idea what I had in store.

"Naw, fuck Vanity's lying, cheating, whorish ass. This is for me."

I took the top off of the beautifully wrapped box, pulling out a pretty piece of steel. This gun was so muthafuckin sweet it made my dick hard. All of Stacks guns were stolen. I didn't care as long as it didn't have no bodies on it.

"Man, I know you didn't just purchase a gun. The last thing you need is a gun. You're going too far."

"Did you see that nicca put a gun in my face?"

"I saw it. I was there, remember? That dude ain't coming back and he's not going to sick his family on you. All he wanted was for you to back up off Vanity and leave him alone. Trust me, if he wanted to do something, he would have done it then."

"I don't give a fuck what that nicca wants. He came over here like he was the Don Dada and shit. Now, it's my turn to show him what I'm made of."

"You doing all this to get back at Stoney, but what about Vanity?"

Everybody Got A Secret 2: A Drama Filled Romance

"What the fuck about her?" Chip was on my last nerve. I was ready to put a bullet in his ass.

"You love her that's why your wildin right now."

Chip was right. My fucking heart was shattered to pieces.

"Why don't you try it my way for once? Apologize and mean that shit. Get her some flowers and put your best game down. Be the Ivan that she fell in love with."

"She ain't gonna let me fuck. Not after all the shit I did."

"I'm not talking about getting pussy, nicca. Where's your romantic side? Women love that mushy shit. Holding her all night. Show her affection by kissing her neck, telling her how much you love her, and wait on her hand and foot. At least until you can get out of the dog house."

"I don't know. Every time I look at her face, man, I see that nicca."

"Just listen to me. If I don't know nothing else, I know women. You might be married, but I've had more women. And I'm still cool with all of my exes. Can you say the same? They all hate your ass."

Chip was wearing me down with his long-winded speech on romance.

"I'm telling you, things aren't as messed up as you think. You do what you need to do and she'll be yours forever. But the moment you fuck up, that's when the next nicca can step in. And let's be real, you been fucking up for a hot ass minute. I'm surprised she hung in this long. Cuz if that was Pebbles, she would have rolled out a long time ago."

Chip chuckled. I supposed he was thinking about how Pebbles left his ass high and dry.

I laughed too. Pebbles didn't take no shit. She will love you and leave your ass in the same breath. "Aight. I'll do it."

Chip grinned. "You will? Well, alright, let me get you something else to wear. You can't be going over there looking like you just finished kicking dirt."

I laughed again, lighting up another blunt. "So, you really think this bullshit is going to get her back?"

"I'm positive it will. Just do what I said and keep apologizing. Lay it on thick and never do nothing this damn stupid ever again."

I hit the blunt a few more times before handing it off to Chip so I could get cleaned up. Chip had some church shit laid out for me. I wasn't digging this look right now. I'd rather rock my camo, but if he thought this is what it was going to take to get Vanity back, then I was all for it. As I showered, reality hit me. I guess I did overdo it. Thinking back, I did some grimy shit to her. I couldn't help it. All I saw was red when I blacked the fuck out.

"Where you going?" Chip asked as I grabbed my keys on my way out.

"Home, to do what you said."

"I'm going with you. Ain't no way I'm going to let you go by yourself. Once I see that you're cool, then I'll roll out."

I was feeling more like the old me and very hopeful that Vanity would forgive me. I tossed him the keys. "Aight. You drive then."

On our way, I stopped at Jewels and picked up some roses. I wanted to hit up a florist, but most of them were closed. I wasn't going out of my way tonight. I'd have to pick them up tomorrow or have them delivered to the house.

As soon as we hit my street, I could have sworn I saw Stoney's ride, pulling off the block. If it wasn't him, it was a whip that looked just like his.

Naw, that can't be that nicca. I know he wasn't stupid enough to be rolling off my block. I'm damn sure he wasn't in my damn house.

When Chip pulled into my driveway, I got butterflies in my stomach. I haven't been this nervous since my wedding day.

"You good?" Chip asked me.

"Yeah. Yeah." I gulped down my spit, hoping that my stomach would stop hurting. It felt like I needed to take a shit. I looked at Chip and he looked at me.

"You getting out? Or you about to stay here and keep looking at me?"

Everybody Got A Secret 2: A Drama Filled Romance

I opened the door and casually stepped out, fixing my pants legs. I saw my reflection in the mirror. I couldn't help but smile. I was too clean.

"Hiya, Ivan," my neighbor, Mr. Gaude said. He was out walking his dog, Fefee, a white American Eskimo.

I hated this muthafucka. I don't know why he was speaking to me. I hit his ass with a head nod and kept it moving. I guess Fefee was offended because she started barking. I didn't give a fuck as long as she kept her ass on the sidewalk.

"How was your day?" Mr. Gaude asked.

Why was he trying to make small talk? See, this shit was all Vanity's fault. She's the one who wanted to be chummy with our neighbors. "I had a long day," I grumbled. I glanced over at Chip who was watching my every move.

"Oh, me too," he replied and went on to tell me about it.

He had me real fucked up if he thought I was going to stand here and listen. I was about to open the door when I realized, I left my keys in the car. I remember taking them out of my pocket because they were stabbing me in the leg through these thin ass dress pants. Jogging down my porch stairs, I went back to the car to retrieve my keys. Fefee was still barking like crazy

"What's going on?" Chip asked, letting down the window.

"I forgot my keys and this damn dog keeps barking at me like she's in heat."

"Damn, how do you manage to piss of every woman?" Chip chuckled.

I didn't see shit funny. "Hand me my keys."

Chip handed me my keys. Meanwhile, Fefee broke away from Mr. Gaude galloping right up to me, sniffing around my leg.

I kicked the dog back. "Aye, Mr. Gaude, get your damn dog, man." Personally, I think he let go of her leash on purpose.

"She's just being friendly, Ivan. I think she likes you."

"Man, I'm serious. Get this damn dog."

Just as I was about to walk back towards my house, this raggedy ass mutt pissed on me. Lifted her leg like I was a fuckin tree and pissed all over my pants leg and shoe. As if that wasn't bad enough, the sucker started biting my damn ankle. Now, I said I was turning a new leaf to win Vanity back, but this shit here was doing the most. Before I knew it, I had retrieved my piece and shot the fuck out of her ass.

"FEFEEEEEEEEEEEEEEEEE!" Mr. Gaude screamed like she was a person. "Nooooooooo! Not my baby. You murderer! Oh my God! Murderer!"

Chip got out of the car, thoroughly disgusted with me. "What'd you do that for? You just created more trouble for yourself."

"I don't give a fuck. I told him to get her ass. She ran up to me, pissed, and then bit me. She deserved to be shot. Fuck her and any other bitch that gets in my damn way."

"Killer!" Mr. Gaude screamed while scooping up Fefee's dead remains.

"He's lucky I didn't shoot his ass. Let's go in the house. I'm sick of seeing this shit," I said, carrying my gift-wrapped guns inside.

Chip stared at Mr. Gaude, shaking his head at what I done, before he followed me in the house. "You dead wrong. You didn't have to shoot that man's dog. He's going to be out of it for the rest of his life."

I laughed. "Too bad. Cuz I don't give a fuck," I said, walking from room to room looking for Vanity. The smell of dog piss lingered everywhere I went. "Where the fuck she at?"

Chip started searching too. "She's got to be here. Her car is in the driveway. Maybe she's hiding from you. She might be scared. Vanity!" he yelled. "This is Chip. Come out. Ivan ain't about to do nothing to you."

I leaned against the wall, while he continued to search. "You make me seem like I'm really a monster."

"From the shit that I heard, you are."

"Fuck what you talking about. I'm going to shower and change. If you don't find her in here, call her ass."

After showering and putting on something more comfortable. I came back out. "Did you call her?"

Everybody Got A Secret 2: A Drama Filled Romance

"Naw, I texted Pebbles. She said she's with Stoney."

I kicked over the glass table in the living room. Then I grabbed my baseball bat and started busting up everything in the living room, cracking all of our wedding pictures. "I'm done seeing things your way." I tossed that bat up against the wall. "Shit just got real."

Chip exhaled, looking at me with pity. "Man, don't do nothing stupid. If Pebbles is with them, then ain't too much happening. She might have been afraid to stay here after the way you put your hands on her."

"That's bullshit, Chip, and you know it. She's still fucking that nicca." I pulled out my phone, texting Vanity. I told her she had twenty minutes to get her ass back here or I was going to come looking for her, leaving a trail of bullet holes behind."

There was a knock at the door. I assumed it was Vanity's cheating ass. I rushed to the door with my gun in my hand. I opened it, ready to crack her in the head. "It's about time, bitch!"

"Are you Ivan Carder?" the officer asked.

I quickly slid my gun behind my back. "Who the fuck wants to know?"

The light skin officer looked at me like he wanted to beat my ass. "Nicca, don't make this harder than this shit has to be. Either you cooperate with us or we're going to make your life a living hell. Your choice." The mug on his face told me that he meant every word of it too.

Chip came to the door. "What seems to be the problem, officers?"

"Who are you?" the light brown officer said.

"I'm his brother," Chip told him. "Is there a problem?"

"Yes, there is," the brown skin one said. "We were called to a disturbance off on 87th where guns were involved. You two wouldn't no nothing about that, would you?"

"Naw, I can't say I do," Chip said, calmly.

"Some of the residents on the block said that is where you live."

Chip looked unfazed staring at the officer. "Yes, I do stay on 87th, but I still don't know what you're talking about."

Meanwhile, I was fuming. I was itching to reveal my gun, and show them what time it really was.

The same officer looked past us in the house. "What's going on here?" He nodded his head towards the trashed living room.

"What can I do for you?" Chip asked, still remaining cool.

"Your neighbor called," the light skin officer said, looking at me. The whole time, he was grilling me. Only briefly taking his eyes off me. "He said you shot his dog. Is that true?"

I cut my eyes at the sky. "That nicca says a lot of shit that ain't true."

"I didn't asked you about a lot of things, I asked you about shooting his dog. There's blood in your driveway. Why don't you step outside so we can talk to you?"

Something about these cops weren't right. I wasn't stepping nowhere. "That's a negative," I said raising my gun to the light skin officer's face.

"What the fuck are you doing?" Chip asked. "Have you lost the little bit of sense you have left?"

I glanced over at Chip. "Let me handle this—"

I felt my gun being kicked out of my hand. The light skin officer got the drop on me. My gun went flying in the air in, landing in the front yard. Before I knew, it, he had grabbed me, tossing me off the porch. I landed on my stomach in the grass. Like a ninja, he jumped off the porch landing in the grass next to me.

"See, you done fucked up now," he told me, forcefully, jerking my wrists behind my back, cuffing me.

"He has a gun too," The brown skin officer said.

I couldn't see them, but I could tell the officer was scuffling with my brother. In a matter of seconds, I saw Chip fall on his stomach, lying in the grass next to me, cuffed.

Chip strained his neck to look at them. "You didn't even read us our rights. Or introduce yourselves. What happened to that?"

146

Both officers laughed.

"I'm Officer Guiliani. And this is my partner, Diaz-Santana. You have the right to shut the fuck up and do as we say or that's your ass."

Chip stared me down as they both laughed again.

I knew what he was thinking. That shit that Dino said was coming back to bite me in my ass. Damn. My wife couldn't find a regular, nicca. She had to fuck a nicca that was connected and shit.

"You can't get away with this," Chip said, struggling to get off the ground.

"I can and I will. Read these little bitches their rights," the light one told his partner.

Chapter 14

Keystone

The last thing I wanted to do was see this nicca Ivan again. It's like this muthafucka wouldn't go away, like a thorn in my side. My aim was to be at home trying to figure out who was going to give me some pussy. All this fighting and shit, it wasn't me. Pulling out guns and busting off, not my thing either. I'm a lover. I preferred being curled up under a woman, enjoying her womanly curves.

I was in a fucked up mood as I made my way from Beverly back to Chatham. I wasn't trying to hear shit from nobody. The girls were quiet. I'm assuming they picked up on my shitty vibe. Vanity sat next to me with a confused look on her face. I didn't tell her what was up. I wanted to see her reaction when we got there. That was going to tell me if I even wanted her ass anymore.

The last thing I planned on doing was risking my life for a woman who clearly wanted to be with another nicca. As it stood right now, Vanity could keep her ass there with her lunatic husband while I roll out with Pebbles.

It's a shame that I couldn't tell Vanity what was up, but I confided in Pebbles so easily. That right there got me to thinking that maybe I made a mistake. What I should have done is left Vanity and her confused ass in the past.

Everybody Got A Secret 2: A Drama Filled Romance

"You mad at me?" Vanity asked, breaking my concentration.

Fuck what she's talking about. I turned up the radio.

She turned it down. "I know you're mad at me."

I glanced at her before looking back at the road. It took everything in me not to let her ass have it. I turned the radio back up, ignoring her.

Vanity sighed.

I know one thing, she better not touch my damn radio again. I looked in the backseat at Pebbles. She looked like she was ready to set some shit off too, wearing the same frown I was. She had on a hoodie, jeans, and Tims. "I see you found my cousin Dutchess' clothes."

I was really feeling her right now. She caught me staring at her in the rearview mirror and smiled. I found myself smiling back. That lightened my mood a little bit.

Turning onto Vanity's block, there were cops everywhere. I think I saw SWAT too. The street was blocked off on both ends. We couldn't even get to her house. I picked up my phone and called Angel. "Yo, we here, but we can't get through."

"Just park. I'll be down there in a second."

"Aight."

I found a parking spot at the very end of the block, almost around the corner. I got out of the car when I saw Angel by the barricade, waiving us over. Pebbles and Vanity got out following behind me. I introduced them to my cousin.

"What's going on?" Vanity asked. "Did something happen to my house?" She looked from me to Angel.

"Your house is fine," he said, ushering us pass the barricade. "It's your husband. He has locked himself inside, threatening to kill himself if you didn't come."

"Wow!" Pebbles said. "If that ain't crazy."

Vanity covered her hand with her mouth and tears immediately began to flow. "Is he ok?"

"For now. This is the last resort. If it doesn't work, and you can't get him to turn himself in, then they are going to rush into the house. Who knows what might happen after that."

Vanity cringed. "I'll talk to him. I'm sure I can get him to cooperate."

Pebbles smacked her lips. "He's only doing all this shit just to get your attention. That's why he asked for you. So damn dramatic."

Vanity asked. "What did he do, officer?"

"He shot your neighbor's dog Fefee."

Pebbles started laughing. "That's crazy, for real, for real."

"And what else did he do?" Vanity inquired.

"Well, he pulled a gun on me so I had to arrest him. If I hadn't kicked it out of his hand, he was going to shoot me. After cuffing him on the ground, somehow he got free, grabbed the gun and put it to his own head, threatening to kill himself. That's when we called for backup. We've been negotiating with him to turn himself in for the last hour. He said he wasn't going to come out unless he saw you. So I called Stoney and told him to get you here before your husband gets himself killed."

Vanity wiped away tears as we walked down the street to her house.

"I know that ain't Chip on the ground." Pebbles ran down the street towards the house. Two cops scooped her up, stopping her from approaching him. She was swinging and fighting like a mad woman. "Put me the fuck down. I'm not no damn criminal. And y'all gonna let Chip go. I know that much."

I knew most of the officers. They weren't family. I'd seen them around quite a few times with Angel or Ecko.

"I'll keep an eye on her," I told them.

They let Pebbles go and she fell into my arms. "Stoney, they got Chip on the ground like a criminal. You gotta do something. I know he didn't do nothing."

What did she expect me to do? This nicca was lying on the ground, probably handcuffed for a reason. "I'll see what I can do, but I need you to chill. Don't do nothing stupid cuz if you get arrested, you might be on the ground right next to him."

Everybody Got A Secret 2: A Drama Filled Romance

She nodded her head, still in my arms.

I approached my cousin Ecko, who was standing over Chip. "What up, cuzzo? What he do?"

Ecko had the most disgusted look on his face. "Trying to help his crazy ass brother."

"Did he have a gun or something?"

"Yes. I had to tackle his ass. He's been right here ever since."

I don't know why, but for some reason, I knew that Chip wasn't insane like Ivan's coo-coo for cocoa puff ass. I kinda felt bad seeing him on the ground like that. I knew that if Dash or Dan did something stupid like his brother did, I'd be right by their side too. Ride or die. We went hard for each other like that.

"C'mon, Ecko. If he didn't do nothing, let him go."

Ecko didn't budge.

I stooped down in the grass next to Chip. The pissy look on his face said it all. "Aye, I'ma see what I can do to help you out. I can't promise nothing, but I'ma try."

Chip just stared at me, unfazed. That's pretty much what I expected. I wasn't doing this for him. I was doing this because my brother always came to my rescue when I fucked up. It was time to pay it forward. Right or wrong, I understood Chip's position.

"I ain't no fan of your brother, as you know, but I don't want to see him killed either. If he doesn't surrender, they are going to shoot him. Does he have any priors?"

"Naw."

"If he gives himself up, they'll take him in, and he can get out on bail. Shooting a dog ain't that bad. I might be able to get his charges reduced. I don't know. Depends on how much he pissed them off. From the looks of things, they're pretty hot with his ass right now. If he's lucky, he'll get community service or probation or something." My ears perked up when I heard another officer talking to Ivan on the phone. "Hold tight, Chip. I'll be back."

The officer had Ivan on speakerphone. "We have your wife out here just like you requested Ivan."

"Send her to the fuckin door then!" Ivan yelled. "And don't try no funny shit. I got a few tricks up my sleeve too."

"We got you what you asked for. After you talk to your wife, you need to give this charade up."

"I'll fuckin think about it, pig!"

Click!

The phone went silent.

My cousin Angelina, Angel's twin sister, we called her Linda for short, signaled Vanity to come over so she could put a bulletproof vest on her.

Vanity rejected the vest. "Do I really need this? I'm positive that Ivan wouldn't shoot me."

"Girl, I've seen this scenario a million times," Linda said. "And sometimes the wife leaves in a body bag. Your husband is pretty emotional. Anything could happen. We just want you to be safe no matter what."

"I hear you, but I know my husband. He's mostly talk."

I know she didn't just say that. This is the same nicca that blackened her eye and put cigarette burns all over her body. Did I miss something? "Vanity?" I yanked her to the side. "Let me holler at you." I was still pissed at her, but I didn't want nothing bad to happen to her. "Be careful and don't underestimate him. This is the same nicca that choked you out. He could have killed you then. Don't think for one minute that he won't hesitate to kill you now."

She looked at me with fear. "You're right. But this is all my fault. I have to talk to him. If they kill him because of me, I'll never be able to live with myself."

This shit was stressing me the fuck out. I had an awful feeling that this nicca was about to do something real crazy. "Aight. Just make sure you come back."

She nodded and slowly walked away. She looked nervous. I ain't gonna lie, I was nervous for her. At least I had a piece on me when I confronted this fucker earlier. She ain't have nothing. I held my breath when Vanity stepped on the porch. I saw the red dot precede her. They were about to take this crazy fool out. I just hoped they didn't miss and hit Vanity by mistake.

"I'm getting a real bad feeling about all this," Pebbles said, standing next to me.

"Me too," I admitted.

Vanity turned the knob. The door opened. Ivan was in plain view. The red dot fell on his chest. I guess he saw it. I'm not sure. What he did next blew my mind. Instead of Vanity talking him into surrendering, she was now being held hostage with a gun pointed to her head.

"I knew this fucker was going to do something stupid like this," Angel said, standing to my left.

"Stand down," the officer next to Angel said to the rest of the squad. "I repeat, stand down."

"OH MY GOD!" Pebbles gasped.

I can't front. I gasped too. Seeing Vanity being held captive did something to me. Being mean and ignoring her earlier only made me feel even worse. If she survived this, I was going to do everything humanly possible to take her away from this crazed animal, and make her my wife. My phone started buzzing. I powered it off. I wasn't trying to hear from nobody at this moment.

Angel reached into one of the cop cars, pulling out a bullet-proof vest. "She should have been left this muthafucka. He cracked like an egg."

"Don't do it, Ivan," Chip yelled from the ground. "Turn yourself in, man. Don't go out like this."

"Fuck that," Ivan said, holding Vanity by the throat with the glock pointed at her temple. "Y'all muthafuckas were going to kill me, right? Well, if I die, she dies too." He kissed her cheek as her tears flowed.

"Let me get one of them vests," I told Angel. I didn't trust this crazy bastard at all. He might let her go, rush out, and pop me. He was insane enough to do something like that.

Princess Diamond

Angel reached in the squad car again, pulling out two vests. "Give that to shorty," he said referring to Pebbles. "Tell her to put one on too."

I handed Pebbles her vest. She hurried up and put it on. Afterwards, she moved closer to me with tears in her eyes. She buried her face against my chest. "I can't watch. If something happens to my sister—" She held me tighter, crying. "This is so fucked up."

"It sure is," Angel cosigned. "I hope he don't do nothing stupid. We got enough senseless violence in the city. And way too much Black on Black crime in Chicago."

I hugged Pebbles close. "Don't even think like that. Everything's going to be ok. Stay positive and keep the faith." I told her that, standing strong, but on the inside I was scared as fuck.

One of the members from the tactical team stepped forward.

"Get the fuck back." Ivan said, shoving the gun into Vanity's mouth. "If you come any closer, I'm pulling the trigger."

Tears cascaded down Vanity's cheeks as she trembled. I can't even imagine how she's feeling right now. I just know it was painful to watch.

"Ivan, I'm Detective Wise. I want to help you."

"You ain't trying to muthafuckin help me. Y'all niccas don't give a fuck about me. I see that red dot. Y'all trying to fuckin kill me."

Detective Wise sat his gun on the sidewalk with his hands in the air. "I'm not going to hurt you, Ivan. I just want to talk to you. Can I do that?"

"It's a free country ain't it?"

"I don't know, Ivan. I'm sure if your wife could talk she wouldn't say it was free right now. You're taking away her right to freedom by keeping her against her will."

"To hell with her free will. She wasn't thinking about me when she fucked another nicca. Now was she?" He jammed the gun further down Vanity's throat. "She needs to be taught a muthafuckin lesson."

154

Everybody Got A Secret 2: A Drama Filled Romance

Detective Wise took five more steps forward while they were talking. "It looks like you already did that. She looks pretty banged up."

"Don't tell me what the fuck she looks like. This my damn wife."

While Detective Wise was being used as a distraction, there were two officers sneaking up on Ivan on both sides.

Ivan kept his eyes on Detective Wise with a steady grip on Vanity. "Don't come any closer."

"I'm just trying to help you, Ivan."

I don't know what made Ivan look to his right, but he did. That's when he saw the officer standing off in the cut. "Y'all must think I'm fuckin stupid." He retrieved the gun from Vanity's mouth pointing it at the officer.

Just then four red dots appeared on him. I don't think they had a clean shot. If they did, I'm sure they would have popped his crazy ass by now.

"Man, this is hard to watch," Angel admitted.

"You think?" I said, being sarcastic.

"I just keep thinking what would I do if this was my sister. How would I react? Or if it was my girl, I'd be stressed the fuck out." Angel must've realized what he just said. He was speculating what he would do, but I was living it. "I'm sorry, Stoney. I wasn't thinking when I said that. I can only imagine how you feel right now."

I glanced at him feeling real fucked up. I wasn't going to tell him, but I was scared that Vanity was about to get shot. I looked at Pebbles. "How are you holding up?"

She didn't speak, continuing to hold onto me, crying.

Ivan was trying to calculate his next move. He was being closed in on. Looking around everywhere, he kept Vanity close, right in front of him so they couldn't shoot.

While Ivan was looking at all angles, Detective Wise pulled another gun out of his suit jacket and took the shot. My heart stopped when Vanity dropped right along with Ivan.

Pebbles screamed. "Noooooooo!"

155

Angel put his hand on my shoulder trying to comfort me. "I'm sure they missed her. She's ok." His mouth said that, but the look on his face said otherwise.

I felt sick to my stomach. "She has to be ok. She just has to."

I started to feel light headed as more officers rushed up to the porch. I saw them jerk Ivan to his feet. He didn't appear to be shot. He was swinging and acting a damn fool as usual. They had a hard time slapping the cuffs on him. He was going hard, fighting off every officer that came at him. Finally, they used the Taser on his stupid ass. That's when he went down.

Seconds later, I saw Vanity pop up. Once she saw that she wasn't in danger anymore, she jetted off the porch as fast as she could, away from crazy ass Ivan. I let go of Pebbles when Vanity rushed into my arms, crying hysterically.

"You were right," she said, balling. "I'm so sorry for not listening to you." She held onto me for dear life, trembling. "I can't believe he just pulled a gun on me. I could have died."

"It's ok. I'm here, baby. I'll protect you."

Pebbles hugged her sister too. "I was so scared," she cried.

Vanity hugged Pebbles tight. "Me too."

I approached my cousin. "Angel, you think you can uncuff Chip. He doesn't need to suffer because of something Ivan did."

Angel nodded. "Yeah, I'll uncuff him."

He walked over to Chip, kneeling down. He took the cuffs off and helped him up. Chip dusted himself off, approaching me like he had beef. "This shit is all your fault. What you did was foul."

"Don't come over here with all that. I didn't make Ivan do none of this."

"No, but you knew Vanity was having marital issues. She was vulnerable. You used it to your advantage. That's why Ivan is so pissed."

I didn't owe him an explanation. And I didn't give two fucks about Ivan's bitch ass feelings. "Is there a point to this conversation?"

Everybody Got A Secret 2: A Drama Filled Romance

Chip looked like he wanted to swing on me. I wished he would. I still had my heat on me. They would be carrying his ass off right along with his looney ass brother.

Pebbles must've known things were about to go left. She stopped hugging Vanity, approaching Chip. "Regardless of what happened, Ivan put a gun to her head. That's not Stoney's fault. That's Ivan's fault. Now, you know I love you, Chip, but wrong is wrong. Ivan didn't have no right to act a damn fool just because she cheated. What if I had done that to you because you cheated?"

Pebbles turned Vanity towards Chip. "Look at her." She pointed to her sister's black eye and the marks on her face and around her neck. Then she revealed the cigarette burns on her arms and lifted her shirt, showing the marks on her stomach. "Ivan did that. Not Stoney. As far as I'm concerned she needs to get as far away from Ivan's nutty ass as possible."

Pebbles must've hit home because Chip's nasty attitude quickly changed. "Vanity, does Stoney make you happy?"

Vanity nodded her head yes with teary eyes.

"You know you're like a sister to me. If he makes you happy, that's all that matters. No woman deserves what happened to you." Chip and I locked eyes. "Speaking man to man, I respect what you did standing up for her. Going hard no matter what. But speaking as Ivan's brother, we ain't cool, and we never will be."

I just looked at his ass. I didn't give a fuck. I told him I didn't have an issue with him. If he wanted to take it there, then I would be ready. Otherwise, I didn't have shit to say.

A swarm of officers were walking Ivan towards the police car, when he fell to the ground. A few of them were skeptical about helping him. I assumed they thought it was another one of his stunts. That quickly changed when blood spilled out onto the sidewalk.

"Get the medics!" Detective Wise yelled. "He's been shot."

Immediately Chip turned around, and tried to approach Ivan, but the officers held him back.

157

"Don't just stand around him watching him bleed to death! Do something!" Chip hollered.

Ecko stepped away from the crowd of officers, around Ivan, moving closer to us. "I'll be damn if I'm giving CPR to his ass."

Angel and I smirked at Ecko's reasoning.

The paramedics pulled up. Two EMT's jumped out with a stretcher running in Ivan's direction. He'd lost a lot of blood in such a short amount of time. As much as I hated the dude, I still didn't want to see him die.

The EMT's and a couple of officer's lifted Ivan onto the stretcher, putting the oxygen mask over his face. I heard them saying that he had a faint pulse and they needed to get him to the hospital right away before they lost him. As they put him in the ambulance, Chip was right there, ready to ride out with his brother. They had tight a bond. That's how it was supposed to be. Family comes first.

"I'm going too," Pebbles said, running over to the ambulance trying to get in with Chip. "No, leave with Vanity."

"No! I'm going with you, Chip."

"Are you going or staying?" the paramedic asked her. "Because we need to leave now."

"She's staying," Chip said, pushing Pebbles back.

The paramedic jumped into the ambulance, closing the door.

"Chip!" Pebbles yelled as the ambulance sped away with sirens. "Chip!"

"Go get her, Ecko."

Ecko walked over to Pebbles, putting his arm around her. "He's gone, baby girl."

Pebbles looked like she was about to cry again. I put my arm around her when Ecko walked her back over to me.

"Is there anything you need out of the house?" Angel asked Vanity. "I advise you to get it now while you have protection. Because if he pulls through this, the last thing you need to be is anywhere near this house."

Everybody Got A Secret 2: A Drama Filled Romance

Vanity wiped her tears. "I just want to get a few things. Oh, and, my car."

Ecko, Angel, Vanity, Pebbles, and I went in the house while the officers were wrapping things up. The news stations were having a field day with this story. I didn't have to tell Angel or Ecko to make sure that the news knew as less about this situation as possible. I'm sure they were already on that. Vanity nor I needed the publicity.

I was helping Vanity pack more of her things when Linda and Enychi walked in. Enychi was Ecko's twin sister.

"We need pictures," Enychi said. "So, y'all guys have to leave."

"Is this really necessary? Can't I do this tomorrow?" Vanity asked. "I'm tired. It's been a long day and a really long night. I just want to go somewhere and lay down."

"Unfortunately, it is," Enychi replied. "We need pictures of your bruises while they're still fresh."

We waited in the living room while all the girls stayed in the bathroom, taking pictures of Vanity's injuries.

"You think Vanity is going to press charges?" Ecko asked, sitting to my left.

"Nah, I think she just wants to get rid of him. She already has to deal with him to get a divorce. I don't think she can deal with a case too."

"You know I can pay Ivan a visit at the hospital," Angel whispered. "If you want me to. All this will disappear."

"Nah, I don't want him to come up missing. Plus, how would that make Vanity feel? She'll never be mine if she found out."

Angel scooted closer to me on the couch. "I'm just saying, he don't have to make it out of surgery. Or maybe he accidently," he said using air quotes. "Slips into a coma and dies. It doesn't have to be sloppy, you know?"

"What you think, Ecko?"

He shrugged. "I don't know, Stoney. Dude seems like a problem to me. If not today, soon. I don't think he's going to let none of this shit go. You stole his girl. You pulled a gun on him. He got shot. He's going to come back blazing."

"But I didn't shoot him," I said, defending myself.

"Yeah, but for some reason, I don't think he sees it that way. I got the strangest feeling that he blames you for everything. And you're at the top of his shit list now. Maybe not number one. From the look of things, Vanity got that spot."

Angel chimed in. "I have to agree with Ecko. This nicca is a problem. You need to handle him now before he seeks revenge."

They both stared at me like I was making a mistake leaving Ivan alive. "I can handle him. I've dealt with much worse."

"It's your call," they both said together.

I had my mind made up. I wasn't going to reach out and touch Ivan unless I had to. "Y'all give this nicca too much damn credit. What can he possibly do?"

They both turned their heads. Angel looked to his left. Ecko looked to his right. I sat in the middle of them thinking that they were both overreacting. It must be law enforcement thinking. Assume the worse.

After Vanity got all her belongings, we got back in my Benz. Angel gave us a police escort back to Beverly. Ecko drove behind me in Vanity's Nissan Altima.

Chapter 15

Pebbles

"I saw that shit on the news." Dash held the door for us as we filed in with Vanity's stuff. "Is everyone ok?"

We all were beat. Stoney mentioned in the car that he had a splitting headache. Vanity was still shook up. I was stressed the fuck out too from texting everyone trying to explain what the fuck happened, and that we were all ok. I needed an immediate release. One of these fine niccas was going to give me some dick. I needed it badly. Otherwise, I was going to be up all night, biting my damn fingernails.

"Daddee! Up." MiMi was standing right by the door in her nightgown with her arms stretched out for Stoney as soon as he stepped into the house. He bent down, picked her up, and kept on walking. Personally, I don't see how he dealt with her. She was too damn much. I would have left her ass right with my parents if I was him.

"Where the boys at?" Stoney asked Dash.

"Still playing video games."

"Did they eat?"

"Yeah, the food came a little after y'all left."

My stomach growled. "That's what I'm talking about. I'm starving." With all this bullshit going on, I forgot that I didn't eat.

Princess Diamond

Vanity, Stoney and MiMi went upstairs while I went into the kitchen. I was warming my plate up in the microwave when I felt Dash ease up behind me. "You ok, sexy?" he asked me, kissing my neck, and then massaging my shoulders.

I smiled. I guess I found who was about to give me some. "I'll bet you push up on every cute girl that you see."

"Naw, just the bad chicks. I don't fuck around with nothing less."

"Can you back up?" I said, sliding out of his embrace. "I'm trying to eat."

Dash stepped to the side, holding my chair out for me. I rolled my eyes at him, sitting down. "Thank you, I guess." I laughed. He was too cute, but I wasn't about to blow his head up. I'm sure he heard that all the time.

He laughed too. "This little attitude that you have won't push me away. If that's what you think. In fact, it makes my dick even harder."

"Good cuz I don't like no weak nicca. If you're weak in person than you're weak in bed. I need a man who knows how to make me cum multiple times. Can you hang?"

He licked his lips. "I can show you better than I can tell you."

I smirked, digging into my food. I piled my plate high. I had pizza, spaghetti, bread sticks, mostaccioli, fish, shrimp, and wings. I licked my fingers. "Where's the hot sauce?"

Dash got up and grabbed the sauce out of one of the cabinet.

"Get me a pop too?"

"What kind?"

"Pepsi."

He sat both items down in front of me before taking his seat across from me again.

"Are you going to sit there and watch me eat?"

"That's not what I'm watching," he said winking at me.

His phone vibrated. He checked it and started texting.

"Look at you, playboy. You can't even get your mack on cuz one of your bitches texting you."

Everybody Got A Secret 2: A Drama Filled Romance

Dash chuckled while he was texting. "Jealous already?"

"Am I lying?"

He chuckled again. "I'm texting my cousin, if you must know. I don't have a girl."

"Yeah, right."

"Don't believe me. I'm not trying to convince you. But I know one thing."

"What's that?" I asked, licking my fingers again.

"You gonna let me hit."

The nerve of this nicca. "Ugh, that was so disrespectful."

He was still texting whoever it was. "Was it? Or did it make your panties wet?"

I can't lie. This little back and forth thing with him was kinda turning me on. I don't know why because normally I would have slapped the piss out of him. But for some reason, this little game he was playing had me intrigued.

His phone rang. "Hello. What's down? Naw, I'm free. I can be there in twenty minutes." He laughed. "I know. Everyone in Chicago always say twenty minutes for everything. Ok. See you then." He hung up. "I gotta bounce, pretty, but I'll be back to see what that pussy do."

"Don't worry about what this pussy do. You just make sure that dick do."

He kissed me on the cheek. "I like that, sexy. I'll be back to show you."

"Yeah, ok." I said, not paying him any more attention. He was about to leave and go see some bitch. I wasn't stupid. His ass was going to be tied up all night. It was all good. I'd play with my own pussy.

"Don't be surprised if you find me in your bed with you in the middle of the night."

"That I gotta see," I said, continuing to enjoy my food.

"I'll be back."

As soon as Dash left, my phone vibrated. I saw that I had several texts from family and friends. I'd get back to them later. Chip texted me. I asked him how Ivan was. He said he didn't know. Ivan was still in surgery. He'd been hit twice that's why it was so much blood. I told him that I hoped he made it. I truly meant that. I didn't want my sister with him anymore, but he was still Chip's brother. I still loved Chip very much, even though we weren't together. Chip said he'd hit me back later. His parents just walked in.

I was taking my last bite when Stoney walked in the kitchen. He looked more relaxed. He had on blue and white pajama bottoms with a blue wife beater. "Are you ok?"

Damn, he looked good. I was trying to keep the sexy images of him out of my mind. "Yeah, I'm ok. I just heard from Chip. Ivan is still in surgery." I put my plate in the sink. "I know you probably don't care. I just thought I'd mention it anyway."

He bit into a chicken wing. "Don't get it twisted, I really don't give a fuck. Dude's a scumbag, but I don't want dude to die either."

"I feel you," I said, trying to get as far away from him as possible.

"You sleepy?"

I was about to walk out of the kitchen. "Not really. I'm wired off Pepsi. What's up?"

"You want to watch a movie with me?"

I don't know why, but I looked behind me at the stairs.

Stoney must've picked up on it. "Vanity's sleep if that's what you're wondering."

"Oh, ok. Is it just going to be us?" I don't know why I was so nervous all the sudden. Stoney just had that kinda effect on me. I don't know if it was my attraction to him or what.

"No, the boys are going to come down too. But I'm sure they'll be sleep before the movie is over. I just don't want to watch it by myself and Dash is gone. He usually watches it with me."

I see tonight had affected Stoney a lot more than he wanted to admit. "Where's crybaby at?"

He laughed. "She curled up next to Vanity, going right to sleep. I could have done a back flip."

Everybody Got A Secret 2: A Drama Filled Romance

"I know you glad. I would punch Emerald in the eye when I saw him if I was you."

He chuckled. "Ain't it. People are starting to think I have a two-year old."

Now, it was my turn to laugh. "True. She looks just like you too. Cute baby. She just cries too damn much."

"Are you saying you think I'm cute?"

He gave me a really sexy look and I almost melted. "Boy, bye" I said leaving the kitchen. "I'll be back."

I went to my room, showered again, and put on Stoney's cousin's pajamas. I looked in the mirror. This shit wasn't me. I liked sleeping nude. I found a cute little short tee that barely covered my ass and let the rest hang out free.

"You're wearing that?" Stoney said, resting on the couch. The boys were on the floor playing with hand-held games.

"Yeah, what's wrong with what I have on?"

Stoney looked me up and down and scooted to the end of the couch. He grabbed a pillow, putting it in his lap. "Nothing. Just sit on that end."

I giggled, purposefully showing him my ass as I sat down. He reached over grabbing a throw off of the chair, tossing it to me. "Put that over you."

"What if I don't want too?" I said, flirting with him. I couldn't help it. I knew I gave him a hard on. It got me hot too.

He looked at me, adjusted the pillow in his lap, and pressed play on the remote. "Just put it on so you don't flash the boys."

I played nice and put the throw over my lower half. I wasn't trying to give the boys a peek. That was sick.

The movie was scary as fuck. Stoney cut out all the lights, the boys put their games away, and it was just the light from the TV. I nearly threw the bowl of popcorn all over the front room when the doorbell rang.

Stoney got up off the couch, laughing at me.

"What up, fam?"

"Sup, actor in training?"

Stoney laughed. "Shut your ass up, nicca."

His voice was sexy. Who was that?

In stepped this gorgeous man that I assumed was another one of Stoney's cousins. They favored.

Stoney cut the light on. "Pebbles this is my cousin Amante. Dom's father."

"Do I know you?"

Amante stared at me. "You look familiar."

That's when I noticed he had pretty eyes too. Damn, is the whole family fine with light eyes? Because I don't have no problem breaking his cousin off too.

"Did you go to Morgan Park?"

"Yeah," I said, realizing that I do know him.

"You know what? I think we had gym together."

"We sure did. I remember you now," I said, standing up. Immediately, Amante's eyes went to my short tee. I pulled my tee down a little, hoping that my goodies weren't showing. I checked him out too. He was fly wearing all white. I assumed he was going to an all-white party.

"What a small world," Amante said, kneeling down on the carpet, next to his son. The boys were knocked out just like Stoney predicted. He pulled off Dom's too big shirt and put on his nightclothes. Then, he picked him up putting him over his shoulder. "You want me to put E to bed too?"

"Yeah." Stoney nudged him. "Get up, E. Go to bed."

I cracked up because E jumped up off the floor with his eyes closed, walking towards the steps. "I'll help him," I offered, holding E by his hand, leading him to his room.

E crawled into his bed, face first, going back to sleep on top of the covers. Amante sat his baby down next to E, putting him under the covers. He kissed his son on the forehead.

"Where's your room?" Amante asked me as we walked out of E's room. I pointed one door over. "Oh, that's what I thought," he said, grabbing a handful of my ass.

Before I knew it, he was tongue kissing me, backing me up inside of my room. Once inside, his hands were all over me. I enjoyed every bit of it. Not only was he a fantastic kisser, he was smooth. He rubbed between my legs as we kissed.

Everybody Got A Secret 2: A Drama Filled Romance

"Sssssss. Damn, you're wet," he said, in between kisses. "I bet you want some dick, don't you?"

If I couldn't get it from Stoney or Dash, then I would gladly get it from Amante. "Yep, you gonna give it to me."

He stopped rubbing me, resting his hand between my legs. "I don't think you're ready for me yet."

"Boy please. I'm sure I could handle you."

He chuckled. "Slow down, little girl. You ain't ready for all this dick."

"Whatever," I said, unfastening his gold belt and then his white jeans.

He had a really nice body too and a tight firm ass. I was thirsty to feel him inside of me. I reached inside his boxers, freeing his dick and nearly passed out. He had the biggest dick I'd ever seen. I thought Chip was holding. Amante had him beat. "Damn, is your dick even real?"

Why did I say that? I just pumped his ego all the way up.

He smiled. "Of course."

"You not putting that in me," I said, pulling my tee down. "You ain't about to bust my coochie wide open. Fuck that. I want some dick, but not that bad."

"Baby, you're not talking to an amateur. I know how to use my dick. I never hurt no woman that didn't need to be hurt."

I gawked at his huge appendage. "How many inches are you? And don't say you don't know. I know your ass measured."

He smirked. "Eleven."

"You don't even look like you'd be packing all that. Where was it hiding?"

Amante definitely had me intrigued. I was excited and scared all at the same time. I was scared as hell to have sex with him, but at the same time, I was really excited to know what he felt like. My pussy was gushy just looking at his huge dick. It was so thick and big that it looked fake.

"Amante!" a woman yelled. "Hurry the fuck up. I don't want to be late."

"Who is that?" I asked.

"Dom's mother."

I smacked my lips. "How you gonna be up here with me trying to fuck when your baby's mother downstairs. That's bogus."

"Because her ass is supposed to be in the car."

I pulled down my short tee again. It kept riding up. "I don't want no problems. I got enough shit to deal with."

"Ain't going to be no problems. I handle all my bitches."

"Oh really? So, I'm a bitch now."

"No, not unless you act like one. Then, you're one too."

"Amante! I know you fuckin hear me," the loud chick said again. She was getting on my damn nerves. "You better bring your ass on. It don't take that long to put Dom to sleep."

He sighed. I could tell his baby's mother was getting on his nerves. His lips touched mine again. "To be continued—"

"I don't think so."

"Well, I do. And I always get what I want."

He squeezed my ass again before he stepped away from me, jogging downstairs. I went to my bathroom to freshen up. I wiped my kitty, and put on some boy shorts, before I returned to the living room. Amante and his baby's mother was gone. Stoney was looking out the window as they left. I peeked too. I wanted to see what he was driving. A white Jaguar.

Stoney yawned. "I'm tired. We can watch the movie tomorrow. I'm ready to turn in."

"Ok," I said about to go upstairs.

"Aye," he said, grabbing me by my arm, pulling me back to him. "What took you so long upstairs?"

I pulled away from him. "Vanity is your girl. Not me. I don't owe you no explanation about what I do. This pussy don't belong to you."

"It don't?" he said, eyeballing me.

I felt so hot under his gaze.

He walked up on me, backing me up against the wall. He pressed his body against mine. I felt myself getting weak. "Stop, Stoney. You know I'm not trying to go there with you," I lied.

Everybody Got A Secret 2: A Drama Filled Romance

"I know I'm right. Look at you. I could have my way with you right now if I wanted to."

"Whatever." I slid down the wall towards the floor, breaking out of his hold. "Goodnight."

He caught up to me as I was walking upstairs, smacking my ass. "We're not done."

"Yes we are. Goodnight."

I went to my room, hoping that Stoney didn't follow me.

*****

I woke up out of my sleep to someone eating me out. The shit felt damn good. It was exactly what I needed. I touched his head as he sucked on my clit bringing me to a climax. He licked and kissed my pearl until I had another one.

"Mmmmm," he moaned, sticking two fingers inside of me, finger fucking me while teasing my clit.

I wanted some dick. After messing around with Amante, and fanaticized about getting some, I was ready to feel something hard. He ignored me continuing to tongue-kiss my pussy. He was going HAM on my clit making me cum for a third time.

Climbing up my body, he rested on top of me, filling me up with his big dick. "I told you I would be back," Dash said. "I was going to get me some of this good, tight, wet pussy."

I kissed him. I didn't care if I tasted my own juices. I was just glad to see him. The last time I was in this situation, it turned out ugly.

"What about your girl?" I asked, grinding my pelvis against his.

"Stop fishing for answers. That was my agent. I needed to sign this contract." He lifted my legs in the crook of his arm. "I told you, I didn't have a girl."

"Ok," I said, not believing him.

"You sound like you want to be my girl."

"Nope. All I want is your dick."

"That's what you say right now. You'll want a nicca after he puts it down on your ass."

"Put it down then."

I didn't want to compare Dash and Stoney, but I couldn't help it. Dash fucked just like him. If I had my eyes closed, I wouldn't know the difference. They felt the same, moved similar, and made me cum back to back. Dash had just as much stamina too.

He put his hand over my mouth. "I know it's good, but you ain't got to scream. You're going to wake up the whole damn house."

"It's so good. I couldn't help it."

He stuck his finger in my mouth, and I sucked it. "Pretty little freak."

"Takes one to know one."

"I admit I'm a freak."

He was pounding me so good. We fucked all over the bed. The covers were on the floor.

"You want to say my name, don't you?"

"No," I lied. I wanted to scream his name at the top of my lungs.

He lifted my bottom, leaning back on his knees. Effortlessly, he scooped my body in the air, bouncing me up and down. I wrapped my arms around his neck, kissing him. Dash was a good kisser too. I rose and fell on his hardness, riding him like a pony.

"Ah! Ah! Ah! Ah! Ah!"

"Is it good?" he whispered in a sensual tone. "Tell me."

"Ah! Dash. Ah! Yes. It's sooooo gooooood." My eyes rolled into the back of my head as I came.

He thrusted into me while I came, giving me back-to-back orgasms. My head fell back and he kissed my neck down to my breasts. "How this dick feel?"

"G-G-G-G-G-Good," I stammered. He was hitting it so damn good that I almost choked on my own damn spit. I started coughing and couldn't stop.

He laughed. "Don't let the dick kill you."

Everybody Got A Secret 2: A Drama Filled Romance

I smacked his arm. "Shut the hell up."

He smiled before sucking my breasts again. "I'ma break that tough girl act you got."

"How?" I said feeling another orgasm coming on.

He picked me up and flipped me onto my stomach, dicking me down. His chiseled stomach bounced off my ass while his balls slapped against my clit. My body jerked a couple of times as I approached another orgasm. Dash pumped even harder as if he knew I was about to let it all go. Burying my face in the pillow, I screamed out as my body shook and shook and shook and shook. He opened my legs wider, gripping my waist hitting my spot continuously.

"Fuck me, Daaaaaaaash!" I cried.

Tears were actually flowing down my cheeks. He was fucking me so good that I started screaming and crying at the same time. I laid under Dash with his dick buried to the hilt, steadily cumming. I wasn't sure how him and Stoney did this, but I ain't never experience dick like theirs before. If anything was going to make me fall for a nicca, it would be getting this kinda dick on a regular.

Dash kept hitting it until I gushed out cum, wetting up the bed. That's when his body stiffened. Then I heard him let out a few grunts before he collapsed on top of me releasing sperm.

"Damn, girl, that shit was incredible. I see why niccas be tripping over you." He smacked my ass hard. "I need to pee. Then I'll be back for round two."

"No," I whined. "I'm tired."

"You can't be," he said from the bathroom, peeing. "I'm not done with you yet."

After he finished using the bathroom and washing his hands, he came back in the room. He picked the covers up off the floor, putting them back on the bed, before he climbed in bed next to me.

"What's up with you and my brother?"

"Huh?" I asked, totally off guard.

"Huh?" he mimicked me, laughing. "You heard me."

"We slept together in the Bahamas. That's it."

"Are you sure?"

"Yeah, I'm sure. Why?"

"He's kinda protective over you. I think he likes you and you like him, but he's with your sister, and you don't want to hurt her feelings. That's what I think."

He had a point. I wasn't going to admit that though. "I guess it doesn't matter because I'm with you now."

"Oh, it matters. Stoney has claimed you as his."

"He can't claim me. I'm not his girl."

"That's what I said. Good pussy got him fucked up," Dash said, rolling over, back on top of me, working his dick deep inside.

"Yeeeeeeeees. Ooooooh! Yeeeeesssss. Daaaaaaaash."

His fingers locked with mine. "Good dick got you fucked up too."

Chapter 16

Vanity

I couldn't breathe. I felt Ivan's hands tighten around my throat. My vision was blurry. I could no longer see his face clearly.

"Bitch! I'm going to fuckin kill you."

His hands tightened around my neck. I gasped for air. "Please don't kill me," I whimpered. I wasn't even sure if he heard me. It felt as if the words got caught in my throat. Never leaving my mouth.

"Oh, there's no need to beg. Your ass is a dead bitch! Believe that. I wouldn't spare your life if someone paid me."

He stopped choking me, pulling out a gun, putting it to my head pulling the trigger.

I closed my eyes expecting to die, but the gun didn't go off.

He laughed as if my fear was funny. "Watching you squirm makes my fuckin dick hard."

"I'm sorry, Ivan. I never meant to hurt you. I really didn't."

"But you did, bitch. You broke my heart in half. Yes, we had our problems but you don't go fucking around to solve them. That's what whores do. Are you a fuckin whore?"

"No. I didn't go on vacation planning to sleep with Stoney. It just happened. I didn't even know he was going to be there."

I felt blood trickle down my face when he whacked me across the forehead with the gun. "That's bullshit, bitch. Nothing just happens. You sound dumb as fuck right now."

"What do you want?" I cried. I couldn't even lift my hands because Ivan's body was resting on top of me. My hands were tucked under his legs. "If you're going to kill me, just do it then."

He smacked me across the face with the gun again. "You don't deserve a quick death. I want you to feel all this shit. You need to suffer like you made me suffer."

"But why?" I cried. "You act like I'm a murderer. All I did was cheat."

"All I did was cheat," he repeated in a girlie voice. "You say that like its ok to fuck up our marriage. Open your legs," He said, moving off my chest.

"What are you about to do?"

"I'm about to show you."

I screamed at the top of my lungs when he shoved the gun inside of me. All this torture. I wish he would just kill me. It felt like my insides were ripping apart as he fucked me with the gun.

Wicked laughter filled the room. It got louder and louder until he pulled the trigger. This time the gun went off. The burning sensation started between my legs, and traveled from my stomach through my digestive system, until it reached my throat. Multiple tears streamed down my face as I choked on my own blood.

I jumped up out of my sleep swinging air punches. Blinking a few times, I realized that it was all a dream. Ivan wasn't anywhere around. Stoney was in the bed next to me, sleeping peacefully with MiMi in his arms. I stared at his handsome face before I broke down crying.

That dream might have been fake right now, but I was sure Ivan was going to come after me with guns blazing. He hated me. I was sure that he wouldn't stop at nothing until I was dead or I felt like I was dead. I couldn't help feeling guilty. I drug Stoney into this fiasco. I almost got us both killed. Knowing Ivan as well as I did, I knew that this was only the beginning. I would feel awful if something happened to Stoney. E would be one more Black child without a father.

I sat in the bed crying my eyes out until my nose stopped up, and I had to breathe out my mouth. Climbing out of Stoney's bed, I went to the bathroom to blow my nose. I guess I must've blown too hard because my nose started bleeding. Drops of blood dripped down my face onto the floor.

Snatching the tissue off the roll, I couldn't remember if I was supposed to hold my head back or forward to stop the bleeding. Holding my head back, I felt blood drip down my nasal passage to my mouth, forcing me to swallow it. Sitting on the side of the bathtub, I held my head down, and the tissue quickly filled up with blood. I tossed that wad in the toilet and grabbed some more. It filled up with blood just as quick. Once again, I tossed it and grabbed another handful, putting it to my face. Finally, the bleeding stopped, but the throbbing between my legs started again.

Ivan really fucked me up.

My coochie hurt. My eye hurt. My neck hurt. The burns all over my body hurt. I suppose he did this to me hoping that another nicca wouldn't want me. Stoney acted like none of this bothered him. I didn't know if he was just being nice or if he really meant it. I know looking battered like this bothered the hell out of me. I couldn't even look at myself in the mirror. I felt my self-esteem drop to the size of a pea.

Between the nightmares, Ivan putting a gun to my head, the fear of him actually killing me, was enough to drive me insane. I slowly rose from the side of the tub, holding onto the sink. My leg was bothering me again. It hurt to walk. If I wasn't so thirsty, I wouldn't even bother going downstairs. The moment I walked out of the bathroom, I noticed that I had blood all over my nightgown.

Marching across the hall, I knocked on Pebbles door. She had all of Stoney's cousin's clothes in her room. I stood there for a moment before I knocked again. Finally, the door opened. Pebbles stood butt naked before me.

"What the hell do you want?" she asked, looking like she just finished fucking.

I looked past her into the room, trying to see if someone was in her bed. "Is that Dash in your bed?"

"Stop being so fuckin nosey. What I got going on in my room don't got shit to do with you. What the hell do you want?"

"I need another gown."

"Clearly," Pebbles said, looking at the blood all over me. "Did you piss Stoney off too?"

"That shit is not funny. You're such an asshole."

Pebbles slammed the door in my face. It happened so quick that I stood there stuck on stupid. As I was about to turn the knob and come in, she opened the door, throwing a really short shirt at me.

"What am I supposed to do with this?"

"I don't know, um, wear it," she said, being sarcastic.

She better be glad I was in pain or I would have slapped her damn face. "I don't want my ass hanging out like yours. Titties and booty bouncing everywhere."

"Well, maybe you should. And while you're at it, maybe you should roll over on Stoney's dick. Your attitude could use a good fuck right about now."

I was getting ready to snatch her up when she closed the door, locking it. "Goodnight, trick."

Who knows what her and Dash were about to do. Knowing her, she probably had his face between her thighs. I wish I could be more confident like her and less like me. If this had happened to her, she would still have the strength to be herself. Right now, I wanted to bury myself under a rock until this shit blew over.

Taking my time, I slowly walked downstairs step by step. When I got to the bottom, I nearly pissed on myself when I saw a shadow sitting on the couch. Instantly, I thought it was Ivan. Fear froze me right where I stood. My hands began to shake. I felt drops of pee about to come out.

Feeling frantically for the light switch, I finally found it, cutting it on. I sighed in relief when I saw that it was a coat. Paranoid wasn't even the word. I was tweaking hard. This man had me so frightened that I was seeing shit. I cut that light out and walked into the kitchen, cutting that light on. I was so distraught that I didn't even remember the last time I ate. Reaching into the refrigerator, I pulled out a piece of cold pizza devouring it. My mouth watered. The pizza tasted like a piece of steak.

Grabbing the pizza box, I sat on the floor eating from it. I stuffed my face until my jaws began to hurt. Then, I washed the pizza down with a cold Pepsi.

Once my stomach was full, I got up. Out of habit, I double-checked the front and back door before wandering back upstairs to Stoney's room. After I changed into the too small shirt, I laid down next to him, closing my eyes.

My phone went off, vibrating. The fear that subsided quickly came back when I saw the text.

Ivan: I'm going to fuck you and that nicca up.

Ivan: You all on that nicca's dick.

Ivan: Fuckin him like he's your damn husband.

Ivan: Your ass is dead, bitch.

Ivan: D. E. A. D. In the ground, bitch. Dead and stinking, bitch. Flies and maggots and shit, bitch. Family crying over your body and paying their respects to you, bitch.

The texts were coming in back to back. I tried to power my phone off. Oddly enough, it wouldn't shut down. Getting out of bed again, I went back downstairs and set the shit on the kitchen counter. I just wanted it as far away from me as possible.

Retreating back to Stoney's room, I climbed back in bed once again. I was lying so close to him out of fear that I was practically underneath him.

In his sleep, Stoney reached over, holding me close with his dick up against my ass.

Chapter 17

Keystone

My dick was hard as fuck. Vanity kept throwing her ass on me. I don't remember her wearing this little ass shirt before I went to sleep, but she was looking sexy as fuck. With her juicy booty all in my face, I was tempted to push her panties to the side and slide my dick right in.

That was until I realized something was on my face. All of a sudden, I couldn't breathe. In a panic, I grabbed whatever this muzzle was on my head, clutching it with both hands. Well, I'll be dammed. It was MiMi. Her little ass had curled up on my face, falling asleep. This crazy ass baby almost suffocated me.

I wanted to toss her little butt across the room. I wasn't used to her and all these antics. E was nothing like this. He slept in his own bed.

Being around MiMi made me think twice about having a baby girl. She was doing the most all the damn time. If my baby girl needed this much attention, I was never going to get any pussy. And that shit wasn't an option. Daddy wasn't going to forgo getting his dick wet because of a spoiled child.

I picked my niece up, laying her chunky butt on the other side of the bed so I could curl up next to Vanity again. I scooted up behind her, resting my dick on her ass, grinding up against her. I couldn't help it. I found her irresistible.

Everybody Got A Secret 2: A Drama Filled Romance

When my lips found her neck, she stirred in her sleep.

"No," Stoney she said, pushing me away. "Not right now."

"C'mon, bae. I'm horny."

"Stoney, what I look like giving you some with the baby in the bed with us."

"I'll put her in the other room."

She sighed. "I'm not in the mood."

"You don't have to be. Just let me stick it in."

"No."

The heat from her body made my dick get even harder. I kissed her neck while I gently pulled her panties aside. "No, Stoney."

"Yes," I said, pushing the head of my penis inside of her.

Her scream scared the shit out of me. It almost made my dick go soft. "What's wrong?"

She moved away from me, grabbing a pillow and blanket, getting out of the bed.

"Where are you going?"

"Far the fuck away from you!"

"Is this how things are going to be? Because you can just go—"

"Go where?" she yelled. "Back to Ivan? Is that what you were going to say?"

I wasn't going to say that, but I could see how she might have thought that. "No, that's not what I was going to say."

"Sure it wasn't. Well, don't think that I haven't thought about it. My marriage wouldn't be in jeopardy if I never fucked around with you."

"Don't get mad at me because you couldn't keep your legs closed."

"Fuck you, Stoney. Fuck you."

I watched her sashay out of my room into the darkness.

I didn't know where she was going. I was still trying to figure out what I did to make her scream. I ran my hands down my face. I was trying my best not to get up and go in the other room

179

with Pebbles. I bet she wouldn't turn me down. I bet she would welcome me with open legs.

I got up out of the bed when Vanity came back into the room, getting back in the bed. I didn't even ask her why she came back. Within moments, she drifted off to sleep again.

Retreating to the bathroom, I decided to jack my dick and take a cold shower. It wasn't going to help that much. Maybe I could calm down enough to go back to sleep.

Standing butt naked in the shower allowing the cold water to rinse over me, I stroked my dick. The more I stroked the hornier I got. I didn't want a hand job. I wanted pussy.

I had a lot of shit on my mind. I loved Vanity with all my heart, but I was starting to feel like being with her was a mistake. My family thought I was making a mistake too. Amante felt like she was still in love with Ivan. That she was going to run back to him as soon as things got rough. Angel said to break her off and move on. Ecko said holler at Pebbles.

Everyone liked Pebbles. I see why. She was mad cool. I felt like she accepted me for me. I didn't have to sneak around and hide shit. It was like she and I were on the same page more than Vanity and I.

My hands rested against the bathroom tile. Was my family right? Was I making a mistake with Vanity? I couldn't help who I loved though. I didn't want to be nobody's fool either. It would crush me if I fought for our love and she went running back to Ivan. I would probably never speak to her ass again. That would just be too much for me to handle.

I stayed in the shower thinking and thinking until I didn't even have the desire to fuck anymore. My dick was soft, my heart was heavy, and my thoughts were running wild. I got out, dried off, and put on a jogging suit. There wasn't no way I was going back to sleep. I needed to work off this anguish. Sweat out my stress.

My phone vibrated back to back. I stepped out of my walk in closet, checking it. I had a long ass text from Kim. She was going on and on about how I don't love her because I never keep my word. I read through the first two text and deleted the rest.

Everybody Got A Secret 2: A Drama Filled Romance

Now, she was calling me. It was time for me to man up and pay her a visit, setting all this shit straight. I texted her telling her that I was on my way over.

As soon as I put my phone down, MiMi sat up in the bed. "Daddee!" She reached out for me.

I reached in the bed, picking her up. "I think you like messing up my life. Don't you?"

MiMi smiled, blowing me a kiss. I kissed her tiny hands. How could I be mad at such a cutie pie? "You wanna roll with me?"

"Yes. Daddee."

"Let's get you dressed."

I dug in her suitcase. I found a pink jumper with a pink and white shirt with some pink and white Nikes. Even her jacket was pink. "You fly now," I said, getting in her face. She grinned when I kissed her chubby cheeks. "Say, uncle, I keep holding on to you because I miss my daddy."

"Daddee."

"I'ma let your daddy know that he has to put in more effort to spend more time with you. Ok?"

She smiled showing off her dimples. "Ok."

I texted Emerald before I went out to the garage, getting into my ride. I put MiMi into Dom's car seat. As I was backing out, I saw Dash's car. I didn't even know he was back. By the time I pulled up to Kim's house, MiMi was sleep. I wished I could have left her in the car. When I came to the door, Kim had on a sexy crotchless get-up. Maybe I should have explained why I was coming. Obviously, she had the wrong idea.

"I'm not here for all that," I said, walking inside with MiMi over my shoulder asleep.

"Oh, I was hoping that we could pick up where we left off earlier," she said, sounding really disappointed.

I really didn't care. I planned on making this short and sweet before Vanity woke up. "Was that before or after you called my brother over?"

She tried not to look too surprised, but I noticed it. "I know you not tripping off that. It was nothing. I just wanted to apologize to him for how things ended. We're going to be family soon."

She was about to be in for a rude awakening. "Yeah, well, that's kinda why I'm here."

"I don't understand."

There was no good way to do this. I didn't like beating around the bush with shit so I just came on out and said it. "I can't do this no more."

"Do what?" she asked as if she didn't know what the hell I meant.

"C'mon, Kim, let's not do this. You knew this day was coming."

"You're dumping me? Why?" Tears came to her eyes. "What did I do wrong?"

See this is why niccas sent texts or made phone calls. The face-to-face shit didn't work. "Because I don't love you. You already know that. It's not a secret."

"I bet this has something to do with that bitch Vanity, don't it?"

"Don't call her out her name. She's done nothing to you."

Kim walked up on me talking with her hands in my face. "Fuck her. I'm not about to respect a bitch that stole my man."

This wasn't going to be as quick and simple as I thought. I sat MiMi down because Kim was getting all emotional.

"I've done everything you asked me to. Everything. And this is how you gonna do me?"

"Kim, save the damn dramatics. We were in this together. We both wanted something out of this relationship—to get back at Cash. It worked. I'm over the revenge bullshit. Obviously, you are too. You just said you called him over here to apologize."

"But I'm in love with you," she said, putting her arms around my waist. "I'll do anything for you. You want me to be more like Vanity? I'll do it."

182

Everybody Got A Secret 2: A Drama Filled Romance

I tried to remove her arms from around me and she held me tighter, kissing my face and neck. "Let me prove it to you, Stoney."

I tried to back away from her. "No. I'm good," I said, avoiding her kisses. "There's nothing to prove."

"You might be good, but your dick ain't." Her hand cupped my erection through my jogging pants. I had on the wrong shit, before I knew it her hands were down my pants, fondling my hard dick.

"Chill." Her hands were all over me like an octopus.

"What's a matter? Vanity ain't giving up the pussy?" How'd she know? Must be woman's intuition. "Let me suck it for you."

My dick really sprung to life. Kim gave great head and her pussy was good too. Get a damn grip. "Nah, we're done." It pained me to say that without at least getting once last hit.

I was trying to pull my pants back up while she was trying to pull my boxers down. I was starting to sweat trying to fight her off. We got to wrestling. Both of us falling back on the love seat. How ironic that she landed on top of me.

"Let's do it one more time. For old times' sake," she said, dry humping me.

I squeezed her ass, ready to fuck. We never had a real issue in the bedroom. As soon as I was about to give in, my phone rang. Vanity's picture popped up on the screen. I knew that was a sign. I needed to get my ass out of here.

"Get off me," I said, pushing her away. I guess I was a little too forceful because she fell down on the floor, landing on her ass.

She sat there crying as if I had really hurt her. I'll admit she did hit the floor kinda hard. Not hard enough for her to be crying the way she was though. Still, her tears tugged at me, making me feel guilty. I'm sure she knew that. I sat up, fixing my clothes, and then reached out my hand for her. "Sorry. Let me help you up."

She grabbed my hand, standing to her feet. "I guess you want the ring back too."

"Well, now that you mentioned it." Honestly, I forgot about it. After she proposed to me, I went out and got her the ring that she deserved.

"Here," she said, taking it off throwing it. It bounced off the door, landing on the carpet.

See, this that petty shit. "And this is why your ass is history."

"Don't come crawling back when this bitch leaves you. Cuz she's going to do you dirty. Watch. That's what bitches like her do. They use niccas like you as the rebound nicca."

"Well, you should know. Ain't that what you did to Cash? Use me as the rebound nicca?"

"Fuck you, Stoney. His dick was bigger and better than yours anyway. That's why I asked him to come over. I was hoping that he would take me back. At least I know he still loves me."

"I ain't got time for this shit." I stepped over the ring on the floor. "You can keep that muthafucka. I don't need it."

I wasn't loaded, but I was balling a little bit. That ring cost me a pretty penny. However, I left it there just to prove a point. I scooped MiMi up, who surprisingly slept through all this commotion, and proceeded to the door. This baby was a trip. Out of all the times for her to stay sleep, this was the one time that she should have woke up.

"Get the fuck out then," Kim said, running up behind me, hitting me in the back. "That's why I never loved your ass anyway. I was pretending the whole time. You ain't mean shit to me."

She backed the hell up when I turned around ready to swing on her ass. I guess she realized that she'd made the wrong move. "Look, I ain't never hit a woman, but you're pushing it. I'm two seconds off beating your ass. Keep fucking with me. You'll keep your hands to yourself if you know what's good for you."

"Just go! Go!"

Everybody Got A Secret 2: A Drama Filled Romance

I walked backwards out of Kim's house onto the porch just in case she wanted to swing on me again. In agony, she fell on the floor screaming and crying as I jogged to my car. I didn't even bother putting MiMi in the car seat. I held on to her with one hand as I drove off with the other. I just wanted to get the fuck away from Kim's crazy ass before I caught a charge.

I called Vanity back. "What's up, bae?"

"This ain't your bae," Pebbles said. "Where you at? Sneaking out to get pussy in the middle of the night, huh? So typical."

She knew me too well. I have done that before. "That's not even possible when I got MiMi's cock-blocking ass."

"Aww, that's the only reason why then."

"Is that what you called to ask me? Or you were hoping that I was all up in your pussy. Knocking it out like I did last time."

She giggled. "Stop playing. I'm off limits."

"Says who?"

"Says Vanity. You trying to get your ass beat."

"I seriously doubt that. But what about you, though? Am I off limits to you? Or have you been thinking about me as much as I've been thinking about you? Pussy wet and yearning for the way I made you cum."

The phone went silent.

It was my turn to laugh. "Look at you, thinking about what I said. I already know you want me to hit it. I hope you still got on that short ass tee. That shit was sexy as fuck."

"I'm not trying to go there with you, Stoney."

"But I'm trying to go there with you."

She exhaled. "Um, anyway, I called because Dash asked me to tell you to bring us some breakfast." I heard Dash in the background say that he was hungry. "He said bring the works from that one place that y'all go to all the time."

"Aight. While I do that, you get ready for me."

I thought about Kim's angry rants. She had me all the way fucked up if she thought I couldn't live without her ass. I had two fine ass chicks that would put her to shame on any given day. Kim was bad, but she couldn't hold a candle to Vanity or Pebbles.

The place that Dash was talking about was downtown. I wasn't going all the way down there. I called my boy that worked at the IHOP in Ford City. He was on his way to work just as I suspected. He said that by the time I got there, he'd have my order ready. I needed to make a stop first anyway.

I picked up my phone dialing the number. "Who is this calling so fuckin early? It better be an emergency."

"Cash, it's me. Were you sleep?" That was a stupid question. He sounded like he was knocked out.

"What you think?" He asked with an attitude.

"Never mind then. I'll call back later."

He breathed all hard in the phone. "Naw, what's up? You must've called for a reason."

"That's ok. I'll talk to you later."

Cash yawned. "Where you at?" He yawned again.

"Not too far from your house."

"Aight. Why don't you swing through?"

"Aight."

Cash came to the door with a toothbrush in his mouth. He let us in while he went back to the bathroom to finish brushing his teeth. "I see you got crybaby with you," he said, coming back into the family room, sitting next to me. "You good?"

My thoughts were all over the place, driving me crazy. I was thinking about that shit that happened yesterday. That was a bold move I made with Ivan and Chip. My temper got the best of me as usual. What if things didn't turn out the way they did? What if Chip's gun went off and I died? What if I shot one or both of them? What if Ivan killed Vanity? What if I did the wrong thing by pursuing her? What if she was meant to stay with him and not me? Why couldn't I stop thinking about Pebbles?

Then the past kept creeping back up too. The death of my father, Karen, and how E was born. Could I have prevented killing Keno? Why did Karen do what she did? Did I lead her on? Did my mother and Carlo do the right thing by adopting E? Was

Everybody Got A Secret 2: A Drama Filled Romance

I a good father? Did E secretly hate me for having him so young and being so inexperienced?

"Stoney? Stoney? Stoney?" I didn't look at Cash until he shook me, snapping me out of my thoughts. "Man, you look stressed the fuck out."

"I am," I openly admitted. I never opened up to Cash. I always viewed him as the enemy. Well, maybe not my enemy, but definitely not someone I could trust.

"Anything I can do to help?"

I took a deep breath. "I've made so many bad choices. So many mistakes. I feel like I'm drowning."

"Hold that thought. I don't want the coffee to boil over like it did last time and Karen threaten to kick my ass."

He strolled into the kitchen and came back with two cups of coffee. He went back and grabbed the cream and sugar for me. He drank his black. I liked a little cream and sugar with mine.

He took a sip. "Now, what were you saying?"

"How did you know Karen was the one? I mean, you were with Kim right before her and it didn't work out. I know I have something to do with that, but let's face it, she definitely wasn't wife material. What was it about Karen that made her stand out so you would pop the question?"

Cash took another sip of his coffee. "Well, speaking objectively, when I was with Kim, I was more in love with the idea of being with her. When I got with Karen, she made me better. She forced me to get my shit in order or she wasn't going to be with me unless I did. As you know, Karen don't give a fuck about my money. She will leave my ass in a heartbeat if I'm fucking up. Also, she rode out with me. She was right by my side during my good and bad days. We had our arguments, but nothing could keep her from me. I couldn't see my life without her."

I nodded my head, staring at the floor. "I broke off the engagement with Kim just a few minutes ago."

"Oh, yeah, how did that go?"

"Not so good. All I wanted to do was make things right." I looked up at Cash. "I want to apologize."

"For what?"

"For getting involved with Kim in the first place. I was so hurt back then. She wanted revenge. I did too. We both just wanted to get back at you. That was the whole basis of our relationship."

Cash looked at me and nodded. I could tell that it bothered him. I saw the hurt on his face.

"I'm not making excuses, but you don't know what I been through when I came to live with y'all. You were so arrogant. So mean. I felt like if I don't strike first, then I'm going to get struck. I'm at a different place in my life now. Especially after this Ivan and Vanity bullshit. The last thing I need is you to be against me too. Will you forgive me?"

"I forgive you. Now, I want to ask you to forgive me?"

"For what?" I wondered

"Well, I didn't know what you'd been through back then but I know now. I overheard you talking to Pops today."

"Oh." That's all I could say. I wasn't prepared for that.

"I heard when you said that you killed Keno. And that Karen was a child molester."

I started feeling myself getting angry. "I don't want to talk about it."

"Hold up, let me finish. So, I asked Mama what happened. She told me everything. That's why I want your forgiveness. You had every right to be angry. All these years, I'd been thinking that it was a home invasion or something. I had no idea what really happened. You went through so much at such a young age. Then, on top of that, you had a child to raise. And not one time did I ever hear you make excuses about taking care of E or having him so young."

I remained quiet. A part of me was glad that Cash knew the truth. Another part of me was so embarrassed. It made me look weak and less than a man. And I hated the word molested. I always thought of the term being associated with women, not men.

"I forgive you," I said standing to my feet. "I gotta go."

Everybody Got A Secret 2: A Drama Filled Romance

Cash sat his coffee down on the end table, hugging me. It wasn't one of those quick one arm hugs either. It was a tight, bear hug that lasted for a moment. When Cash stepped away from me, he sniffed, blinking away tears. "I just want you to know that I'm truly sorry. Instead of picking arguments with you, I should have been more supportive. Had your back like a big brother is supposed to do."

"C'mon, man," I said, feeling myself getting emotional. I refused to cry. In fact, I don't even remember the last time I did.

Cash chuckled, wiping his eyes. "Only you could make me bitch up like this."

We both let out a hearty laugh.

He promised to work harder on our relationship. I promised the same.

He kissed MiMi and hugged me again before I left.

Chapter 18

Pebbles

After Dash and I had sex, I went downstairs to get something to drink. I found Vanity's phone on the kitchen counter. That was odd. I went to Stoney's room to return it, seeing Vanity in bed alone. Where was this nicca at? I looked around the house, going from room to room. Still no Stoney. That's when I decided to call him on her phone.

As usual, he was trying to push up on me. We had this lustful back and forth thing that we did. I'm sure he got off on it just as much as I did.

"But what about you, though? Am I off limits to you? Or have you been thinking about me as much as I've been thinking about you? Pussy wet and yearning for the way I made you cum."

That brief conversation left me wet, willing and waiting. It's like he knew exactly what to say to have me sitting in a puddle. That moment we shared in the Bahamas was so fuckin sweet. Truth be told, I never stopped thinking about it. I know he was my sister's man but I had a Jones for him. And I needed to be with him at least one more time.

Once the call ended, I went back in Stoney's room, putting Vanity's phone on the dresser beside her purse. I made my way back to my room, getting back in bed next to Dash. He had his back turned to me, snoring. Instead of curling up next to him, I faced the opposite direction. I had no emotional connection to Dash whatsoever. He made it clear that he didn't want a relationship. I respected that. It was all about sex.

Unfortunately, I felt very connected to Stoney. It wasn't just sex like I thought it was going to be. Something was developing between us. I wasn't sure what it was. I just knew that I liked spending time with him. I liked the way he looked at me. The way he held me in his arms. And I loved the way he fucked me until I nearly passed out. I didn't know what it was about Stoney, but I wanted that feeling from him again. I knew it was wrong. Still, I couldn't help it.

I just stepped out of the shower with another short tee on with no panties when Stoney walked in the kitchen carrying MiMi.

"I see you're wearing what I asked you too." When I looked over my shoulder, he kissed my lips. "I'll be right back." He grabbed a handful of my ass before going upstairs.

I assumed he was putting MiMi down. I was surprised she was still sleep. He came back downstairs, and went back out to the garage, carrying in breakfast. "You need my help?"

"Yeah. Come out to the car."

I went back to my room, stepping into my slippers, before I went out to the garage. When I didn't see him, I opened the car door. "What you need?"

"You," he said, pulling me inside. I landed on top of him, straddling his lap.

"Stop," I said, weakly. Stoney knew that I liked it. That's why he kept on touching me all over.

"How long are we going to play this back and forth game? You know as well as I do that we both want it." His kisses were so sweet and tender. "I can't stop thinking about you."

As much as I wanted to deny it, I couldn't. "I can't stop thinking about you either."

"Tell me you want it then."

"I want it in the worst way."

He pulled my shirt over my head, tossing it into the backseat. I sat before him nude. He kissed from my neck down to my breasts, holding them together, sucking them at the same time.

"Mmmmm. I bet you're real wet, aren't you?" He didn't wait for me to answer. While sucking my breasts, he reached in between my legs, touching my wetness. "You want this dick?"

I didn't even answer, tugging at his jogging pants until I freed his dick. As soon as I slid down on his pole, the car door opened, startling both of us. I jumped. Stoney kept cool, but I felt his heart rate speed up.

"It ain't no fun if Dash can't have none," he said, jumping into the car. His hand caressed my backside before slapping it. "We should do a threesome."

I didn't say anything looking from Dash to Stoney.

"Nah," Stoney said, holding me closer to him. "Plus it ain't enough room."

"Let her answer," Dash said calmly. "That's your fantasy right? Being intimate with two niccas."

"Yeah," I replied bashfully.

It wasn't that often that I blushed. This was one of those rare occasions. Fucking two fine ass niccas had been my fantasy for the longest. Actually, I wanted to fuck twins. Dash and Stoney were just like twins. Sex was incredible with both of them.

Being desired by both men had me feeling extra. I could definitely get busy with both of them.

Dash kissed the back of my neck down my back. "Let me see you ride that dick," he said smacking my ass. When I didn't move fast enough he smacked my ass three more times, leaving a hot sting on my backside and a new fire burning between my legs. "Ride it."

I began working my hips seductively. Slowly, I rode Stoney's dick, staring deep into his eyes. I could tell that he wasn't feeling this. I guided Stoney's hands to my waist, tongue-kissing him, while rocking my hips as Dash kept smacking my ass with a sweet sting. I got so lost in my fantasy that I forgot we were in the car.

Everybody Got A Secret 2: A Drama Filled Romance

Dash's hands were all over my body. "You like this?" he whispered in my ear before licking my lobe.

"Yes." Damn, Dash was a freak. I thought I was freaky, but I think he's got me beat.

"I can't do this shit," Stoney said, pushing me away from him. "Get up."

"Cool. I'll take your place then." Dash literally pulled me off of Stoney's dick, into his lap.

Before I knew it, I was straddling Dash's lap with his hardness deep inside of me. He locked his arms around my hips with his face buried in my chest. I should have felt nasty, trifling, and slutty, but I didn't. I loved the attention. It made me feel desired.

Stoney stared at us for a moment. "When did you two start fucking?"

"In the middle of the night," Dash replied in between kisses.

Although, Stoney didn't show it, I could tell he was heated. "Just so you know, that pussy is mine."

"It's all good," Dash replied. "I'm just keeping it warm for you."

I was feeling Stoney, but I had to check his ass. Nobody owned me. "Just so you know, this pussy is mine. It don't belong to no man. Especially not you. I can't claim your dick. It got my sister's name written all over it. So, either you're staying and joining in or you can beat it."

Stoney remained quiet, eyeballing me. And I gave him something to look at too. I began bouncing up and down on Dash, showing off my riding skills. Arching my back, I rolled my hips with the seduction of three big booty strippers. Stoney adjusted himself, tucking his dick back inside of his pants, and got out of the car.

I stopped riding Dash when the car door closed. "I'm not trying to come in between you two."

"Never that. Bros before hoes. Always. That'll never change."

193

I smacked his arm. "Are you calling me a hoe? Cuz you climbed in bed with me."

Dash chuckled and smiled. "No. I wasn't calling you a hoe. I was just using that term to express that me and Stoney are Gucci."

"So, he's not mad?"

"Oh, he's pissed the fuck off, but he'll be ok. He likes you. That's why."

"Maybe I went too far."

"Don't trip." Dash began grinding inside of me. "Let's enjoy the moment and cum together."

There was a tap on the window. Dash cracked it at eye level. It was Stoney. "Don't be all day. Marcel is going to be pissed if we're late."

"We won't be that much longer."

Stoney eyed Dash and then me. I felt so transparent under his gaze. I was so glad when he stormed away. Dash rolled back up the window. "Now where were we?"

"I don't know if I can do this."

"Let me convince you," Dash said. "Turn around."

I switched positions, putting my ass in his face and my palms on the dashboard. He jerked me back onto his lap, making me cum after only a few strokes. Dash lasted a few more minutes before he busted off too.

Dash got out of the car, walking in through the front door. I walked in through the back into the kitchen. Dom and E were sitting at the breakfast table eating. Vanity was sitting there too feeding MiMi.

"Where you coming from?" She asked, eyeing me suspiciously.

I ignored her, eating a piece of bacon. I wanted more, but I needed to hit the shower first. I was too sticky to sit down and eat. I needed to wash my ass first. Dash walked into the kitchen, washing his hands as I walked out. I wondered where Stoney went. I thought he'd be in the kitchen with everyone else, but he wasn't. I peeked in his room across the hall. He wasn't in there either. Maybe he was in his bathroom.

Everybody Got A Secret 2: A Drama Filled Romance

I stripped out of my clothes, throwing them in the hamper, and stepped into the shower. I had flashbacks of what happened in the car between me, Stoney, and Dash. A smile spread across my face. It would be nice if it went a little further. I liked messing with both of them. Although, Dash seemed a little more cool about all this. Stoney seemed more territorial. I can't believe he had the nerve to put dibs on my pussy. I wasn't his woman. We were just fucking.

I stepped out of the shower, drying my body with a towel. Shuffling through his cousin's smell-goods, I found my favorite scent from Bath & Body Works; Sweet Pea. I stood in the full-length mirror, putting lotion all over. Staring at my flawless body in the mirror, I saw Stoney walk up behind me. He was just as nude as I was.

"What do you want?" I said, pretending that his presence didn't make my nipples hard and my pussy drip.

"You still think that pussy ain't mine?"

"Boy, bye. Is that why you're in here? I can tell you right now, you don't have no—"

Stoney grabbed me by my neck, shoving me over the vanity style sink, ramming into me hard and fast. One hand pressed down on my back while the other hand gripped my leg, lifting it up on the sink too. My ass was tooted upward while my face was pressed down against the porcelain sink.

Slap! Slap! Slap! Slap! Slap! Slap! Slap! Slap!

He was fucking the hell out of me.

"You thought that shit you pulled in the car was cute. Didn't you?"

"Ah! Ah! No! Ah! Ah! Oh my God! Oh my God! Oh my God! "

"Yes, you did," he said, steadily fucking me hard while slapping my ass too. "Didn't you?"

"Oh, shit! Oh, shit! Oh, shit! Oh, shit! Oh, shit! Oh, shit! "

"You always popping off at the mouth. Talk that shit now." He grabbed my hair, making my back curve into an S. "Say my name, dammit."

"Stoooooonnnneeey!" I screamed cumming.

He kept hitting it at super speed. "Say it again."

My body shook so hard that my legs stiffened, my toes curled, and I had drool coming out of my mouth. "No!" I said, hoping that would piss him off even more so that he would continue to prove himself with his dick.

"I see you don't learn shit."

He removed his hand from my hair, lightly gripping my neck, applying the right amount of pressure. I came immediately. My face contorted in all these ugly sex faces as I called out his name over and over in the throes of passion. It felt like I couldn't breathe. Still, I didn't want him to stop fucking me.

"Tell me this pussy belongs to me."

"It's yours. Oh gawd, it's all yours. Just keep beating it up. Please, don't stop. Oh gawd, don't stop. Yes!"

He let go of my neck, jerking my hips with quick spurts that left me speechless. I felt myself cumming again. This time, my body shook uncontrollably like I was having a seizure. Stoney kept pounding me, giving me another intense orgasm. My eyes rolled so hard into my head that I thought they got stuck. I gripped at the sink almost breaking my nails. "Fuck! You got the best dick. I sweeeeeeeeeeeeear."

He slowed down, hitting my sweet spot in a sensual way. I felt a bunch of mini spasms before I had the urge to pee, and then I squirted cum.

He grunted thrusting into me super deep. It felt like his dick was in my throat. A low guttural moan escaped from his lips and then I felt his seed up inside of me. He kept pumping in and out until he unloaded every drop.

He pulled out. "Turn around." I turned around facing him. "Look at this."

I stared at his hard dick that was covered with white sticky cum.

I smirked asking him a question that I already knew the answer to. "My pussy did that?"

Stoney smirked and, stepping away from me, wiping his dick off.

Everybody Got A Secret 2: A Drama Filled Romance

I sat up on the sink, sliding to my feet. "I agree, but you know like I know, this has to stop. We can't keep doing it."

"Why?" he asked as he dressed. "We both want it."

"Because I don't want to hurt my sister. What happened in the Bahamas is different from now. I can't keep doing this with you."

"But you want to. You like fucking me just as much as I like fucking you. Quit acting like you don't."

He was right. I absolutely loved it. "Stoney, I'm coming clean. I love it, but you don't belong to me. I don't have your heart, just your body. I deserve a chance at happiness. A real chance with someone. That's why I left Chip."

"I'm not ready to give you up yet," he said walking out of the bathroom. I guess he left so he didn't have to keep hearing the truth.

I followed him into my room ready to finish our conversation when Dash walked in. I paused, waiting to see the interaction between them. Dash said Stoney was cool about everything. He seemed a little heated about it to me. I was pleasantly surprised to see Stoney and Dash chopping it up like everything was all good. Dash knew his brother better than I thought he did.

When Stoney left, Dash kicked off his shoes, flopping across the bed. "Baby, I'm so damn full."

I giggled. He was sprawled across the bed looking like a child who overate. "That's what you get for being such a pig."

"I know right. I'm so sleepy now." He grabbed a pillow, folding it under his chin. "Man, I swear, if this wasn't for Marcel, I would cancel. I'd be right here curled up until y'all came back."

"Damn, how much did you eat?"

"Baby, I straight smashed on everything. All that fucking had my eyes bigger than my belly."

"Naw, your ass just greedy as fuck." I laughed, looking at Stoney's cousin's dress clothes, trying to find something to wear. She had some real nice stuff. Nothing I could rock at this event though. "I hope you know you have to take me back home. I can't find shit up in here to wear. And I refuse to look like a goofy."

"I got you." He stretched, standing to his feet, stripping out of his clothes.

"What you doing?"

"I'm about to shower." He walked around the room naked with so much confidence.

Damn, I loved that in a man. I was starting to see Dash in a new light. He was growing on me. "But I need to get back in there."

"It looks like we about to be sharing. Marcel reserved a spot for all of us. He won't be cussing me out because we're late. That shit carries over to practice. I can't take that kinda heat. It's brutal. Marcel's cool, but he got this other side that is ugly."

"Oh, I'm with you when you're right. He came down hard on me too. I don't wish that on nobody." We both walked to the shower. I got in first. "Don't be trying nothing while we're in here. We're on a time limit, remember?"

Dash grinned. "I'm going to leave you alone this time. I'll beat it up later," he said, smacking my wet ass.

"Quit," I said, pushing him away from me. "You play to damn much."

He smacked my ass again, laughing.

Secretly, I eyed Dash as we showered. He had this wild yet controlled personality. I was really starting to like him. His vibe was so damn cool. It's like he didn't sweat shit. No attitudes. No stresses. No jealousy. Nothing but positive energy. Just the type of dude I needed to spend my time with. Not to mention, his dick game was right too.

I still had a strong itch for Stoney, but I was going to try my best to leave him alone and focus on Dash.

Being pressed for time, I got out of the shower and threw on some leggings, a tank shirt, a leather jacket and some ankle boots. I looked like I was going to audition for a video. Meanwhile, Dash was dressed to the nines. He was suited up, wearing a black Armani suit with a crisp white shirt and tie.

We gathered our stuff and headed downstairs, where everyone else was waiting. Stoney was dressed up too, wearing an Armani suit as well, but his shirt and tie were gray. Vanity was sitting on the couch, looking disoriented. She was pretty though. The heavy makeup covered up her bruised eye and neck. Her attire complimented Stoney. She had on a silver shimmer mini dress with sparkling glass-looking slipper shoes.

The boys had on their uniforms and backpacks. Ready for school. MiMi had on the same clothes with her suitcase nearby. I assumed she was being dropped back off at his parent's house.

From what Dash told me while he was getting dressed, Marcel's conference was a big deal. He's accepting the money awarded to him by the Chicago Police Department. Also, he's giving a speech, and we will be having lunch with the mayor. The city's elite will be in attendance for this high-end luncheon.

"Is everyone ready to go?" Stoney asked, taking charge like he usually does. This is what I loved and hated about him. He was controlling. At least that's what I saw.

Dash popped in a piece of gum. "I need to take Pebbles home. She's going to get dressed right quick and we'll meet y'all there."

"Let me get a piece," Stoney asked his brother. Dash gave him a stick of gum. "Ok, we'll meet you there then. Don't take all day though. Meanwhile, I'm going to take the boys to school. After that, I'm going to drop MiMi off. Then, we'll be on our way."

"Sounds like a plan," Dash said as we all marched into the garage.

This was the first time that I noticed that Dash had the same car as Stoney. "You two have the same ride? How ironic is that?" They both had fully loaded silver Mercedes Benz S-Class Sedans. The only difference was the license plates. Stoney had personalized plates that said Eternal.

Princess Diamond

"It's not ironic. I got mine first." Stoney opened the car door for Vanity and the kids. "Damn, I forgot, I don't have no damn gas. Shit. Marcel just texted me, asking me to come early. I ain't got time for this shit."

"Let's switch then." Dash tossed Stoney the keys. "I got a full tank."

They made their way over to Dash's ride, while we got into Stoney's.

"Thanks, bro."

"Ain't no thing, bro," Dash said, getting behind the wheel. Stoney was about to take Dom out of his car. "Aye, why don't you leave him? His school is right across the street from the gas station. I can drop him off. That should save you time."

"Aight. Good looking out."

Stoney backed out of the four-car garage first.

Dash backed out right behind him, cranking the sound system up as loud as it would go. Blasting Nasty Boy by Notorious BIG.

"Am I nasty?" he asked me, humping on the steering wheel. "You like that, don't you? How I just rolled my body like that?"

I smiled, watching him roll his entire mid-section like a stripper. Yep, that shit was sexy. "Why you stupid?"

We both laughed.

At the stop sign, Stoney honked at us before turning onto 103rd Street, making a right towards Beacon Therapeutic to drop E off.

Dash hit the horn back, turning left on 103rd Street towards Western, headed to Small Strides Academy and BP gas station.

Chapter 19

Ivan

I can't believe these sons of bitches shot me. Not once, but twice. I didn't even know I was hit until I collapsed on the sidewalk. My aim was to get at my wife and put hot lead in her ass. Cheating ass hoe. She didn't even bother to see if I was dead or alive. Her main concern was running into that nicca's arms. Like he could really save her from me. She's more stupid than I thought if she even thinks I was going to let any of this shit slide. Ain't no fuckin way. Oh, she was going to pay. One way or another. Nobody betrays me without suffering from my wrath.

I was conscious the whole time even though it looked like I was out cold. I saw that punk ass cop uncuff Chip. I saw him walk over and talk to Vanity and that sweet-looking nicca Stoney. That nicca came from a long line of sweet-looking niccas, if you asked me. They all played hard, but they were soft like girls. I wouldn't be surprised if they took it up the ass too.

Chip seemed concerned about me. I'll give him that much. He jumped in the ambulance and rode out, but it was too late. I didn't trust his ass anymore. He'd gotten too fuckin chummy with the enemy. Agreeing with him and shit. Repeating shit he said word for word. Then, he was always trying to change me. Like he didn't accept me for who I was. I'm muthfuckin Ivan, nicca. That's who the fuck I am. That's all the fuck I shall be. Since this Chip didn't seem to understand that shit, I was putting his ass in time out. He could wonder what my next move was going to be, like the rest of these played out muthafuckas trying to one up me.

The ambulance ride was quick. It's like they were putting me in the vehicle, and then the next moment, I was being taken out. I kept hearing Chip tell me to hold on while the paramedics worked on me, trying to save my life.

I lost a lot of blood by the time I got to the hospital. My clothes were bloody. Nurses and doctors came from every direction. The police stormed in shortly after I was wheeled in. I guess to keep an eye on me. Like I was going to get the fuck up and walk out of this bitch bleeding to death. They be doing too damn much. I'm fighting for my damn life, and all they can think about is arresting me once I'm well enough. Too bad they don't know me very well. I'll go on the run before I allow them to escort me off to jail.

A nicca was feeling weak. For the first time in my life, I was having serious doubts if I was going to make it. Between feeling lightheaded, woozy, and the excruciating pain, I wasn't so sure of the outcome. One thing I knew for sure, if I made it out of this incident alive, I was going to raise hell on earth.

*****

Opening my eyes, I looked around. I was in a hospital room. Chip was sleep in a chair on one side of my bed. My parents were sleep on the other side. I saw a duffle bag sitting on the floor by them. I assumed it was my things. I always told Chip if I ever got admitted to the hospital to make sure someone went to my place and got my bag. I see Chip was paying attention. Funny, he never asked me why I needed it or what was in it. I kept it packed just in case. It was times like these that I was glad I was one step ahead. Just in case I got hemmed up and needed to escape, I had my get away bag.

The first thing I felt for was my dick. You know how they make stupid ass mistakes in these hospitals. I come in with gunshot wounds, and they amputate my dick because they mixed up the charts. Shit like that happened all the time, especially to people of color.

While I was staring off, thinking about how crazy today was, I spotted my phone. It was lit up. I swung my legs over the bed and doubled over in pain. I was shot in my chest and twice in the arm. Whoever shot me needed to go back to the gun range. I was thankful that they had a fucked up shot or I would be dead right now. However, I couldn't help but think that if I needed protection, this would be the nicca firing off sloppy ass shots. Missing muthafuckas and shit. The first bullet hit me in the chest and went out of my side, hitting me in the arm. So I have three holes from that one bullet. The second shot hit me in the arm. So, my left arm and shoulder were real fucked up right now.

I endured the pain just so I could reach for my phone. After a few attempts, I finally grabbed it before settling back in the bed in pain. Taking deep breaths, I hoped that the throbbing would end soon. Still, that didn't stop me from checking my phone. I had a numerous amount of texts. Everybody and they daddy sent me a message. As I scrolled through, I got real heated when I didn't see one from Vanity. I could only imagine what she was doing right now. I know what I would be doing at three am if she was laying in my bed.

So this is how she wants to play me? I could be dead right now and this bitch is fucking the next nicca. I've known Vanity for a very long time, since we were kids. I never had to question her motives. She might be a little naïve, or downright clueless, but she was always loyal to this dick. Right now, I wanted to bash her head in. I would never do her dirty like this.

Pissed off at her, I texted the first thing that came to my mind. And I meant every last word too. She had me tight as fuck. I sent about fifteen or twenty texts before I felt a sharp pain shoot up my left side. It started at my shoulder and shot down to my foot. Agonizing, debilitating, and excruciating pain. I threw my head back against the pillow, quickly pushing the call button for the nurse to come. The shit was so bad it brought tears to my eyes. I pressed the button again. Shouldn't this bitch be in here by now? I'm muthafuckin dying in here. Still no damn nurse.

If I wasn't in so much pain, I would yell out. It hurt so fuckin bad I didn't even want to blink. I'll teach her ass. I pressed the call button with my thumb, and laid on that muthafucka until I saw someone rush in. Seconds later, two nurses came rushing in, waking Chip and my parents. I quickly closed my eyes, mumbling that I was in pain.

"Oh, hurry up and give him something. He's in pain," my mother said. She was out of her chair and by my bedside trying to oversee my care. "It's bad enough that the police shot him. He shouldn't even be here. Do something. Why aren't you moving faster? Can't you see he's been hurt?" She gently touched my forehead. "Everything's going to be ok, baby. Mama's here."

"Mrs. Carder, I understand your concern, but I want you to know, we are taking great care of him. His pain medicine wore off. That's all. I assure you that once he gets another dose, he'll be just fine."

My mother didn't say anything else. She stood on the side watching them like a hawk. Making sure they did what they were supposed to do. That's how she treated all of us. Me and my brothers, we were all her babies.

My father's eyes popped wide open. He got up and stood next to my mother, holding her hand.

"What's going on?" Chip asked, stretching in his chair.

The morphine kicked in. I could have nutted from the euphoric feeling. Just what I needed. Relaxation. My mother was talking to me as well as the nurse. I didn't hear shit they said. I was floating in the sky. At least that's what it felt like.

"Hello, there," the doctor said, walking in, grabbing my chart. "I'm Dr. Brandon. And you are one lucky young man. With all the blood you lost, you almost didn't make it." The doctor looked down at me smiling.

I was so high all I could do was nod and smile back.

"Will he be okay, doctor?" My mother asked.

Everybody Got A Secret 2: A Drama Filled Romance

I turned my head towards my dad and smiled some more. These drugs were awesome. They had a nicca feeling like a brand new person. I wish I could feel like this every day.

"Yes," the doctor replied. "He'll be good as new once he's all healed up. It's amazing that the bullets didn't do any permanent damage."

The relief showed on my parent's face.

"Doc?" Chip asked. "Will my brother be able to use his arm? I mean, like he used to. He used to be a football all-star. He still plays from time to time while teaching the kids."

"Most likely. There wasn't much damage. The worse part will be all the pain because of his injuries. He might be in pain even after his injuries heal. Weeks or even months."

Fuck my left arm. As long as my dick still worked. My right arm was my dominant arm anyway.

The doctor left and Chip stood in his place. "Man, you scared me to death. I just knew you were gone. You flat lined like three or four times before we got here. I was afraid you weren't going to make it."

"You should know better than that. I'm not going no fuckin where."

"Blood was everywhere though." He stood back giving me a view of all the blood on his clothes. He was covered in blood. Even on his shoes. "Before they could get you into surgery, you tried to get off the stretcher, slinging blood everywhere."

"Damn. I don't even remember that."

Chip leaned in closer. "Look, I know all this has been rough for you—"

"Naw, save the speech."

"Just listen, man. You my brother. I don't want to see you hurting."

"I'm good, though," I lied. Truth was I planned on mending my broken heart with retaliation.

"You not good. I know you too well. I think you should just divorce Vanity. Let her be with that nicca. We'll find you a new

205

woman. Someone who loves you for you. How does that sound?"

I was speechless. Chip didn't know me as well as he thought he did. If he did, he'd know that I wasn't letting Vanity go. Only death would keep me from her. She was the love of my life. I'll be damn if I allowed another nicca to take her way from me.

We took vows. Until death do us part. Well, if I ain't dead, she still belonged to me. Forever. Even if I had to pretend that I was cool with everything, I would. I was going to do whatever it took. Whatever I needed to say. Whatever I needed to do. Anything to carry out my plan. Vanity would be mine again. I closed my eyes with a smile on my face, dreaming of sweet, sweet revenge.

*****

Not sure how long I slept. When I woke up, everyone was gone. I heard Chip say something about changing his clothes before I went to sleep. I assumed my parents went to the cafeteria to get something to eat. My father was going to eat regardless of what was going on. Me getting shot wasn't going to change that.

They would be back any minute.

I took off the oxygen, and reached over, cutting all the machines off that I was hooked up too. Swinging my feet over the side of the bed, I ripped the IV out of my hand. It stung a little, leaving droplets of blood. With my arm in a sling, I hurried to the other side of the bed where my duffle bag was. I'm sure my parents would have never brought this bag if they knew what I wanted it for.

Going into the bathroom, I hurried up and changed, dropping the hospital gown right on the bathroom floor. Slowly, I put on my jeans, shirt, gym shoes, and fitted cap. It hurt to put my jacket on without the sling. I didn't have no choice. I had to. Rocking this sling was a dead giveaway.

Swiftly, I looked in the mirror checking myself out. I looked more like a visitor rather than a patient. I walked back out of the bathroom, fluffing up my pillows. I molded them under the covers to make it look like I was still in bed with the covers over me. I'm sure it wouldn't take that long for someone to notice that I wasn't there. Hopefully, it would buy me enough time to get far away.

I threw the duffle bag over my good shoulder and walked out of my hospital room, right pass the officer waiting by the door. He glanced at me as I confidently strolled pass him, going in the opposite direction. The idiot didn't even recognize me. That's what happens when you put a rookie on the door of a smart nicca. Stepping in confidence, I walked past the nurse's station as they gossiped about reality TV. This was easier than I thought. Nobody was paying me any attention.

It must've really been my lucky day. Three bottles of morphine with needles were sitting in the hallway as soon as I passed the nurse's station. I looked back at them as they continued to talk, scooping all three bottles up, putting them into my pocket along with the needles. I wasn't worried about getting more. As soon as I figured out my next move, I would hit the streets and get some more. One thing about Chicago, there wasn't nothing you couldn't find. The black market was endless. I just so happened to know the right connections. As long as I had the money, I could get anything I wanted.

I knew I had to move fast before hospital security figured out I was missing. Once that happened, I was going to be a wanted man on the run. I wasn't taking no fuckin bus. I needed a ride. I scoped people out as I walked through the halls. I needed a gullible female. Someone I could kick game to. I planned on spending a lot of time with this woman so she needed to be easy on the eyes with a hot body, just in case I wanted to fuck. All I saw were beat up bitches though. Where was all the bad bitches at? This shit didn't make no sense. I've seen some of the ugliest broads I'd ever seen in my life, travelling through these hallways

I was just about to give up and settle on stealing a car when I laid eyes on a real dizzy bitch walking out of the pharmacy. In the few minutes that I watched her, she dropped the pill bottle three damn times. She was fine as fuck though. Her exotic beauty made up for the lack of brains.

She had on a sexy black one-piece fitted jump suit, showing off cleavage with really high heels. I knew ladies fashion because of Vanity. There was no way I could be involved with Vanity all these years, being drug to the mall shopping and shit, and not know what women liked. I could tell this chick was some kinda model or video vixen by the way she was over dressed. And the fact that she had no problem stepping in those high heels.

I decided to approach her when she accidently dropped her jacket. This girl was a hot fuckin mess. Perfect for me though. Just what I needed. "Let me get that for you." It hurt like hell to bend down and pick up her expensive jacket. I grimaced all the way down and back up.

"Thank you so much." She stuck out her hand. "I'm Kimaya, but you can call me Kim."

I shook her hand, looking into her red puffy eyes. "Nice to meet you, Kim. I'm Ivan." I was running out of time so I needed to move this thing along. "I hope I'm not too forward when I ask, why is a beautiful woman like you crying?" The compliment seemed to lift her spirits a little. She was going to be a lot easier than I thought. All she needed was some attention.

"I'm having man problems," she admitted.

I could tell that whatever went down happened recently. Like yesterday or this morning. "Let me guess. You found him cheating or he left you for another woman. Am I right?"

Her slanted eyes widened. "How'd you know? You must be psychic." She laughed. "Or was it that obvious?"

Even her laugh was sexy. I smiled, continuing to lay on the charm thick. "No. I just know men. We can be stupid sometimes. Not realizing what we had until it's gone."

She looked down at my hand, noticing my wedding ring. "Oh, you're married?"

"Sort of."

She frowned. "Aww, see, don't tell me you about to be on that bullshit too. You were doing good."

Everybody Got A Secret 2: A Drama Filled Romance

I kept smiling although I wanted to scream out in pain. My arm was killing me. "No, beautiful, I'm not on no bullshit. Can I be honest with you?"

"Sure," she said, anticipating what I was about to say next.

"The truth is, my wife cheated on me. Then, her and her lover sent the cops to my house and they ended up shooting me." I showed her my bum arm for added emphasis.

She gasped, putting her hand up to her mouth. "Oh, my goodness, I heard about that. It happened last night, didn't it?"

"Yeah," I said, holding my head down. When I looked back up, I had crocodile tears in my eyes. "She did me so wrong. I loved that woman with all of my heart and she did me so dirty."

"C'mere," Kim said, putting her arms around me.

While she fell for my story, I was taking it all in. Another weakness—she was real nurturing and willing to please.

"Say, it wouldn't trouble you to give me a ride home, would it? See, I was brought here by ambulance and I don't have a way back."

"Yeah, sure, Ivan. I'd be glad to help you."

I'll be tapping that ass in no time.

Chapter 20

Ivan

I followed Kim out the hospital to her car. I was tripping when we approached her ride. "Get the fuck outta here," I said, amazed that we drove the same car. A BMW 4 Series Gran Coupe. It was the same year and the same color too. I was starting to think that maybe meeting her wasn't just by chance. Maybe it was fate.

"You're kidding?" She gave off a sexy giggle. "Looks like we have more in common than I thought. You know, I'm kinda liking you, Ivan."

"Likewise," I said, flashing my perfect teeth.

I gave her my address and sat back while she drove. As we were leaving the hospital grounds, I saw a few police cars pulled up. I'm assuming that they now knew I was gone. My phone vibrated too. It was a text from Chip asking me where I was. He confirmed what I already knew. That the police were looking for me. I cut my phone off. I wasn't about to talk to him or anyone else.

"So, I told you about my marital problems. Tell me what your boyfriend did to you?"

Kim exhaled as if talking about it took every last breath that she had. "We were together for five years. Engaged for two. I loved this man with all of my heart. I just knew we were getting married. In the middle of the night, he dumped me. No warning or nothing."

"Wow! It sounds like your heart was broken just like mine."

She grabbed some tissue out of the glove compartment, dabbing at her eyes. I guess she was trying not to mess up her make up.

"You know," I said, feeling such a strong connection to Kim. "I probably shouldn't even be saying this, but I really want revenge. I feel like I was done wrong and I want my wife to pay."

Kim glanced at me. "You know, I thought I'd never say this, but I want Stoney to pay for what he did too."

I nearly passed out when she called out that nicca's name. "Wha-what did you say your man's name was?" It just couldn't be. I really needed to hear her say it again.

"Stoney. Why do you know him?"

"I'm not sure," I said, calculating my next move. "Do you happen to know the woman's name that he left you for?"

Kim huffed and puffed. "How could I forget that bitch? He openly told me that he loved her, and not me, time and time again. Her name is Vanity."

My head started fuckin spinning. I set out on this journey to find a woman that I could use. I just so happened to bump into Stoney's fiancée. What are the odds of me hooking up with his ex? "I think today is your lucky day, Kim."

She smiled again. "Why do you say that?"

"Because I'm Vanity's husband."

Now it was her turn to say, "Get the fuck outta here. You gotta be kidding me?"

"No. And this has to be fate. It just has to be."

Her whole demeanor changed. The tears that once were, were now gone. "Yes, we were definitely meant to meet. That's for sure."

"Listen, now since we are connected by the two people who betrayed us, will you help me seek revenge?"

"I sure will. Not only will I help you, you can come and stay with me if you like. If I know Stoney the way that I do, his family will be all involved. And trust me, you can't go up against them. It's too damn many of them. They have connections everywhere."

"Well, that's where you come in, gorgeous. What can you tell me about them?"

"I've been around for a long time. I know some things. I don't know everything. Stoney kept most of his family business from me, but I will tell you whatever I do know."

"That's good enough."

I had Kim pull up in the back of my house. The last thing I needed was for the police to pull up out front right next to her. I knew I was on borrowed time. I rushed inside gathering all the things that I need. I wasn't sure if I was going to be able to come back anytime soon.

The first thing I got was my gun. I planned on using it ASAP. The next thing I got was all of our bank account information. Next, I got my car keys. I noticed Vanity's car keys weren't on the hook next to mine. I didn't see her car in the driveway anymore. That's ok. I was about to show this bitch whose the muthafuckin man up in this piece. Last, I loaded up my duffle bag and suitcase with a few other possessions and clothes.

I heard sirens in the distance as soon as I came out of the house. That meant the police were nearby. Hearing sirens wasn't something new. I heard them all day long. The fact that I was on the run meant they might be for me.

"Scoot over," I told Kim, dropping the nice guy charade. "I need to drive. She didn't give me any lip, like Vanity would have, sliding her sexy self over to the passenger's seat. "I need to make a few stops. I hope that's okay."

"Yeah, go ahead. We're on the same team now."

I chuckled. I was really feeling Kim. She was my type of chick. "I like the sound of that."

"Me too," she said, holding her hand up for a high-five. That was some girlie shit, but I slapped her hand anyway.

Everybody Got A Secret 2: A Drama Filled Romance

My first stop was the bank. I emptied out our joint account, my personal bank, and Vanity's account. It might have been her account, but I put all the money in that bitch. She spent her checks on bullshit.

My next stop was the chop shop. "What up with it, Tank?" He was a real grimy muthafucka. We were cool as long as he never crossed me though. I didn't care how wrong he did others. That shit was their problem.

"Ivan, my man. What up with it?"

He got up ready to give me a one arm hug, when I put him on pause, backing up. "My arm is fucked up, man."

"That's right. Them fuckin pigs did it."

"Yeah, them bitches. Listen, Tank, I'm in a bind. I need to chop my BMW. What can you give me for it?" Vanity could sleep on me if she wants. If it wasn't for me and my money making skills we wouldn't have two brand new cars that were paid in full.

"Um, let me see." He pulled out this old raggedy book. I wasn't sure what he was about to do. "I can give you twenty for it."

"Twenty?" Did this man think I was a sucka? I knew the value of my car. "Tank, we go way back. Don't try to con me, joe. I thought we were better than that. My car is practically new. Six months old to be exact. It's in excellent condition. I can get thirty-eight for a trade in."

Tank let out a hearty laugh. "I see you did your homework."

"I always do." Muthafucka!

"Thirty. That's as high as I can go. You're hot so your car is even hotter."

"That's more like it. Throw in a chopper and some heat and we have a deal." I needed a getaway car and two more guns.

"Deal."

I gave Tank my car keys and the combination to my garage so he could go and pick the BMW up. I still felt like he was cheating me, but I didn't have time to stand here and argue with him. If need be, I'd just come back and take what I felt he owed me. Being on the run, I needed all the cash I could get. Especially since I can't go back to my work no time soon.

I walked back out to where Kim was parked. "Pull your car in."

Kim looked at me like I was crazy. "I'm not leaving my car here."

Playing nice guy was overrated. Bitches didn't understand nice. They only understood when you man-handled their asses. I opened the car door, pulling her model ass out. She nearly fell, but she quickly caught her balance in those high ass heels. Jumping behind the wheel of the car, I drove it into the garage.

"What are you doing?" Kim asked, standing there pouting.

"Listen, pretty girl, you're either rolling with me or you're not. Now you said you wanted payback. That's what I'm on. But make no mistake about it, I'm getting mine with or without you. So, what's it going to be?"

I got into the souped-up old school Chevy, cranking the engine. I looked over at Kim and she was still standing there looking dumb. I ain't got time for this shit here. Just as I was about to pull off, Kim rushed over, jumping her ass in. That's what I thought.

"Where are we on our way to?" Kim asked, looking uncomfortable in the hooptie. She held onto her purse as if the car was about to swallow it up. I could tell she was high-maintenance and not used to hood shit.

"On our way to Stoney's crib. Where he live at?"

"In Beverly off 103rd and Seeley. But you can't roll up on him like that. His family is everywhere. Even when you don't see them, they see you."

I turned onto 87th and Western. "I bet they won't see me coming. Not this time." What I had planned was going to be so sweet. It made my dick hard just thinking about it.

"I know you're not going to hurt him."

SKIRRRRRRRRRRRRT!

Everybody Got A Secret 2: A Drama Filled Romance

I slammed on the brakes, quickly pulling over, throwing the car in park. "Get the fuck out. I don't need no fraud ass bitches on my team."

She held her purse to her chest, looking around the area we were in. Yeah, I can't lie. It was a little suspect. If I was a pretty bitch, I wouldn't hop my ass out. Then again, I wouldn't go against a nicca like me either.

"Get the fuck out!" I yelled, startling her. She wasn't 'bout this life. I needed me a ride or die bitch. When she didn't move, I shoved her ass, intimidating her. This tactic always worked on weak women. "Bye! I thought you were leaving. Be on your way, bitch. Cuz I don't fuckin need you. I'll get this shit done regardless."

"I'm nobody's fraud." She looked like she was about to cry. "I said I would help you so that's what I'm going to do."

I wanted to laugh. "Then, sit your pretty ass down and shut the fuck up. Only one nicca is in charge in this bitch. That's me. So follow my lead before or become causality."

I didn't feel bad intimidating Kim. If I didn't hate Stoney so damn much, I'd understand why he dropped her annoying ass. Her beauty was all she had going for her. After a couple of hours with this saditty bitch, I was ready to drop her ass too. She would have been canned if I didn't need her. I wasn't going to let her know that I needed her ass. I wanted her to think that she needed me. That way I stayed in control.

I must've made my point because she sat back and shut the fuck up the rest of the way down Western. Gave me a chance to really think. I was going over my plan in my head about to make a left turn onto 103rd when I thought I saw Stoney's car across the street. "Ain't that that nicca right there?"

Kim perked up. "Where?"

"Right there?" I asked, pointing to the silver Benz that was in the BP gas station at the pump. "That's definitely him. You see the license plates, Eternal."

"I think," she said, squinting. "Yeah, that's definitely his ride. He's the only one that I know with those plates."

"Aww, hell. Is that Vanity in the car with him?"

"It looks like her."

"Fucking bitch. I got something for that ass," I said, making a left in the opposite direction. I had to. I was already in the middle of the street. I pulled into Patrick Plaza, turned around, and came back onto 103rd again.

As soon as the light turned red, I sped across Western, making another left into 7 Eleven right by the gas station. I threw the car in park, getting out. Going into the backseat, I pulled out one of the guns I got from Tank.

"Oh my God! You got a gun. What are you going to do with that?"

That had to be the dumbest question I ever heard in my life. Then again, look who I was talking about. Dumbass Kim.

Kim rocked back and forth in her seat. "I said I wanted to get him back, not kill him. Please say that you're only going to scare him."

"Yeah, sure," I lied, telling her whatever she wanted to hear.

Kim took a deep breath. "Good. For a minute there, I thought you were going to do something stupid."

If she thought that I was going to pull out a gun and not use it, she was dumber than I thought. I got back in the car, sitting both guns in my lap for easy access.

I made my way back onto 103rd Street, making a sharp right into BP. Some dude was standing there on the driver's side talking to Stoney. I didn't give a fuck. He could get it too. Slowly I crept through driving pass Vanity's side. I rolled down the window just enough to stick my gun out, busting off.

POP! POP! POP! POP! POP! POP! POP! POP! POP!

The passenger's side window shattered. Then I heard Vanity scream before slumping over. I hope I killed that bitch. Stoney hit the ground. I was sure he got popped too. Damn, I wish I could have checked. I was about to let off more shots when all of a sudden shots rang out. Someone was shooting at me.

POP! POP! POP! POP! POP! POP! POP! POP! POP! POP!

Everybody Got A Secret 2: A Drama Filled Romance

That's when I saw dude that Stoney was talking to busting off at me. I stepped on the accelerator, peeling out of the gas station as fast as I could.

POP! POP! POP! POP! POP! POP! POP! POP! POP! POP!

Kim screamed hysterically when a hail of bullets hit the car and the back window got shot out.

Damn these muthafuckas going hard.

I looked back as I made my way onto Western into traffic again. Two people were shooting at us. A guy and a girl. Must've been Stoney's family.

Damn. I hate to admit. Kim was right. They ain't no joke. I'm going to have to come at them on some sneaky shit. Otherwise, I'm going to be in a body bag.

Made in the USA
Columbia, SC
28 September 2022

68122771R00122